AMANDA EYRE WARD is the a~~~~~~~ ~~~~~~~
Be Lost and *Sleep Toward Heaven*. She lives ~~~
with her family.

Visit her website at www.amandaward.com

By the same author

How to Be Lost
Sleep Toward Heaven

AMANDA EYRE WARD

Forgive Me

HARPER PERENNIAL

London, New York, Toronto, Sydney and New Delhi

Harper Perennial
An imprint of HarperCollins*Publishers*
77–85 Fulham Palace Road
Hammersmith
London W6 8JB

www.harperperennial.co.uk
Visit our authors' blog at www.fifthestate.co.uk

This Harper Perennial edition published 2008
1

First published in Great Britain by Harper*Press* in 2007

A catalogue record for this book is available from the British Library

ISBN 978-0-00-723386-1

Typeset by Palimpsest Book Production Limited,
Grangemouth, Stirlingshire
Printed and bound in Great Britain by Clays Ltd, St Ives plc

Mixed Sources
Product group from well-managed
forests and other controlled sources
www.fsc.org Cert no. SW-COC-1806
© 1996 Forest Stewardship Council

FSC is a non-profit international organisation established to promote the
responsible management of the world's forests. Products carrying the FSC
label are independently certified to assure consumers that they come
from forests that are managed to meet the social, economic and
ecological needs of present and future generations.

Find out more about HarperCollins and the environment at
www.harpercollins.co.uk/green

For Liza
Who made me climb Table Mountain

*The real beauty and power of forgiveness
is that it can deliver the future to us.*

RICHARD HOLLOWAY, *On Forgiveness*

One

■

Nadine hears the parrots. So picturesque in the evening, floating over the courtyard while she sips tequila and deciphers the day's notes, the birds make the hot dawn intolerable. Two thin pillows cannot block the cacophony. Nadine's sheets press against her body. She remembers the warm lips of a local journalist, but wakes alone.

A room at La Hacienda Solita includes breakfast. Slowly, Nadine makes her way to the wooden table outside the kitchen. She orders eggs, beans, coffee, and juice from the girl. The juice arrives in a ceramic glass filled with ice cubes, and Nadine drinks it, though she should not. The girl—no more than ten—stands next to the table, her bare feet callused. She watches Nadine.

There is a communal shower. Nadine uses Pert Plus shampoo, bought in an American Rite Aid on her way back over the border: she was in a Laredo police station when the news of the twelve dead boys came in.

Nadine travels light: a comb, shampoo, lotion, lipstick. Two T-shirts, two pairs of pants, lace underwear—her one indulgence. She has an apartment in the Associated Press compound in Mexico City, but hasn't been there in a month.

On the dashboard of her rental car, Nadine finds a rubber band. She pulls her black hair back with both hands, affixes the band, and puts on sunglasses. She opens her topographic map. Today, she will find and interview the boys' families. The mother of one boy told a local TV reporter that her son had worked in a seafood restaurant. Her large, two-story home and expensive clothes told a different story.

The car's air-conditioning is broken. Nadine punches the radio on and begins to drive. Her Spanish is good; languages have always come easily to her. She plays the music loudly and hums along. It's a song about a man who wronged a woman. "If you come back to me," the man sings, "I will never stray again." She thinks of the journalist's spicy cologne, his breath against her ear as they swayed to jukebox melodies at the cantina. She smiles. It took half a bottle of Herradura and a few kisses to get directions to the boys' tiny village.

Nadine drives slowly down the narrow streets. Men unlock metal doors and heave them upward, exposing bright fruits and vegetables, rows of shirts, videocassettes. Women sweep the sidewalk and children walk to school, holding hands. A donkey cart blocks Nadine's way, then lurches down a side alley.

Finally, she reaches the outskirts. Passing squat homes protected by latticework concrete, Nadine accelerates. The air blazing through her open window is little comfort. She heads toward the mountains. Ian made her promise to wear the bulletproof vest, but Nadine reasons that having it in the backseat is good enough. It's heavy and bulky, and for Christ's sake it's got to be a hundred degrees.

Nadine reaches the place she's marked on her map with an X and pulls off the road. At a gas station, she fills the car and takes out her list of names. The man behind the counter, old and overweight, looks at Nadine without expression. He sells her a warm Coke. When she asks to use the bathroom, the man gestures with his hand. She walks behind the store, positioning her feet on either side of the fetid hole.

The village does not have paved roads, and Nadine's head begins to hurt as she drives over uneven ground. She sees a group of men gathered outside one thatched-roof home. The men stare as Nadine approaches. Nadine slows the car and tries a smile. She is met with stone faces.

The thoughts flood her—*Something is wrong. You should have told Ian where you were going. You should not have come alone. Back away, put on the vest*—but the thoughts will fade. Nadine sets her jaw and keeps driving.

The men look at one another, at the approaching Honda. By some consensus, they rush the car, and Nadine tries to stop, to reach the locks. It is too late, but she grabs the gearshift, smoothly putting the car in reverse.

As she presses the gas, a tall man wearing a Cookie Monster T-shirt opens the passenger-side door. His sweat smells metallic as he climbs in the car. He unlocks the driver's-side door, reaching across Nadine. The door is opened from outside. Two men drag Nadine out of the car and into the street. She fights—clawing at the men with her fingernails, screaming that she is *periodista*, a journalist. Their fists hit her stomach, and then her rib cage.

Two

N adine woke in a blue-and-white hotel room. There was a mini fridge by the bed, a painting of a sailboat on the wall, and a telephone with instructions in English. The window framed a familiar ocean. Nadine closed her eyes, then opened them. Her body ached. Her left arm was bandaged, so she lifted the phone with her right and dialed 0. A woman's voice answered, saying, "Oh my Lord!"

"Hello?" said Nadine. "Where am I?"

She heard footsteps on a staircase, and then the door opened. "Oh, honey," said a stout woman with a mushroom cap of blonde hair.

"I'm sorry," said Nadine. "Who are you?"

"Oh dear," said the woman. "Didn't your daddy tell you?"

Nadine had not spoken to her father in months, maybe a year.

"Where am I?" said Nadine.

"Why, honey," said the woman, "you're at the Sandy Toes Bed and Breakfast."

Nadine touched her temple. The last thing she could remember was a man who smelled like rust. "You've been in a terrible accident," the woman said, putting a fat hand on Nadine's wrist. "Thank goodness you had your daddy's card in your wallet."

Nadine stared at the hand.

"He'll be here any minute," said the woman. "By the way, my name is Gwen." Nadine did not answer. Gwen bit her lip and then released it, leaving a bright pink spot on her tooth. "Your daddy and I are in love," she informed Nadine.

"Is there room service?" asked Nadine.

"What?"

"Is there room service," said Nadine, "at the Sandy Toes Bed and Breakfast?"

"Well," said Gwen, "of course there is."

"I'd like a tequila on the rocks, please."

"It's the middle of the day, dear," said Gwen.

"A ham sandwich, as well," said Nadine.

Nadine had not seen her father, Jim, since her journalism school graduation a decade before. After the ceremony, Nadine had taken him to the Oyster Bar for dinner. It was her favorite restaurant: dark, smoky, and, to Nadine, glamorous. She ordered oysters and an expensive bottle of wine.

"I think you'll like this," said Nadine when the waiter began to pour.

"I'll have a Coors," said Nadine's father, covering his wineglass with his palm. He looked around at the businessmen and well-heeled New Yorkers. Jim wore jeans, a green windbreaker, a cap that said FALMOUTH FISH.

"So I've decided," said Nadine. "I'm going to Cape Town."

"Cape Town?"

"I'll be freelancing, of course, but maybe it'll lead to a job with the AP, or the *Times*. People are fighting the pass laws, standing up to the government. Remember that kid from Nantucket? Jason Irving? He was killed outside Cape Town last month. Everything is changing in South Africa. There's so much to write about."

Jim sighed. "That kid from Nantucket," he said. "Poor kid comes home in a coffin. This is your role model?"

"Dad," said Nadine, leaning toward him, "I could be in South Africa for the fall of apartheid!"

"Nadine," said her father, "for all I know, you're speaking Chinese."

"Come on, Dad," said Nadine. "Don't you get *The New York Times*? I renewed your subscription, I thought."

"I'm busy, honey," said Jim. "I get home late. It's just so much paper."

"So much paper."

The waiter returned with a tray of oysters and horseradish sauce. "Flown in this morning," he said, "from Buzzards Bay." He stepped back with a smile and a nod.

"If oysters is what you want," said Jim, "I've got a rake and a pair of waders for you in the garage."

Nadine looked down at her napkin. "I wish you could try," she said. She swallowed. "It's not that Woods Hole isn't great. I just—"

"What about working for the *Cape Cod Times*?" said Jim. "Your mom used to read the *Cape Cod Times*."

Nadine sighed. She drained her wine and poured another glass. For forty minutes, they talked about housing prices on the Cape, the new pizzeria on Main Street, and the traffic problem at the Bourne Rotary. Declining dessert, Nadine gave her father a quick embrace, walked him to his Midtown hotel, and took the six train downtown. At McSorley's, she argued passionately about the future of Romania with a grad student who smoked unfiltered cigarettes. They agreed that Ceauşescu's regime was on the verge of collapse, and then pressed against each other in a dim corner, the boy's tongue hot in Nadine's mouth.

She moved to Cape Town the following week.

Ten years later, her father stood before her, his hands in what could have been the same jeans. "Hey, now, Deanie," he said, reaching out to touch Nadine's hair.

"What am I doing here?" said Nadine.

"You were in some Mexican hospital," said Jim. "You were

beaten real bad. Your wrist and ribs got bunged up, you've got a nasty concussion."

"How long—"

"You'll be in Woods Hole awhile," said Jim.

"Woods Hole?" said Nadine.

Jim put his arm around Gwen. "You can stay here as long as you need. Gwen and I own this hotel. We open for business in May, soon as the summer folks get here."

"The Sandy Toes," said Gwen. "I thought of the name."

"So the closest airport is Hyannis?" said Nadine.

"What?" said Gwen. She looked nervously at Jim.

"Nadine," said Jim, "you likely can't feel it, but your wrist is still very weak. Not to mention head trauma. You were *attacked,* Nadine, by Mexican *thugs.*"

"Mm-hmm," said Nadine. She reached for the phone, murmuring, "So Logan would probably be just as easy, or Providence—"

"You can't go anywhere!" said Gwen. "You're very ill, dear!"

"What the hell was she doing down next to Guat-e-amala, is what I'd like to know," said Jim.

"May I make a long-distance call, please? In private?"

"Deanie," said Jim. "Can't you give it a rest?"

"I'll pay you back, of course," said Nadine.

"No, it's fine," said Gwen, flustered.

"Thanks," said Nadine. She picked up the receiver.

"Maybe we can visit later," said Gwen. Jim snorted.

"Okay," said Nadine, dialing quickly. Her father and Gwen exited the room, and Jim pulled the door shut with a thud that shook the Nantucket basket on the windowsill.

"You are on mandatory vacation," Ian said when Nadine finally reached him. In the background, Nadine heard the sounds of the New York office: typing, shouting, televisions tuned to CNN.

Nadine sighed into the phone. "I've got to get out of here," she said.

"You've been beaten within an inch of your life by Mexican drug traffickers. I talked to your doctor. You can't even use your left arm for two weeks."

"You think they were traffickers?"

"Whoever they were, they didn't want you nosing around," said Ian. "Some shopkeeper called the embassy. You were found in a ditch. They could have killed you."

Nadine looked out her window, at the placid sea. A large vessel, the *Atlantis*, was docked in the harbor. "How long?" she said.

"Six months."

"Ian!"

"Three months. You need to rest."

"I know you don't believe me," said Nadine, "but I feel fine. I do, really."

"Wander along the beach. Have an affair with a lifeguard. Whatever it takes, Nadine. Don't call me until March."

"I can't believe this."

Ian was silent. Nadine could picture him stroking his snow-colored moustache. "I've known you a long time," he said, finally. "And I've told you this before. You let the wall come down, you can never go back."

"I didn't let the wall down," said Nadine.

"Nadine, I'm trusting my gut on this one."

"What am I supposed to do all winter on Cape Cod?"

"Write a novel," said Ian. "Write a memoir about your hair-raising adventures around the world. If all else fails, watch TV."

"Lord help me," said Nadine.

"Talk to you soon," said Ian. "Not that soon," he added.

Dr. Duarte had olive skin and a rich voice. Nadine hit MUTE but continued to watch *Law & Order* as he listed her many bruises and lacerations. "When can I get out of here?" she asked when he stopped talking.

"Out of bed? A week, maybe ten days. I'm most concerned about the head trauma, and we'll just have to keep an eye on that."

Nadine lay back and sighed.

"Can you turn off the television, please?" said Dr. Duarte.

Nadine hit the POWER button as Dr. Duarte told her how lucky she was to be alive, how her body needed time to heal. She nodded, eyes on her intertwined hands. There was a pause, and then Dr. Duarte said, "What's it like?"

Nadine looked up, into his brown eyes. "Sorry?"

"What's it like?" he said. "What does it feel like, being a reporter, putting yourself in danger? I guess I've always wondered what that feels like."

"You just think about what you need to do," said Nadine. "Warnings, they come into your head, but they go away. You do your job." Nadine's voice sounded confident. She did not say that some evenings, after her story was filed and she was safe in a hotel room, taking a shower, her legs shook so hard she had to sit down, letting the water rain over her until she calmed.

"You get used to being terrified, basically?"

Nadine looked out the window. She still remembered the dark winter days of her childhood, the sense that life was happening elsewhere. The thought of staying on Cape Cod was unbearable. "When's the last time you were terrified?" she asked.

"Senior year," said Dr. Duarte. "Right before I called to ask Suze Phillips to the prom. No, wait, my boards." He paused. "No, Suze was scarier."

"What did she say?"

"She said yes," said Dr. Duarte. "I hung up the phone and almost cried with happiness."

"That's it exactly," said Nadine.

"So being a globe-trotting journalist is like asking Suze Phillips to the prom," said Dr. Duarte.

"It's like asking her, and having her say yes."

He nodded, pleased. "Well," he said, "I'll be back tomorrow. I can bring you some books, if you want. Might help pass the time."

"Thanks," said Nadine. "But I'm fine, really."

"How many *Law & Order*s do you think you can watch?"

"Seven?" said Nadine. "Maybe eight."

"Wow," said Dr. Duarte. "My limit would probably be six."

Gwen ministered to Nadine as if she were a child home from school. She made chicken soup and lasagna. She brought gossip magazines and crossword books. She went to Wal-Mart and returned with a nightshirt featuring a grinning cat. "I'm thirty-five," said Nadine when she opened the bag.

"No one's too old for Garfield," said Gwen.

Nadine slept and watched television. Fellow journalists and off-again lovers sent flowers. Nobody called, however: what had happened to Nadine was the thing you didn't allow yourself to think about. All of them were playing a game of chance, and even the best luck ran out eventually. There was a point at which many took a desk job, for love or family. But Nadine, with the exception of Jim, had no family.

As for love, there had been Maxim, shot by a stray bullet in Cape Flats. One love, one bullet. Nadine learned her lesson.

Three

■

Woods Hole, Massachusetts, where Nadine had grown up, was a small and strange town. It was located in the armpit of Cape Cod, an old fishing village now populated by drunks and scientists. In the winter, most of the shingled houses stood empty, barbecue grills sheathed in plastic, porch steps hidden by dull snow. Buttery summer gave way to lead skies by November, skies that barely brightened before June. Winter on the Cape was a time of resting, reflection, and deep depression. After two days in bed, Nadine defied Dr. Duarte's orders and walked to School Street to visit her oldest friend, Lily.

"Holy guacamole," said Lily, opening her front door with her shirt unbuttoned. Nadine tried not to wince at the sound of children shrieking over a loud television.

"It's me," said Nadine.

"Hm," said Lily.

"Can I come in?"

Lily folded her arms across her giant breasts, but nodded.

"I'm sorry," said Nadine, when she was settled into a couch that smelled like pancake syrup and diapers.

"So you said," said Lily, "on your *postcard*." Lily's newest baby—a girl, by the looks of her pink pajamas—was asleep in the crook of Lily's arm, and her two-year-old twin boys were watching a video called *Hooray for Dirt*. On the screen, a fat man in a construction helmet drove a bulldozer.

"It was a year ago," said Nadine. "Can't we forgive and forget?"

"Nadine," said Lily, "I have three children under three years old. There's nothing else to fixate on. Breast milk, crayons, and how much I hate you."

"But didn't you have fun in London?"

"Fun?" said Lily. "I took a boat ride down the Times. I had half a gross warm beer in some pub. The sun never came out. I went to the Tate museum by myself and I was late for the changing of the guard. I was three months' pregnant, Nadine. I missed Bo and Babe—I came home a day early."

"Thames," said Nadine.

"What?"

"It's pronounced *Thames.*"

Lily bit her cheek and glared at Nadine. The baby had to be six months old, but Lily still looked pregnant. Her hair was pulled into a French braid, and her roots were showing.

"Have you lost weight?" said Nadine.

"Go to hell," said Lily.

"Listen," said Nadine. "Please. It was an important story. I didn't have a choice. It's impossible to get an interview with Marcos. It's funny, Lily, actually. He wears this black ski mask . . ."

Lily widened her eyes and shook her head. "I don't know what to say," she said.

"I didn't plan on it," said Nadine. "I got us show tickets."

"Mommy!" said one of the boys—Bo? Babe? Lily ignored him.

"Do you know what I had to go through to get my mom to take the twins?" said Lily. "I left my babies with a senile witch to fly over and see my best friend—"

"Let's have lunch. On me, Lily. We can go up to Boston. I want to tell you all about it. I had to go to this jungle hideout. Marcos comes out wearing a freaking Kalashnikov—"

"Mom-eeee!" said a twin.

"I need watch Big Bird!" said the other.

"I need watch *Fraggle Rock!*" said the first. "Please, Mommy, pleeeease!"

"I'm sorry you got hurt, Nadine," said Lily, "but I don't give a flick about Marcos and his kala-whatever."

"It's a gun."

Lily expertly changed the tape in the VCR, the baby still asleep in her arm. The boys settled down with their hands in their laps. "I don't know who you're trying to impress, Nadine," she said. "I'm busy, if you don't mind."

"What's *gun,* Mommy?" asked one boy politely.

"I need watch Thomas Train!" repeated the other.

"I need watch Big Bird!"

"I need gun!"

The din was getting to be a bit much. Nadine stood. "Lily," she said, "my interview was on the front page of *The Washington Post.*"

Lily laughed and sank back down on the couch. Both boys climbed on top of her. The baby slept on. "Meanwhile," said Lily, "how are the kids, Lily? Do you miss the library? You're staying home with your children. That's really wonderful." As she spoke, her eyes filled with tears. She spit out the words. "Do you still love Dennis? How do you breast-feed twins? I'm interested. Tell me about your life. You're my best friend, Lily. I care."

"Right," said Nadine. "I do care, Lily. Your new baby, she's so beautiful."

"What's her name?" said Lily, staring at Nadine.

Nadine looked at the sleeping child, her mouth a tiny gum-drop. "Jesus, Lily . . ."

"How old is she?" said Lily. Her boys moved around her like squirrels, burrowing into her skin. All hell would break loose, Nadine realized, if Lily had an injured wrist.

"Lily," said Nadine.

"Flick you," said Lily, cutting her eyes toward her boys, to make sure they hadn't heard her swear. "Come on, sweetie peeties, let's make some peanut butter and jelly."

"Flick me?" said Nadine.

"You heard me," said Lily. She placed the baby in her bassinet and took one boy in each hand. In the kitchen, she bent over the counter. Nadine watched Lily's back for a while, then turned and walked slowly out the door. Her head ached, and she felt weak. The wind whipped and tangled her long hair. Nadine stood on the snow-covered lawn and gazed at the line where the ocean met the slate-gray sky.

Clearly, it was time to start smoking again.

Four

On Water Street, Nadine headed for the Woods Hole Market. She walked across the drawbridge, her right hand wrapped in the long sleeve of her father's coat, left arm bound to her chest. The coat would be perfect for work, she thought. It was warm and had enough pockets for a notebook, pen, and plastic bag. Nadine kept her passport and plane tickets in a ziplock and close at hand. Until the year before, Lily, who had been the reference librarian for the Woods Hole Public Library, had sent a small Moleskine notebook with information about every place Nadine was headed: a hand-drawn map of Ciudad Vieja with a history of the Guatemalan National Revolutionary Unity, tips on finding the best cheeseburger in Tulum.

Nadine and Lily had grown up like sisters, as they had no siblings of their own. Jim worked late at Falmouth Fish, so Lily's mother would take Nadine in after school, feeding her Chips Ahoy cookies and strawberry milk. On Sunday, his day off, Jim took Nadine and Lily hiking along Sandy Neck Beach. Though both girls dreamed of being detectives like Nancy Drew, Lily fell for Dennis and went to Cape Cod Community College. Nadine went to Harvard and then traveled four continents before NYU journalism school.

Until the twins were born, Nadine and Lily still wrote and called constantly, reveling in the differences between their lives. But something changed after Lily's frightening childbirth. The babies were early and sickly, and Nadine—traveling with the Zapatistas—couldn't make it home in time to help out. By the time

Nadine visited, Lily had already become someone else. She wasn't interested in Nadine's stories or the La Reliquia mezcal Nadine had brought from Mexico. Nadine spent the weekend cold and miserable, trying to feign interest in Bo and Babe's sleeping patterns and weight percentiles. There was a new alliance between Lily and Dennis, too. Where once Lily had laughed about his dream of a McMansion and six kids, now she seemed to have bought in hook, line, and sinker, showing off her mini van and giant TV. Was Lily happy? Nadine couldn't bear to believe it. She drank the mezcal herself on the bus back to Logan and made out with the man next to her on the flight to Mexico City, fondling him under the thin polyester blanket.

Nadine missed the Moleskine notebooks.

She bought a pack of Merits and made her way back to the Sandy Toes, jumping when she heard a loud rapping sound. It was someone inside The Captain Kidd, pounding at the window to get her attention: Dr. Duarte. He came outside wearing a yellow T-shirt with a salmon printed on it, his arms folded across his broad chest. "Nadine," he said, "what are you doing out here?"

"I could ask you the same."

He nodded quickly, his cheeks turning red from the cold. When he spoke, his words were frosted. "Left my coat inside," he said. "Nadine, I'm serious. You need to be in bed."

"You'd have to buy me dinner first."

He looked bewildered. "It's a joke," said Nadine. "I'm sorry. I'm going back right now. I just needed—"

"Some cigarettes?"

Nadine looked down at the pack, visible through the plastic bag.

"Anyway," said Dr. Duarte. "Please go home, Nadine. I don't need a dead woman on my conscience."

"Jesus," said Nadine. "I'm not that bad off. I'm headed back to Mexico next week."

"The hell you are," said Dr. Duarte.

"I want a second opinion."

"All right," said Dr. Duarte. "You need to lie down and eat. Go home and get in bed. I'll bring you some fried clams in an hour."

Nadine blinked.

"Onion rings or fries?" said Dr. Duarte.

"I don't—"

"It's freezing, Nadine. Give me an answer."

"Onion rings."

"Fine," said Dr. Duarte. "See you soon." He raised his bushy eyebrows and smiled, then darted back into The Captain Kidd.

At the front desk, a package from La Hacienda Solita waited. Inside, Nadine found her dirty backpack. She sat on the floor and emptied the pack with her right hand: rubber sandals; Pepto-Bismol and antibiotic tablets; three tamarind candies; a roll of toilet paper; condoms; a jar of Nescafé (when coffee was hard to find, she stuck her finger in the jar and sucked the crystals off); a Nalgene bottle; a headlamp; a Swiss Army knife; three lined notebooks; two Bic pens; an envelope of tobacco; and a tin of rolling papers.

And taped inside a composition notebook, the photograph of her mother, Ann, sitting on Nobska Beach. Even when she was sick, Ann had loved hiking to the lighthouse with a picnic dinner. She wrapped a warm blanket around her diminishing frame, a Red Sox cap covering her bald head. They would walk at sunset, the sky rippled with color. "I've never been outside New England," Ann told six-year-old Nadine, "but there can't be anywhere more beautiful than this."

In the photo, Ann was young and healthy. Her black hair was tucked behind her ears, and her hand shaded her violet eyes. She wore a green bikini and smiled at Jim, who was taking the picture. Ann's stomach was slightly rounded with baby Nadine.

"Knock, knock," said Dr. Duarte, rapping on the door to Room 9.

"Oh, hi," said Nadine.

"Why's there trash in the middle of your room?"

"That's not trash," said Nadine. "It's all my worldly possessions."

"Oh," said Dr. Duarte, "wow. I'm sorry."

"It's a reasonable mistake," said Nadine, easing into bed.

"It really looks like trash," said Dr. Duarte, taking a Styrofoam container from a paper bag. The smell of onion rings filled the room. "They were out of clams, so I got you a scrod sandwich."

"Fried seafood. What kind of a doctor are you?"

"Believe me," said Dr. Duarte. "Fried seafood is nothing compared with an amputated arm."

"Come on," said Nadine. "It doesn't even hurt that much."

"You're on Demerol."

"Right."

"Eat your sandwich," said Dr. Duarte.

"Speaking of Demerol," said Nadine, biting into the soft Portuguese roll, savoring the hot fish, the melted cheddar cheese.

"No," said Dr. Duarte. He sat on a chair in the corner of the room and turned on the television with the remote control.

"You don't even—" said Nadine, wiping her lips with a napkin.

"Yes I do," said Dr. Duarte. "You want some extra Demerol to add to your—" He gestured to the backpack. "—your worldly possessions."

"But what if my wrist starts to hurt in the middle of the Sierra Madres?"

"Stop showing off," said Dr. Duarte. "We'll talk about it when you've sat in that bed for a while longer."

"Right," said Nadine. "By the way, this is fantastic."

Dr. Duarte cracked open a bottle of beer. "You think I'm kidding," he said. "Next time I come, Nadine, I'm bringing an X-ray of your arm. Haven't you ever read *A Separate Peace*?"

"The boarding school book?"

"Phinneas dies," said Dr. Duarte, pouring into a glass. "He dies of a broken bone."

Nadine dipped an onion ring in ketchup. "Dr. Duarte, how about a beer?"

"You can call me Hank. And no, no beer for you. I got you an iced tea." Hank handed Nadine the bottle, then settled back into his chair.

"What kind of beer is that, anyway?" said Nadine. "Looks delicious."

"It's my favorite, Whale's Tail. They make it on Nantucket. Ever been to Nantucket?"

"No," said Nadine. She thought for a moment of Jason Irving, who had grown up on the island. Then she forced Jason—and his sad story—from her mind.

"Too bad," said Dr. Duarte. "The fast ferry only takes an hour. It always surprises me how many Cape Codders have never been. Ah, fourth quarter," he said, finding a Patriots game on television.

"I hate football," said Nadine.

"Well," said Hank, stepping from his boots and propping his stocking feet on the ottoman, "it seems I have the remote."

"To tell you the truth," said Nadine, "I don't get football."

"You want me to teach you?"

"No," said Nadine, "I have some research to do anyway."

"Suit yourself," said Hank.

Nadine opened the newspaper and scanned the headlines. "Damn!" she exclaimed.

"Beg pardon?"

"Damn Kit Henderson! He got my story." Hank hit MUTE,

came over to the bed, and leaned in. Nadine pointed to a picture of three men in handcuffs. "These guys, they shot twelve little boys. That's why I was in Mexico, looking for them. They were drug traffickers, like I thought. Cleaning up their boy smugglers." She scanned the story. "Kit's a stringer. He must have followed up with my contacts. Goddamn it."

"Nadine," said Hank, "you're lucky you made it home."

"Home," said Nadine, bitterly. "Kit Henderson got the front page."

"The front page," said Hank. "That's what it's all about?"

"Now you're a therapist?"

"No," said Hank. "I'm a generalist."

"Teach me about football," said Nadine. She folded the paper and put it in the trash.

"Well, to begin with, that's the tight end," said Hank.

"You're telling me," said Nadine.

Five

"**P**lease," said Nadine. "I'm going. Send me to Lima. I can get in with the Shining Path." Nadine's hand rested on the newspaper spread across her lap. Her room was filled with papers, and news blared on the television. She had pulled the gingham curtains closed, and she fought to ignore the searing pain between her temples.

"It's a standoff, Nadine," said Ian. "Nobody's coming in or out. And I'm not sending you anywhere until you get your doctor to give the good word. Nadine, honestly. Are you listening?"

"Ian . . . ," said Nadine. She drained her soda and stacked it on top of the other Diet Coke cans on her bedside table.

"We've already sent Clay anyway. By the time it's in the paper, we have someone there. You know that."

"Well where, then? Where do you need someone?" Nadine opened another soda.

"Where do we need a nutcase with a broken wrist?" said Ian. "We'll talk next year, okay? I've got to run."

"Next year?"

"It's Christmas," said Ian. "It's Kwanzaa. Hanukkah. The holiday season. Kiss someone under the mistletoe. Recover, Nadine. I'll be in touch."

"You can't—" said Nadine.

"Happy holidays," said Ian.

Tucking the phone under her chin, Nadine clamped a cigarette between her lips and lit it with her right hand. She swallowed, and decided to play her final card. "How about sending me back to

South Africa? When I took the Mexico City job, you made me a promise." She tapped her cigarette on the scallop shell she was using as an ashtray.

"And I intend to keep it. I know your heart's in Cape Town, Nadine, but you're not strong enough to go anywhere yet."

"My heart? Ian, please."

"Do you have any idea how much you talk about it?" said Ian.

Nadine laughed, blowing smoke. "What?"

"Will Mandela bring peace to South Africa, what about the townships, the Truth and Reconciliation Commission . . . and on and on."

"Really?"

"Everyone has a story that sticks in their craw," said Ian.

There was silence, and then Nadine said, "But seriously, Ian? I need to get back to work."

"Dear?" Gwen's voice was tentative from the hallway.

"One second!" said Nadine.

Ian's tone was kind. "Talk soon, Nadine."

"But—"

"Good-bye," said Ian.

"Wait," said Nadine, but Ian had hung up.

"Nadine?" said Gwen.

"Come in."

"Are you still on the phone?" said Gwen, opening the door. She came into view wearing a sweatshirt with a reindeer appliqué. In her ears were tiny ornaments, and she held an old shoe box.

"No," said Nadine. "I'll pay you back for the long distance," she added.

"Don't worry about that, dear," said Gwen. "How are you feeling?"

"I'm fine."

"I brought you something," said Gwen.

"For the love of God," said Nadine. "Please, no more cross-word puzzles."

"Well," said Gwen. She stood in the doorway for a moment, and then she said, "There's no need to be nasty."

"I know," said Nadine. "I don't mean to be. It's just . . . Gwen, I don't need mothering. I'm happy for you and my dad, and I'm just ready to get back to Mexico."

"Speaking of lovebirds . . . ," said Gwen, settling on the corner of Nadine's bed, tracing a circle on the coverlet.

"Hm?" Nadine put down *The New York Times* and opened the *Boston Tribune*.

"What about you settling down? Getting married? Babies?"

"Don't think babies are in the cards for me."

"You still have time," said Gwen. "Well, a little."

"I guess I'm missing the mommy gene," said Nadine.

"You're so pretty," said Gwen. "And you have lovely panties. Are they French? You could get a man, Nadine."

"I don't want a man," said Nadine. "I want to get back to work."

"What about that nice Dr. Duarte?" said Gwen. "Everyone has a past, you can't fault him for that."

"What?"

"Poor Dr. Duarte," said Gwen, leaning in. "I really shouldn't gossip."

Nadine was silent.

"Okay," said Gwen. "Twist my arm. His wife ran off with a Greek man she met on a cruise ship!"

"Jesus," said Nadine.

"A Carnival Cruise," said Gwen in wonderment. "Now she lives on Mykonos and has two children. Both Greek. So Dr. Duarte moved here."

"I'm missing something," said Nadine.

"Oh, he used to work in the city. Some terrible emergency room. He worked all day and night." Gwen warmed to her story. "So Maryjane finally convinces him to take a break. They go on a Caribbean cruise. A Carnival Cruise, did I mention?"

"Yes, Gwen, you did."

"So who knows? I heard she met the Greek in the buffet line. I keep telling your father: they have really good food on those cruises. Everybody says so. And things like Tex Mex night, sushi night, what have you."

"I am really tired," said Nadine.

"Tex Mex night with margaritas. He'd like it, don't you think?"

"Gwen," said Nadine, "I'm going to take a nap now."

"Oh." Gwen was quiet for a moment, and then said, "Well, I just had to show you what I found in your daddy's things." She held out the shoe box.

"Sneakers?"

"No, silly," said Gwen. "It's all your articles." She lifted newspaper clippings. "He saved every one," she said.

One of the clippings fell from her hand, and Nadine held it up. It was a story she'd reported from South Africa: EVELINA MALEFANE: MURDERER OR MARTYR? Nadine's stomach clenched.

"That is the most terrifying story," said Gwen. "That little African girl! How could she have killed an American? And a boy from Nantucket, no less."

"Jason Irving," said Nadine.

"Right. What a sicko. Did she get executed? I certainly hope so."

"She's in jail," said Nadine.

"I would have voted for execution, myself," said Gwen.

"She was fifteen," said Nadine.

"A bad apple," said Gwen, standing, "is a bad apple, any way you slice it."

"Actually, she's getting out of jail, if you really want to know," said Nadine.

"Out?" said Gwen, sitting back down.

"The Truth and Reconciliation Commission. TRC, for short."

"You have lost me, Nadine," said Gwen.

"Under apartheid—" Nadine began.

"Oh Lord," said Gwen, holding up her palm to stop Nadine. "What?"

"Well, to be honest, sweetheart," said Gwen, "I'm just not interested in history."

Nadine sighed.

"What? A bunch of people over in Africa killed each other. I mean, what can you do?" She lifted her hands, a gesture of helplessness. "Anyhoo, I just wanted you to know about this shoe box. Your daddy's cut out every article you've ever written. He cares, Nadine, is what I'm saying."

"Evelina's appearing before the TRC," said Nadine. "She could be given amnesty."

"You're like an onion," said Gwen. "Lots of layers. I mean that."

"Okay," said Nadine.

"An onion," said Gwen. "Seems all rough, but then it's tender underneath. Makes you cry. Best when softened up a little . . ."

"I get the picture," said Nadine.

"Anyhoo," said Gwen, "I'm real glad we had this little chat."

When she was alone, Nadine stared at the article, which she had written almost ten years before.

Six

■

The summer she flew from JFK to Cape Town International Airport, Nadine was twenty-five, her hair in a long braid down her back. On her face, Nadine wore only sunscreen and ChapStick, and she was often mistaken for a student. But the lines in her forehead and the coldness in her eyes, her angry cynicism, betrayed her experience. By twenty-five, Nadine had been to Bhopal, India, where she had seen and reported on hundreds of dead bodies, victims of a slow, lethal leak in a Liberty Union methyl-isocyanate plant. She had comforted dying children in an emergency feeding center on the edge of Ethiopia's Danakil Desert, filing detailed accounts for the *Boston Tribune*. Her articles about the torture wrought in Haiti by the Tonton Macoutes won her a five-hundred-dollar award, which she put toward credit card bills. She didn't shy away from the gruesome details. In fact, as her *Tribune* editor, Eugenia, said, Nadine was "hot for gore."

Nadine was ready to stare the worst in the face. But a steady paycheck still eluded her. It was part of the job: stringers paid their own way, hoping to sell enough stories to cover plane tickets, hotels (or crummy apartments), meals. Sometimes Nadine was forced to share a room with a more established reporter. Eugenia often bought Nadine's stories, but Nadine dreamed of a steady position. Or the ultimate prize: paid expenses.

Eugenia called Nadine first when something unimaginable happened in a far corner of the world. "I don't know how she handles it," Nadine once overheard Eugenia telling another editor, "but she handles it. For now, anyway." Eugenia had a foul mouth and a nose for ratings. "Nadine, babe," she'd say, "I'm FedExing tickets to Haiti. Can you smell the blood?"

In Port-au-Prince, Nadine met Padget Thompson, the bureau chief for *The New York Times.* One night, as they drank whiskey at the Hotel Oloffson, Padget fixed her with a stare. "May I give you some advice, my dear?" he said.

"Of course," said Nadine. She sipped her drink quickly, trying to pry her mind away from the boy she had seen that morning, killed in a voodoo ceremony.

"Your work is shocking. It's fresh and energetic."

"Thanks," mumbled Nadine.

"But there will come a day when shocking people will grow tiresome. You'll want to teach, to change things."

"I'm hardly a tabloid reporter."

"Oh?" said Padget. He ran a hand over thinning hair. "I don't have a daughter," he said. "Indulge me my fatherly tendencies."

Nadine sighed, but revolved her hand to say *go on.*

"What you do is good. You rush in, detail the facts. You're courageous. But to get better, to become a great reporter, you're going to have to learn what it is you're doing. You need to take it apart and put it back together with thought. You need to go to graduate school, and then stay in one place for a while. Your work needs perspective. Yes, horrible things are happening, and thank you for telling us. But *why,* Nadine? And what can we do about it?"

Nadine ordered another drink. She was quiet.

"For example," said Padget. "When Duvalier flees the country, which he will, what's going to happen? He's a vicious asshole, yes. But who's going to replace him? And what will become of Haiti then?"

Nadine looked up. "Whatever comes," she said, "it will be better than Baby Doc."

"Are you sure?" said Padget. "In '57, Baby Doc was the great hope."

Nadine sipped her drink. "I never . . . ," she said. "I guess I hadn't thought."

"Thanks for listening," said Padget. "Just a few words from an old man."

"You're not old," said Nadine.

"Got to pass the torch sometime."

In the morning, Nadine called the NYU School of Journalism, Padget's alma mater.

Nadine studied writing, photography, and history at NYU. One of her professors was South African, and she urged Nadine to head to Johannesburg or Cape Town for the summer. "I'd give my arm to go back," said Renata. "The Young Lions are changing the world. They're braver—and dumber—than we were."

Nelson Mandela's struggle for a nonviolent takeover had come to nothing, Renata explained. Mandela was in prison, and many of his ardent supporters—including Renata, a white journalist who had questioned the mysterious deaths of jailed activists—were dead, missing, or exiled. Black youth, born and bred in the townships that surrounded South Africa's cities, stripped of rights, material pleasures, and education, had grown up angry. "Their parents were too scared to fight. They had jobs, and they didn't want to lose them," said Renata. "But these kids? They've got nothing. They don't have one thing to lose."

They called themselves the Young Lions, and they were coming of age, embracing violence as a way to take back their county, which had been ruled by whites since 1948. South Africa was going to ignite, Renata said, "like a fucking bomb.

"For God's sake, they just beat that American boy to death for being in the wrong place at the wrong time."

"I don't get it," said Nadine. "I mean, why did they kill him? How could that help anything?"

"It's the mind-set," said Renata. "These kids feel like violence is the only way. Maybe they're right. If they kill people, blow things up, the government will have to take notice. Everyone will stop ignoring apartheid. Jason Irving's face was on the front page of every paper in the world."

"But Jason Irving was American. He was teaching in the townships—"

"This isn't subtle, Nadine. It's not about thinking actions through. If you see a white person, kill them. If you announce a strike—nobody go to work for the white man—and some people take the train to work, blow up the train. It's cut-and-dried, desperate. The kids who killed Jason, they had just left a rally. They'd been told to kill. One settler equals one bullet. A simple equation, in a country where there's no room for nuance."

"It's insanity," said Nadine.

"It's *news,*" said Renata.

Nadine went to Boston to meet with Eugenia, who was skeptical. "First you ditch me for graduate school," she said disdainfully, lighting a cigarette in her cluttered office, "and now South Africa? I don't know, babe. What about Sudan? Starving orphans, Nadine. Hundreds of 'em. We've got Bill there, but you're better at the misery and death stuff. Hell, Nadine, orphans are your specialty."

"But I know I could do great work in South Africa," said Nadine. "My professor, Renata Jorgensen, she fled the country with her notes on Steve Biko—"

"Spare me," said Eugenia. She touched her springy red curls and then stubbed out her cigarette. "I'll advance you the plane ticket and one month's rent. Find something cheap."

"Thanks, Eugenia. I promise, you'll be glad."

"Yeah, yeah," said Eugenia. "Let's go pig out on pizza."

. . .

From the moment she stepped outside the airport, Nadine was entranced by Cape Town. She loved the way the city wrapped itself around majestic Table Mountain, embracing the peak on three sides and spilling out to Table Bay and the Atlantic Ocean. Sun-drenched vineyards climbed the eastern slopes of the mountain, their picturesque wineries wreathed in oak and pine trees.

Nadine took a rare day to herself, heading south of the city, to the Cape of Good Hope, and hiking out to its craggy point. High above two oceans, she breathed deeply. In the nature reserve, she saw a zebra and ostriches. Small but fierce baboons grabbed at the remains of her picnic lunch.

For the first time on assignment, Nadine looked just like the locals around her: black Cape Townians were not allowed in white areas after dark, and Nadine blended in with the white South Africans as she wandered among the Dutch and British colonial buildings, the cathedrals, shops, and the old slave market, now a shady square lined with upscale restaurants. Only Nadine's American accent gave her away.

Nadine studied guidebooks and maps of the city. A blank section on most maps between the peninsula and the African mainland was designated CAPE FLATS. Nadine knew this bleak place plagued by wind-driven sand was where the city's millions of non-whites lived. She visited District Six, once a thriving mixed-race neighborhood in one of the most beautiful parts of Cape Town. It had been "bleached" by the government, its buildings bulldozed, its residents sent to the Flats. Now it was a wasteland of rubble, plans for its revival mired in red tape.

Nadine stayed at a hostel on raucous Long Street for a week, examining the classified ads in the white edition of the *Cape Argus*. She'd heard there was a "native edition," but no one was selling it on Long Street. Finally, Nadine called the number on an index card tacked to the hallway bulletin board: OBS HOUSE NEEDS ROOMIE. 17 NUTTHALL ROAD. CALL MAXIM AT 448-6363.

She spoke with Maxim, who was short on the phone. "Come see the place," he said in a strong Afrikaans accent. "Then we can talk," he said.

Nadine tried to take a bus to Observatory, but all the buses were labeled NON-WHITES ONLY, and the drivers wouldn't let her on. Finally, she took a taxi to 17 Nutthall Road, a ramshackle house with a sagging front porch. Nadine climbed the steps and pressed the buzzer. Nothing happened. She wiped perspiration from her brow: the southeast wind the guidebooks called "the Cape Doctor" was hot as hell and she was tired. She carried a bulging backpack. Finally, she banged on the door, and it opened. A guy her age stood in front of her, wearing only a towel.

"Uh," said Nadine, "are you Maxim?"

"No, darling," said the guy. "I'm George." He was lean and muscled, his shoulder-length dark hair combed back from his boyish face. Even his accent was charming—almost British, but not quite. Nadine would later learn that he was American: the accent was complete artifice. He held a cigarette. He leaned against the doorjamb and crossed one leg over the other. He watched Nadine, a smirk playing across his face.

"Can I have a cigarette?" she asked.

"That depends," said George.

"On what?"

"Well, who are you?" said George. "And why are you wearing an enormous bag on your shoulders?"

"I'm Nadine Morgan. I'm a journalist, and I need a place to live. I saw the ad and spoke with Maxim."

"Good enough," said George, holding his towel while he turned. "Come in," he called, and Nadine followed him. The floor was cracked linoleum, and the apartment reeked of pot and beer.

"Three bedrooms off the hallway," said George. "Shared bathroom and kitchen. And one common room." The apartment was filled with photographs: chilling scenes of beatings and people lying in the street, dead or dying. Peaceful pictures of rolling South African farmland—Maxim's home, George explained—and a beautiful blonde woman: Maxim's mother. There were photos of dancers. One girl had her head thrown back in ecstasy, her muscled leg kicking high. The power of her body brought her joy, it was clear. Nadine was unnerved to see a similar facial expression in another photograph: a woman in an angry mob, beating a man to his death.

George walked briskly and turned a doorknob. "My love," he called, "can you bring a cigarette for my new roommate?"

"Of course," came a voice from inside the bedroom.

"Um," said Nadine, "is Maxim here?"

"He's at work," said George. "Taking pictures in Cape Flats."

"And you . . ."

"Oh, me," said George, still holding his towel. "I'm waiting tables and writing a novel. It's terrible. I'm also trying to convince this woman to marry me." He extended his arm, and a stunning black woman in a gray dress came into the hallway. Her hair was cut short. Unsmiling, she handed a pack of Marlboros to Nadine. With her perfect posture, she seemed six feet tall, though her lips only reached George's bare shoulder, which she kissed. "Nadine," said George, "this is Tholakele."

"Put on some clothing, George," she said. "It's nice to meet you, Nadine."

"Your wish," said George, touching her hair, "is my command."

"Do you live here as well?" Nadine asked. Tholakele laughed. "I could go to jail for spending the night," she said angrily. "Or for loving that boy."

"Aren't I worth the price?" said George, coming back into the hallway wearing a terry-cloth robe, his hair in a red rubber band at the nape of his neck.

Tholakele rolled her eyes. "I must get back to work," she said.

"Thola is a dancer," said George.

"I am a maid," said Thola.

"And a maid," said George, his face darkening.

"Good-bye, new roommate," said Thola to Nadine, and she walked hand in hand with George to the door, where they kissed chastely. Then Thola opened the door, looking both ways nervously.

"There are men who watch us," said George simply. Nadine was to find that this was not a paranoid delusion: the government employed security police to keep an eye on questionable liaisons.

"Good-bye, Prince Charming," said Thola. She slipped into the warm evening, shutting the door behind her.

In Woods Hole, Massachusetts, Nadine closed her eyes and saw her friend Thola. Perhaps she was alive and well, married to George at last. It was possible.

Seven

Another gloomy day dwindled into brittle night. Nadine watched scientists exit the Marine Biological Laboratory from her hotel window, willing herself to get out of her pajamas, wrap herself into a parka, and walk down Water Street to get the paper. Her father and Gwen had decided it would be best for her mental health to avoid the news. Gwen had taken away her television while she slept, replacing it with a ceramic whale.

"Sweetheart?" said Gwen, rapping on the door.

"I'm asleep," said Nadine.

The door nudged open anyway. "Nadine," said Gwen, "I wanted to see if you'd join us tonight for the Christmas tree lighting at the library."

Nadine sat up.

"You're not asleep," said Gwen accusingly.

"I'm in my nightgown," said Nadine, pointing to Garfield's smiling mouth.

"And it suits you," said Gwen. She nodded, and the holiday bells on her headband jingled.

"Thanks for inviting me," said Nadine. "I appreciate it. But I'm a little tired." She did not add, *I'm a little tired of you trying to make a daughter out of me.*

Gwen pursed her lips and blew air from her nose.

"Gwen, I'm sorry," said Nadine. "I guess I'm just not a holiday person. I'd like to be alone, if you don't mind."

"It's not fair," said Gwen. "She took Christmas right away from you both."

"What?" said Nadine sharply.

"Of course she couldn't help it," said Gwen. "But dying the week before Christmas . . . I cried when Jim told me about your mother."

Nadine bit her tongue.

"And I've been wanting to be a mother to you ever since," continued Gwen. "I never had a baby of my own, but God sent me you, Nadine."

"Please stop," said Nadine.

"She was beautiful," said Gwen. "I've seen the pictures of your mom. That long dark hair, just like yours. And she was smart, all those books."

"I said *please stop,*" said Nadine, raising her voice. She avoided meeting Gwen's eyes, staring out the window instead. It was snowing, fat wet drops. Nadine had not seen snowflakes in a long time.

"This isn't the way I had planned—"

"I'm sorry you had a whole scene laid out for yourself," said Nadine, turning back to Gwen. She tried, and failed, to keep the bitterness from her voice. "A big hug and a brand-new daughter to love. I suppose you wanted me to be in the wedding, right? Maybe wanted to get married on Christmas, make up for my mother's death?"

"Nadine."

"I'm sorry," said Nadine, stopping her tirade with effort. "I just . . . I don't think you have any right—"

"I thought we could go to the tree lighting," said Gwen. "I thought, maybe, eggnog . . ." Her voice trailed off.

"Everyone has a fantasy," said Nadine. "Sorry, Gwen. No offense. Mine doesn't include a new mother. Or eggnog, for that matter."

"We could sit by the fire—"

"Gwen—"

"Nadine," said Gwen. "I'm reaching out. Honey, I'm here."

Nadine was overwhelmed with fury and unhappiness. "You know what," she said, "I've got to go." She pulled her father's overcoat off the floor, awkwardly draped it over her nightgown. She tugged on jeans and took her prescription bottles from the bedside table. With her good hand, she stuffed her backpack and slung it over her shoulder. Gwen watched silently. Then, with little aplomb, Nadine walked out the door.

"Oh, honey," said Gwen, but Nadine was down the stairs already, feeling stronger with each step.

Under a full-moon sky, Nadine walked toward Surf Drive. The wind was painful on her face and her wrist ached. Cold burrowed inside her coat, chilling Nadine to the bone. After about fifteen minutes, she saw the familiar outline of her childhood home.

The house had been built for a whaling captain, and had a turret with dizzying views of the sea. Jim and Ann had bought it in complete disrepair as newlyweds, spent every weekend working on the foundation, the floors, the nursery.

Ann died when Nadine was six, but Jim and Nadine stayed put. The house was miserably quiet without Ann's noisy cooking, the records of Broadway shows she'd played day and night. Ann had filled the freezer with home-cooked dinners when she still felt well, but they eventually ran out. On the night they ate the last dinner, a turkey potpie, Jim finished his meal and then stood. "Going to have to work late from now on," he said, his eyes red and his voice unsteady.

"Can we play Chutes and Ladders?" Nadine asked.

"Hannah's going to stay and have dinner with you," said Jim. "She'll put you to bed, et cetera." Hannah was the first nanny, a young Irish woman who gazed at Nadine and said "You poor wee one" all the time.

"Daddy," said Nadine, "can we play Chutes and Ladders?"

"One round," said Jim, "then it's the bathtub for you."

Jim and Nadine rarely ate together on weeknights after that potpie. Hannah was followed by Hillary, Clare, and then Laura. Sometimes Nadine heard her father come home after she had gone to bed. He would open a can of beer—Nadine could hear the pop of the tab—and sit in front of the television. Many mornings, Nadine found him asleep in his easy chair, still dressed. She would climb into his lap, and he would let himself hold her. She rested her head on his shoulder and made her hair spread across his face. He breathed deeply, and Nadine knew that he still loved her, though when he woke, he pushed her away, saying, "Off me now, monkey."

Nadine loved Sunday, when Jim brought her to dinner at The Captain Kidd. They walked into town and ate scallops by the fireplace or at a table overlooking Eel Pond. The walks from their house to town were Nadine's favorite times. Jim would ask her about her homework, offer suggestions. All week, she thought of funny stories to tell him. And when the sidewalk narrowed, he took her hand.

Nadine stood in front of the house for a moment, then drew a breath and walked across the lawn, her boots making footprints in the snow. She treaded gingerly up the front steps, felt the icy doorknob. She tried the handle: the house was locked. Now that Jim had found Gwen, 310 Surf Drive was empty. Gwen had tried to convince Jim to sell it, she told Nadine, but he had resisted, saying he wanted to wait for the market to pick up.

Snow crunched as Nadine made her way to the back sliding

glass door. As always, it was unlocked. Nadine flipped the light and looked around the kitchen. The fireplace was clean, the cabinets empty. She moved through the high-ceilinged dining room to the staircase. The house smelled familiar, a faded fragrance of talcum powder and wood smoke.

In the second-floor foyer, Nadine fumbled in the dark for the cord that would bring down the steps. She found it and yanked. The ceiling door protested with a rusty groan. Nadine climbed the steps to the turret.

The circular room was lit with a soft glow. This had once been the place where a woman would sit and watch the horizon for her husband's—or son's—ship to sail home after years at sea. As a child, Nadine dreamed of being the one on a boat, heading toward adventure and away from her lonely house.

She sat in the rocking chair by the bookcase, where Ann had loved to spend evenings reading. Outside the window, waves crashed to shore. Nadine knelt on the floor and ran her fingers over her mother's books until she came to *The Lying Days* by Nadine Gordimer. On the back of the book was a picture of an elegant woman with gold hoop earrings and twinkling eyes. Ann had named Nadine for the author of her favorite book, a story of a South African girl trying to find her place in the world.

The book was scribbled in, a few pages folded down. Nadine opened it. On page 366, her mother had underlined, "I'm so happy where I am." Nadine was surprised to find, when she read the book herself, that the narrator speaks this line on the eve of her departure to Europe. The narrator accepts "disillusion as a beginning rather than an end: the last and most enduring illusion." But Ann had not underlined that realization.

"I guess I won't get to see the whole world," Ann had said in the hospital, her violet eyes luminous in her sunken face. "But you'll see it for me, won't you? Send postcards to me in heaven." Nadine accompanied her mother to all the chemotherapy treatments, and grew to hate the chicken soup stench of the hospital, the sickly people, the useless fight against death.

"Is Mommy going to be okay?" Nadine asked her father the last, long night.

"Don't ask questions," said Jim hoarsely, "and I won't have to lie to you."

Nadine rubbed her tender wrist. She heard footsteps coming up the turret stairs, and dropped the book. A voice rose: "Nadine?" It was Lily, walking up with effort. When she appeared, she smiled. "I knew it," she said.

"Hey," said Nadine.

"Your dad called me," said Lily. "He thought I might know where to find you."

Nadine shoved the book back in its place, but Lily sat down heavily on the floor and said, "Nadine Gordimer?"

"Don't make fun of me," said Nadine.

"I'm not," said Lily. "It's freezing."

Nadine sighed. "Fucking Gwen," she said.

"She's all right," said Lily.

"Please," said Nadine. "Have you seen the holiday outfits?"

"She means well," said Lily.

"I just don't belong here," said Nadine. "I never have."

"I'm here, though," said Lily.

Nadine put her head on Lily's shoulder. When Lily reached for her hand, their fingers laced together. They sat in silence, watching Vineyard Sound.

Eight

Nadine spent a sleepless night on Lily's couch. Dennis, flushed from cans of Budweiser, had sat with his giant hands covering his knees and told Nadine which septic systems in town his company had installed. "And underneath the coffee shop?" he said. "Wait till you hear this, Nadine."

One baby or another screamed all night long. By morning, Nadine was on the edge of a nervous breakdown. In a bathroom covered with celebrity magazines and plastic bath toys, she combed her hair with her fingers and tried to make a plan. She had to get back to her quiet apartment in Mexico City. Bo burst in and screamed, "Nadine going peep in the potty!"

"I'm going to need some time by myself," said Nadine. "Okay, honey?"

"Nadine going poop in the potty!" cried Bo, bouncing on the balls of his feet.

Without thinking, Nadine tried to push the door closed, but Bo's fingers were in the way. He looked at his hand, stunned, and then began to wail.

"Oh, shit," said Nadine. "I'm really sorry, Bo. Can this be a secret?"

Lily came upstairs, carrying a basket of clean laundry. She looked at Nadine quizzically, then put down the laundry and gathered Bo in her arms. Bo sobbed, "Nadine go peep in the potty! Nadine hurt me!"

Nadine stood and pulled up her pants. "Time for me to head on out," she said.

. . .

"Sorry," said Hank, as Nadine sat on an examining table in a borrowed T-shirt and jeans. "Did I hear you correctly? You want money for a bus ticket?"

"I need to get to Logan," said Nadine, "and they don't take credit cards at the bus station."

Hank crossed his arms and leaned back against a counter lined with glass bottles of tongue depressors and Q-tips.

"Anyone going to meet you at the airport?" he asked.

"Sure, yes. I don't need to remind you, Hank, but I am an adult."

"I don't need to remind you, Nadine, but I don't have to give you bus fare."

"Fine," said Nadine, sliding off the table. She turned and banged her left arm, sending pain shooting to her wrist. Nadine gritted her teeth.

"I have a house on Nantucket," said Hank. "I'm headed there for the holidays. Why don't you join me?"

"Thank you," said Nadine. "That's nice. I'm fine, though. I just need to get back to Mexico City." She tried to catch her breath and ignore the dizziness, the dark patches at the edges of her vision.

"I love to cook," said Hank, "and there's a bar with good burgers downtown. I can push you there in my wheelbarrow."

Nadine tried to smile, and shook her head.

"You won't make it to Mexico City," said Hank. "Nadine, you're still on some strong painkillers, and your body has undergone a serious trauma. You'll pass out at the bus station."

"I have friends who can help me." Nadine wasn't sure this was true, and the room did look fuzzy. *Oh hell,* she thought. She envisioned the long security line at the airport. She thought about her empty apartment, the meaningless flirtations with the fact checker next door. She wanted so desperately to get back to work, but she couldn't travel, not like this. She had to sit down, just for a little while.

"Okay," said Hank. "Thought I'd give it a shot. It's lonely out there. You take care, Nadine. Have a great holiday."

"All right," said Nadine. "All right, fine."

"Let me help you to the door," said Hank. "Do you want to take your records, or should we fax them to your doctor in Mexico?"

"I said fine," said Nadine.

"What?"

"Let's go," said Nadine. "I don't . . . I said, okay. Let's go to Nantucket. But I'll need . . . I need some clothes."

"They have clothes on Nantucket," said Hank.

"I shudder to think," said Nadine.

"You're my second-to-last appointment. I was planning on catching the four PM ferry."

"I'll be in your lobby," said Nadine.

The receptionist did not appear to notice as Nadine sat down in an orange plastic chair and paged through the *Cape Cod Times*. She finished the paper, three old *People* magazines, and one *Travel + Leisure* before Hank appeared.

Nine

Sun shone on the water as the ferry moved out of Hyannis Harbor and past expensive gray homes. Next to Nadine and Hank, an old woman petted her dog. The dog's collar was printed with tiny lobsters.

"Look," said Nadine, "a yacht." She pointed. It was a lovely boat, its sails bound in blue cloth. "Or I guess you'd call that a sailboat."

"Definitely a sailboat," said Hank. "Didn't you grow up here?"

"Sort of," said Nadine.

"What does that mean?"

"I don't remember it much," said Nadine. "My life started after I left."

"Coffee?" said Hank.

"Great."

Nadine watched his red T-shirt as he walked away. The shirt had an ice cream cone on the back. His jeans were faded, and his hiking boots looked well worn. Hank's thick black curls needed a trim.

The ferry rocked slowly. Hank returned a few minutes later, balancing a cardboard tray of coffees in one hand. "Cream and sugar?" he said.

"Neither," said Nadine.

"I figured," said Hank, handing her a paper cup.

"At what point does a sailboat become a yacht?" said Nadine.

"Hm," said Hank. "Fifteen feet? Twenty?"

"Oh," said Nadine. "Well, you learn something every day."

"Do you?"

Nadine sipped her coffee. "You know," she said, "I do."

"I envy you, then."

"I love my job," said Nadine.

"Yes," said Hank, "you've said that."

"Why do you sound as if you don't believe me?"

"I used to work in an emergency room in Boston," said Hank. "At first, it was great. You know, it was what I was trained to do. Someone ODs, or comes in with a broken leg, I know how to handle it. At work, I was happy. I guess it was somewhat like you said. I felt alive. But I couldn't . . . I couldn't switch it off. I mean, you walk out the door, you know, you walk outside, but those patients are still . . . you're supposed to go on home, have a beer, relax. I'd take the T, twenty minutes, and then my wife would be opening the door, wanting to go see a movie or talk about new paint for the living room . . . it was strange. It got to me. I felt as if I couldn't stop, not for a minute. I didn't like who I turned into. I didn't like who I was, outside the ER."

"I could stop," said Nadine.

"Okay," said Hank.

A man began to spray bright yellow cleanser on the ferry window, wiping it afterward with a thin blade. He wore a jacket that read STEAMSHIP AUTHORITY. There were two patches on his jacket: an American flag, and his name, JEFF. Jeff was sweaty and had a pimple in the center of his forehead. He sprayed the cleanser and wiped it away.

"Gwen told me your wife, um," said Nadine.

The old woman began patting her dog and talking to it. "We had a wonderful morning, didn't we?" she said. "You saw your friend Austin, didn't you?" The dog, like Hank, did not respond.

"Gwen told me your wife, well, went on a Carnival Cruise ship . . . this can't be true . . ."

"No," said Hank, "it is true. We went on the cruise together. It was a theme cruise."

"I don't want to ask," said Nadine.

" 'Bring Back the Zing,' " said Hank, staring at Jeff, who sprayed and wiped.

"Pardon?" said Nadine. "The zing?"

"You heard me," said Hank. "It was for couples. 'Bring Back the Zing.' It was my idea."

"Oh, Hank," said Nadine.

"I'd been working around the clock. I knew Maryjane was unhappy. I thought that maybe if I got far enough away, I could shut off. I could . . . talk about her, pay attention to her." He rubbed his forehead with his fingers. "I got us tickets on 'Bring Back the Zing.' We were supposed to make love from Miami to Bermuda."

"But Gwen said . . . and again, this cannot be true—"

"Oh it's true," said Hank. "Hercules Kalapoulou."

"Hercules?"

"You might ask yourself, as I did, why a divorced Greek businessman booked a room on 'Bring Back the Zing.' But Maryjane didn't ask any questions. When the cruise was over, so was our marriage."

"I don't know what to say," said Nadine.

"I went back to the ER for a year, and then decided I wanted a quieter life. A small community. I guess I wanted a home. Falmouth needed a generalist. And that's the story."

Nadine shook her head. "Wow."

Hank nodded. "I suppose I can see the humor in it now," he said, one side of his mouth turning up. He continued to look out the window. Nadine couldn't tell if he was seeing Jeff or the water beyond Jeff. The glass did not look any clearer.

"I've never been on a cruise," said Nadine.

"So I sold my place in Falmouth after a year," Hank said, forging ahead. "I rent a condo now. And I bought the house on Nantucket. It has a fireplace. I love it out here."

"You love Nantucket, too, Marlo," said the woman next to them. She was talking to her dog again. "Don't you, Marlo? Don't you love Nantucket?"

A man with red hair walked by. There was a comb in his back pocket. "Aren't you a good boy?" said the woman, scratching her dog's belly. "Aren't you a good, good boy?"

"So that's my saga," said Hank. "What's yours?"

"Oh, you know," said Nadine.

"No," said Hank. "I don't."

"Well," said Nadine, "what have you heard?"

"Jim Morgan's daughter," said Hank, sitting back in his seat. "Difficult as a kid. Crazy in high school. Always looking for trouble. Ran away with a guy who came through town on a Harley-Davidson. Called her dad from Sturgis, wanting money to come home."

Nadine smiled. She had met Sammy after the Senior Dinner Dance, which had been held on a spring Saturday night under a tent overlooking Old Silver Beach. Tiny white lights twinkled along the edge of the canvas fabric, and the temperature was a perfect seventy-five degrees. The strains of "Wonderful Tonight" played as Nadine's date, Liam Baker, spun her too fast. Over his shoulder, Nadine saw a girl she barely knew crying by the punch bowl. She saw Lily dancing with Dennis, trying to look happy as Dennis, too drunk, staggered around the parquet floor.

"This is perfect," whispered Liam in Nadine's ear. Poor Liam, who thought they would get married and stay on Cape Cod forever. Suddenly Nadine couldn't bear it: Liam's overpowering cologne, the crying girl, Lily pretending so fiercely. The sun set, an orange orb, and the gap between the reality of imminent heartbreak all around her and the cheery illusion of a perfect summer night was too wide for Nadine to straddle. She twisted free of Liam's embrace and ran. She ran until her legs wore out, and then she sat on the back porch of someone's empty summer house and watched the stars. She fell asleep on a teak lounge chair.

In the morning, walking home, she saw Sammy parked by the side of the road, smoking a cigarette. He was short and ugly. He was real. When he offered to take her for a ride, she accepted. As they sped around the Sagamore Rotary and then over the bridge toward freedom, Nadine pressed her cheek to his leather jacket and held on tight.

"Oh my God," said Nadine. "Hank, who have you been talking to?"

"Wrote about the biker underworld for the school newspaper. Wins some contest—"

"The Young Writers' Fellowship," murmured Nadine.

"Heads to Cambridge, never looks back. Turns out she's not just crazy, but brilliant."

Nadine smiled and looked at Hank. "I hang out at The Captain Kidd," said Hank. "Jan the bartender went to school with you."

"Jan Hallnet."

"Yes."

Nadine looked down. "Did he tell you about my mother?"

Hank didn't answer. An older man wandered by, leading a sheepdog on a leather leash. The sheepdog stopped next to Marlo. "Who's this?" said the man.

"This is Marlo," said the woman.

"This is Roady," said the man. The dogs sniffed each other.

"So," said the man, "how old is Marlo?"

"We don't know," said the woman. "My daughter rescued him from a farm. They were going to shoot him. He ate the eggs and scared the chickens. Maybe around eleven. But he acts like a little puppy."

"Roady here is five," said the man. "I got him from a breeder in Wellesley."

"Don't you?" said the woman. "Don't you act just like a little puppy?"

Hank moved close to Nadine. She could smell him, and it was a comforting smell, like butter, like gingerbread. "No," said Hank finally. "Jan didn't tell me about your mother."

"Oh," said Nadine. A woman made her way to the bathroom, sipping from a bottle of beer. Jeff moved to another window. The sun broke through a bank of clouds and spilled across the waves. Nadine leaned over and kissed Hank. He kissed her back.

"Hey, hey," said the man with the dog. "What have we here? Somebody falling in love right here on the slow ferry?"

Ten

I t was dark by the time they pulled into Nantucket Harbor. From the outdoor deck, Nadine and Hank watched the island come into view: the row of neat houses with windows lit, cargo trucks lining up, readying for the shipments of food and fuel. The wind was fierce, and when Hank put his hands in his pockets Nadine slid her right hand inside the warm wool of his coat, entwining her fingers with his. Hank looked at her and smiled.

"We can grab a burger in town," he said, "and then take a cab to the house. I've got an old Volvo there. Hope it starts."

"Great," said Nadine.

"Or there's the Straight Wharf. A little snazzier. Candlelight, et cetera."

"No," said Nadine, "a burger's fine."

They lined up above the metal staircase leading off the ferry. Pink-faced passengers wrapped in mink and North Face parkas stood elbow-to-elbow with heavyset women gossiping in Jamaican patois. At the ferry dock, construction workers waited for the last ship out, empty lunchboxes in hand. Nadine and Hank strolled across the gangway, then past a lively taco stand and a bicycle rental shop, closed for the day.

"Come," said Hank, leading her by a basket museum and a whaling museum, then into town, where the streets were made of cobbled stone and holiday lights twinkled from every lamppost. "How are you feeling?"

"I'm okay," said Nadine, though she felt completely dislocated, even anxious. "This is beautiful. Really. I guess I thought the streets were paved with gold."

Hank laughed. "Quaint isn't cheap," he said.

On Broad Street, after a store specializing in French cookware, Hank stopped. "Here we are," he said. "The Brotherhood of Thieves." He opened the door to a warm underground restaurant. "This was a hangout for whalers back in 1840." In the dim space, a fire blazed and people sat around wooden tables. "Two for dinner," Hank said to the teenager in a polo sweater and cargo pants who stood behind a wooden reservation stand. The boy's overgrown hair and burgeoning beard testified to his decision to stay on-island for the winter.

"Forty-five minitos," said the boy. "Maybe an hour."

"How about a drink?" said Hank, inclining his head toward a bar where men in knit hats and baseball caps watched television intently.

"Sure," said Nadine. She took a few steps, then said, "You know, I'm going to go get some fresh air, actually."

"What?" said Hank. "Are you okay?"

"Just some air," said Nadine, as she rushed past the host and to the door. Awkwardly, she yanked it open and the cold wind hit her. She started to walk. Something about the dark space, the rumble of voices, the tinny sound of the television. She turned a corner and saw a church, sat down on the steps. Underneath her jeans, the stone was cold. Nadine felt her temples throb. It was something about the fire, the smell of meat. Memories rushed forward, vivid and painful.

During her summer in Cape Town, Nadine often drove from her manicured neighborhood to Sunshine township. With her housemates and fellow reporters, she drank beer at a bar called the Waterfront, listening to the Moonlights and JC Cool on the jukebox. Some nights, the tinny sound of soccer games won out over the music.

Nadine was working on a piece about the parents of boys who had run away from home to join the Mandela United Football Club. The "club" was really a gang that roamed the township streets, using fear and brutality to stamp out resistance to the anti-apartheid cause. Rumors had begun to spread about Winnie Mandela, the wife of jailed leader Nelson Mandela who would later be released and elected president of South Africa. Winnie, it was said, was housing young men in her mansion. The men called her "Mommy" and carried out any orders she gave, no matter how illogical or violent. Nadine was having a hard time finding people willing to speak out against the Football Club, and finding proof of Winnie's involvement was simply impossible.

Still, Nadine loved talking to her subjects for hours, drinking tea and picking the locks of their minds. She was always amazed at how much people would tell her, a stranger, even as she held a pen in her hand. They seemed so eager to be seen, to be recognized. But Nadine had to listen carefully for the narrative beneath the façades they constructed for themselves.

Sometimes Nadine felt interviewees pulling back from her, as if they thought she could not understand their reality, or might judge them. She used her own secrets then, handing over personal tidbits like bargaining chips, creating a sense of intimacy that almost always led subjects to reveal deeper truths about themselves.

Nadine relished the drive home with pages of scrawled notes. She would pour a glass of wine, play some jazz, and type on her antique Olivetti—she had bought it in a Station Street pawnshop—finding the arc of the story in the process. The hiss of the fax machine, the thrill of snapping open a paper to see her name, the way people lit up when they realized she had written an article they had read and thought about: Nadine loved it all.

But then there was the night they heard gunfire outside the Waterfront. A large bottle of Castle beer in front of her, the lights in the bar going dark, the music stopping abruptly. There were shots, and then screams. Around her, the murmur of voices speaking in Xhosa.

Nadine didn't have to go outside. Her work was slow and cunning. But the photographers stood in the dark, wrapped their cameras around their necks, and raced toward the action. Nadine sat in the warm *shebeen,* her hands pressed to her eyes. The gunfire stopped, and there was an eerie silence from the garbage-strewn streets. Something made her stand up, leave the bar. Notebook tucked in the pocket of her shorts, she ran outside, cutting through dirt alleys. And then the gunfire started again.

It hadn't been a premonition that had made her run outside. It had been the silence. Now, on an island far from war, she was enveloped by terror.

"Nadine?" Hank sat next to her on the church step. He looked concerned as he bent down to see her face.

"My head," said Nadine. Her hands were shaking. "I don't know," she said. "I'm sorry, I'm just feeling . . ."

"Continuing headaches are completely normal after head trauma," said Hank. "Maybe this trip was too much for you."

"No," said Nadine. "I'm fine. Just some air, you know?" She looked into Hank's eyes, and watched him decide whether or not to believe her.

"How about a burger?" she said, her voice controlled.

"There's soup at my house," said Hank.

"Really," said Nadine. "I'm fine. Maybe I just need some food." He nodded warily. She smiled, and took his arm as they walked back to the restaurant, wrapping around him tightly. She did not think of Maxim, the way his lips had felt on her skin. She did not think about returning to Nutthall Road the next day, staring at Maxim's clothes abandoned on the floor.

Eleven

∎

For four days, Nadine woke early in Hank's guest bedroom. The winter sun streamed through the panes of the upstairs windows; even when Nadine closed the white shutters, the light worked its way underneath her eyelids. Besides the hissing of the steam heat, the house was utterly quiet. Nadine's dreams—which had always been blissfully blank—were filled with images like shrapnel: the clay Madonna on a sick child's bedside table, the knot of skin where a Haitian boy's ear had been. Ann's wedding ring, nestled amid Jim's spare change in a glass dish on his dresser in the Surf Drive house.

In her pajamas, Nadine made coffee and drank it in on the front porch, looking over the large yard, which led to a dirt road and then the beach. The yard was made for dogs and children, thought Nadine, but there was only Hank and his fragile patient, drinking coffee, wrapped in a scratchy red blanket. By the front door was a row of fishing rods and a green plastic tackle box.

In the afternoons, they would read in the living room. They had visited Nantucket Bookworks and bought each other books for Christmas. Hank was working through *War and Peace* and Nadine was revisiting *Cry the Beloved Country.* They sat at opposite ends of the couch, propped up by pillows. Once in a while, Hank would read a sentence to Nadine, or she would look up to find him focused on her, not his reading.

"What?" she said once, catching him staring.

"Oh," said Hank, "I just hit a boring part. You thought I was gazing at you?"

"No," said Nadine, smiling.

"Good," said Hank.

After a lunch of cheese, sliced apples, and bread, they shopped in town and then sat on the beach. They told each other ribbons of stories: Nadine's summer in South Africa, Hank's mother in Florida, who was growing forgetful, the young girl he'd just diagnosed with diabetes. "That must have been tough," said Nadine, when he described telling the girl's parents.

"She's fine," said Hank. "Diabetes is a cakewalk compared with the worst things." Nadine wanted to ask about the worst things, but stopped herself: she didn't need nightmares about pediatric health disasters. Instead, she changed the subject.

"I had a boyfriend once with diabetes," she said. "Cameron. He was from Vermont."

"Cameron," said Hank.

"Yeah," said Nadine. "I loved his family. I loved his house. His parents built it themselves." Nadine had met Cameron her freshman year at Harvard. He was tall, with brown hair and green eyes. He had to give himself an insulin shot before every meal, taking the bottle from a mini fridge in the corner of his dorm room. He taught Nadine how to give him the shot, and he taught her about writing music, his passion. They went to jazz shows in the city, Cameron's fingers tapping the beat on Nadine's knee.

He brought her to Vermont for Thanksgiving. Cameron's house, filled with skis and musical instruments, was never quiet. He had five siblings, and none sat still. Something was always cooking—bread, apple pie, vegetarian lasagna—and someone was always telling a story or practicing an instrument. Nadine threw away a bread bag, and Cameron's mother, who wore fleece tops and athletic pants, fished it out of the garbage. "We can use this again," she said kindly, her hand warm on Nadine's shoulder.

Cameron's home could not have been more different from Nadine's. Jim never saved a bread bag to refill with a homemade loaf, or cooked at all, for that matter. Nobody ever trailed through Nadine's house wearing a wet suit and flipper fins, the way Cameron's brother Horace did after swimming in the nearby pond. Even when the whole family was finally assembled at the table for tofurkey Thanksgiving dinner, Cameron's house buzzed with noise: clattering plates, scraping chairs, booming classical music. Nadine held the butter dish, which Cameron's mother had made and painted with butterflies. She soaked in the noise of a happy family, and thought, *It is possible. I could have this.*

"What was it like?" said Hank. "The house Cameron's parents built?"

Even after Cameron dumped Nadine for a willowy oboe player, she thought of his family: a table of loud people who belonged together. She looked at Hank. "It was wonderful," she said.

Nadine tried on clothes at the Lilly Pulitzer store, refusing to even exit the dressing room in the bright outfits. Finally, she found a store she liked, and charged jeans, slim black pants, leather boots, and two sweaters—more clothes than she'd bought in years.

Hank made elaborate dinners, which they ate in front of the fire: clams and linguine, lobster Diablo, steaks on the grill for Christmas. While he cooked, Nadine sat at the kitchen table and watched. "Where did you learn how to cook?" she asked.

"Maryjane could have been a chef," said Hank. "When we broke up, I couldn't peel a garlic clove. In fact, I had lost every skill she had—remembering people's names, keeping up with Christmas cards, knowing where to hang a picture. One day I was in the grocery store, throwing ginger ale in the cart, and I stopped and asked myself, *Do I even like ginger ale?* Learning how to cook was a way of making my own life. I took lessons, actually, at Cape Cod Community College."

"Do you?" said Nadine.

"Do I what?"

"Like ginger ale?"

"You know," said Hank, "I prefer Pepsi."

That night, Nadine dreamed of dinner at her favorite restaurant in Mexico City. It was a small, neighborhood spot called Alejandro's. Alejandro's wife, a slight woman named Marguerite, made a chicken dish with a rich sauce from her native Oaxaca. The sauce was called *mole,* and Nadine loved it so much she decided to feature Marguerite in an article. She arrived at Alejandro's with her notebook and convinced Marguerite to take her into the kitchen. The resulting story was a huge success, and Nadine committed the *mole* recipe to memory.

In the morning, Nadine decided to make *mole* for Hank. She presented him with a list of twenty-six ingredients and told him dinner would be late and fabulous, just the way it was at Alejandro's. Hank stared at the list. "Chocolate?" he said. "I thought you were making chicken."

"It's a sauce with chocolate and chiles," said Nadine. "You're going to love it. Might as well get some sipping tequila, too."

"Nadine," said Hank, sinking into a kitchen chair, "You think the Nantucket Stop & Shop is going to have—" He paused, counting, and then continued. "—five kinds of chiles? I'll be lucky if I can get tortillas."

"Right," said Nadine, sitting down next to him. "Well, do your best."

Nadine cooked all day, and around nine PM they ate. "Spicy," said Hank appreciatively.

"That would be the Ortega taco seasoning packet."

"Hm," said Hank. "And these——" He held up a forkful of something crunchy.

"Fritos," said Nadine. She shook her head, imagining Alejandro's horror at her creation. He'd like Hank, though, she decided, watching him pour another glass of tequila.

"Fritos," mused Hank, swirling the smoky liquid in his glass. "Well, Fritos were tortillas once, right?"

On their last night, Nadine and Hank sat on the couch in front of a roaring fire. They shared the red blanket, spreading it over their knees as they balanced bowls of shellfish pasta in their laps. "Well," said Nadine, "this week has been wonderful."

"It's been nice to have the company," said Hank. "How are you feeling?"

"Fine, actually," Nadine lied. Her wrist felt better—by the third day she could use her fingers without trouble—but her headaches were worse. "They won't send me out for a few months," she said. "So I guess I have some time to . . . visit friends."

"You're going to Mexico, then?"

"I'm steering clear of the Sandy Toes, that's for damn sure." Nadine had tried to call her father but reached only a cheery answering machine announcement about the Sandy Toes' summer season opening. She had left a message saying, "Dad, I love you. It's Nadine. I just . . . I needed to get back to work. I'll call soon."

"You know," said Hank, "you're welcome to stay here. It's empty all week. I come out most weekends, but the guest room's all yours."

Nadine looked at Hank. "That's so nice," she said. He shrugged. "Maybe I will stay a few more days. Are you sure?"

"Absolutely."

"I could do without a city for another week," said Nadine. "My apartment in Mexico City. Jesus, Hank, it doesn't even have a couch! A futon and some milk crates to rest the printer on. It's awful."

"Do you ever want . . . I don't know how to phrase it."

"A boxspring? Some pots and pans? To tell you the truth, no. That's just not for me. I'm happiest in the thick of things." Even as she spoke, Nadine wondered whether she was telling the truth. She had repeated the same story about herself for so long that it was hard to admit how much she was enjoying afternoons reading in a cozy house, the smell of a real dinner being prepared as opposed to a bowl of Raisin Bran and a glass of wine, her usual repast.

That night, after he had gone to bed, Nadine watched the fire die down to embers. She didn't want to leave the living room: the plum-colored glow, books on the shelf, Hank's teacup on the counter, the blanket that held his dusky, molasses smell. She touched the rough wool and felt tranquil. She breathed in the house, the week they had spent there. A house held on to the moments lived inside its walls, she thought. And Nadine had only her mind to hold her history. She had always been able to keep the unhappy memories at bay, but her brain, jammed full, was beginning to sabotage her. She was so tired.

Nadine walked barefoot across the living room floor. Hank's room was off the kitchen, a large bedroom facing a vegetable garden. In the kitchen, the dishes were piled in the sink. The ticking of the grandfather clock. A heavy wind buffeted the house, but Nadine was warm inside. She cradled the knob to Hank's room, and then she turned it.

Hank was asleep with his book in his hand, the light still on.

Nadine watched his chest rise and fall. His skin held the caramel color of his Portuguese parents; his lips were full. He had not shaved all week, and there was stubble under his cheekbones: half black, half gray. Nadine slid her pajama pants down, pulled her shirt over her head. Naked, she approached the bed, folded Hank's book, and placed it on the floor.

Nadine pulled back the covers and eased herself next to Hank. She pressed her lips to his, and something inside her relaxed. Her head stopped hurting, and Hank woke and said, *Is this a dream?* and Nadine said *Yes* and moved on top of him.

In the morning, it was snowing, the trees blanketed in white.

Twelve

■

Hank didn't leave for two more days. "I'll tell them it snowed," he said, lying next to Nadine, twirling a strand of her hair in his dark fingers.

"It did snow," said Nadine.

"It did snow," said Hank.

Nadine drove him to the ferry, carefully piloting the Volvo through slippery streets. The car had no heat, and cold air blew around the edges of the convertible top. "I'll be back on Friday night," said Hank. "I can catch the seven o'clock."

"Okay," said Nadine.

"You think you'll be all right by yourself?" said Hank. Though he said she should start seeing another doctor in his office, Hank had examined her pupils and prodded her arm and pronounced her self-sufficient. Nadine had not mentioned the terrible pain in her head, or the dizziness.

"Of course," she said.

He ran into the Nantucket Juice Bar for a drink and came out with a copy of the local high school newspaper, the *Whaler*. "I thought this might interest you," he said. "And fudge," he said, handing over a waxy paper box and leaning over to touch his lips to her cheek.

"You're too good for me," said Nadine.

"Obviously," said Hank.

. . .

Nadine watched him run to catch the ferry, a slow pleasure test-
ing itself in her body. He turned and blew her a kiss, and she
waved. When she put the car in gear, she caught herself smiling in
the rearview mirror. She stopped at the bookstore and bought *The
Joy of Cooking,* planning to practice for a few days before attempt-
ing a welcome dinner. "You staying awhile?" asked the store
owner, ringing up the cookbook on an old cash register.

"Who knows," said Nadine.

"It gets in your blood."

"God forbid," said Nadine. The woman laughed. Nadine
drove to Quidnet Road, blowing on her cold hands at every stop.
She was sore from lovemaking and ready for an afternoon nap.
She brewed a cup of chamomile tea, smiling and thinking of
Hank, his body, his fingertips.

Nadine hummed as she walked into Hank's room and climbed
into bed. She sipped her tea. Next to her, the *Whaler* beckoned.
Still, she resisted for a moment, looking out at the snow, tasting
the sweetness of the two spoonfuls of local honey she had stirred
into her mug. Then she opened the paper. She was calm until she
saw the headline.

Local Couple Heads to South Africa for Son's Murder Trial

And the sickening thrill ignited in her chest. She scanned the
article. *Jason Irving* she saw, and *bludgeoned to death* and *gang of
street children* and *beat his head with a rock* and *body flown back to
Nantucket* and *Sophia and Krispin Irving.* Nadine held her breath.

She had always felt a connection to Jason, though they had never
met. They were from the same corner of the world, after all, and had
both ended up in South Africa. But Jason had never come home.

The *Whaler* article was written by a Nantucket High senior
and featured a grim picture of Jason's parents: Krispin, a wealthy
entrepreneur, and Sophia, his blonde wife. Nadine had seen pictures of the Irvings before, splashed over the papers after Jason's
murder. They looked completely different now—old and broken,
sipping coffee and looking away from each other.

In Hank's warm bed, Nadine read.

This holiday season, Krispin and Sophia Irving are not buying
ornaments at Nautical and Nice. They aren't walking off too
much turkey on Madaket Beach, either. Instead, the Irvings, who
founded Cranberry Creations, are packing for their first visit to
Cape Town, South Africa, where their son, Jason, was bludgeoned to death by a gang of street children ten years ago, his
body flown back to Nantucket for burial.

Jason, valedictorian of Nantucket High School Class of
1984, went to South Africa to fight against apartheid, the shocking system of separating blacks and whites. Jason taught English
to black children in the impoverished townships where blacks
were forced to live in filthy conditions, often without water or
sanitary facilities. He really loved his students, said his father.
"Jason felt it was his life's goal to fight the injustice of the
apartheid government," said Krispin Irving in an exclusive interview with the Whaler held in the high school cafeteria during
free period.

But the young black children in South Africa had grown up
persecuted by whites, and some adopted the saying, "One settler,
one bullet," which they yelled as they killed Jason Irving, who
was not, obviously, a white settler, but a young man from Nantucket who incidentally once wrote for the *Whaler,* too. "They
didn't designate between different white people," explains
Krispin. "These children thought that any white person deserved
to die. They believed that killing white people would end
apartheid."

On April 7, 1988, Jason was driving a student to the student's
home in Sunshine township. Some kids, all riled up from a polit-

ical rally, surrounded the car and smashed the window with a brick. They dragged him out of the car, and jumped on Jason as he tried to run. A group of boys and a young girl kicked him and beat his head with a rock. They murdered him with their bare hands and the aforementioned rock.

Three of the boys and the girl were sentenced to eighteen years in prison each. But then things changed in South Africa. In 1992, Nelson Mandela (who is black and who was jailed for twenty-seven years) was elected president, ending apartheid. But the hatred between the races continued. Like a terrible motor-boat, whites and blacks had committed heinous crimes, leaving a giant wake behind. Nelson Mandela's party, the African National Congress, is handling the wake of these actions in a new way.

The Truth and Reconciliation Commission (also called the TRC), headed by the charismatic Archbishop Desmond Tutu, has invited victims and persecutors to come forward and tell their stories. The commission has already spent almost a year traveling to more than fifty public hearings all over the country to take statements.

If people's crimes were political, and they tell the truth and ask for forgiveness, they can be given amnesty. In other words, they might walk free! "This process is not about pillorying," Archbishop Desmond Tutu said. "It's actually about getting to the truth, so we can heal."

(Author's note: Desmond Tutu did not say this to me, but I saw it in The New York Times. I wrote Desmond Tutu a letter but have not heard back as of yet.)

Jason's murderers say that they thought killing Jason Irving would lead to the end of apartheid. They will appear before the commission on January 10, and Jason's parents will be there to watch them explain what they did to Jason and why.

Krispin and Sophia Irving could make all the difference when they speak at the TRC hearing. If they support amnesty, their son's killers might walk free into the sunshine. On the other hand, if they fight these children's pleas for forgiveness, they could send them back to jail.

"I support their application for amnesty," says Krispin Irving, eating the Dove bar I bought him. "They were young and angry, and they deserve a second chance. I am going to South Africa to tell Jason's killers that I forgive them."

Sophia Irving disagrees. While my parents and the Irvings were having cocktails on the Irvings' yacht, Bogged Down, I was undercover, and I asked Mrs. Irving what she thought about Jason's killers' applications for amnesty. "I hope they rot in hell," she said.

—Janine Lewis, senior editor, the *Whaler*

It was time to go back; Nadine knew it in her bones. She told herself it was an important story—she had to see the TRC, to write about Evelina's hearing. But there was more: a part of Nadine was still stuck in South Africa, still living the night she had betrayed Maxim. Nadine picked up the phone. A ticket from Nantucket Memorial Airport to Cape Town, South Africa, cost $2,301. She could leave in the morning. Nadine put the ticket on her Master-Card and began to pack, her chamomile tea growing cold on the kitchen table.

Thirteen

Nadine met Maxim on her first day in the Nutthall Road house. After she dropped her backpack in what would be her bedroom, Nadine sat at the kitchen table and shared an afternoon beer with George. George was writing all day, but his words, he said, weren't adding up to much of a novel. He was clearly jealous of Maxim, whose photographs were selling well. Maxim, George told Nadine, worked his ass off, driving his car into the townships and documenting the bloody battles there. Blacks were attacking blacks, blacks were attacking whites, and Maxim was making a name for himself, signing with a prestigious agency and garnering paid assignments for newspapers and magazines. George looked wistful as he described his successful roommate.

"And Thola?" asked Nadine. "How did the two of you meet?"

George grinned. "It's a long story."

The beer was cold in Nadine's mouth. She hadn't spoken to anyone in a week. "So go on and tell it," she said, relaxing into her chair.

"I was ten years old when I first saw her," said George. "Her leotard was the color of orange sherbet."

"Very dramatic," said Nadine. "I'm guessing you've told this story before?"

"Be quiet, you," said George.

The program was called Dance for All, and it was one of the few ways a child could get out of the townships. "They hold auditions every year," said George. "Kids come barefoot, hungry, whatever. Kevin Holderman, Thola's teacher, he chooses the ones with talent, and he trains them. One of Thola's classmates is in the London Ballet."

"Fantastic," said Nadine, smelling a lifestyles feature.

"So Thola came to San Francisco," said George.

"In an orange leotard," said Nadine.

"My mother took me to the ballet," said George, ignoring Nadine. "I fell in love with her by the end of the first dance. That night, I lay under my Batman bedspread and dreamed she was in the top bunk. In the morning, I begged my mother to find her and invite her to lunch."

"What's your mother like?"

"Rich, confused, beautiful. Anyway, she found out that Tholakele was staying in the Stanford dorms. She thought my crush on a little African girl was adorable, at first."

"Is she still alive?"

"What? Who?"

"Your mother," said Nadine.

"Of course she is," said George. "Will you zip it and listen?"

Thola arrived late. She wore a starched dress and plastic jelly sandals. She told George her teachers had made her wear the stupid dress. She much preferred jeans, she said, and she was going to be a Freedom Fighter.

Ten-year-old George fidgeted behind his plate of turkey sandwiches. Thola hadn't turned out to be the quiet ballerina he had imagined. He wasn't sure what a Freedom Fighter was, and he didn't know what to say. His strategy of impressing Thola with his collection of butterfly wings seemed increasingly ill conceived.

"These little sandwiches are fab," said Thola, who had put away four already and was slathering mayonnaise on a fifth.

George watched the way expressions came and went quickly on her face: enthusiasm, anger, delight. She took a bite and sat back in her chair, one arm across her chest and the other holding her food aloft. "So, George," said Thola, "I hear you love me."

George's heart hammered in his chest. This was not going according to plan. He could feel his palms and his armpits grow damp. "I . . . ," he said.

"It's okay, man, no worries," said Thola. "You're not the only one, let's leave it at that."

"Oh," said George. His food sat in front of him on his plate. He never wanted to eat again.

"I don't have time for boys," said Thola. "My cousin Albert's in the MK. I want to be in the MK, too. But I'm only nine, so I must wait. There are more important things than boys, you know?"

"I thought," said George. "I thought you wanted to be a ballerina."

"Dancing's okay," said Thola. "I love to dance. And I can go places. Here I am in America! It's great, but I miss my mom. Someday I'll go back to dancing. When my country is free, I will be a ballerina. It will happen, you know, whitey."

George was speechless, completely flummoxed. Was there a chance for a hug? He looked at her brown arms, and imagined them around his shoulders. Did she wear perfume? He couldn't tell from across the table. He wanted to get one milk shake with two straws. Then they could both sip at the same time, as George had seen in movies.

"What are you staring at, boy?" said Thola. "Don't look so unbelieving." She finished off her sandwich and leaned across the table. Her face was very close to George's. Was she going to kiss him? George looked into Thola's brown eyes. Thola opened her mouth and sang joyfully, "Free Nelson Mandela!"

. . .

"Did you have any idea what she was talking about?" said Nadine, opening two more cans of beer.

"Fuck no," said George. "But she did kiss me after lunch. She tasted like Reddi-wip."

"Whipped cream?"

"We'd had banana splits for dessert," said George. He shook his head. "She ate most of mine."

Nadine laughed.

"I wanted to stay in touch. She gave me Kevin's address. I wrote her for months."

"Did she write back?"

"Not for a long time. The company went to LA, New York, Boston. I started researching South Africa at the library. Can you imagine? There I was, this sheltered kid from Pacific Heights, learning about apartheid. I'd never really understood how . . . how big the world was, how horrible and exhilarating. It blew my mind."

"It was the same for me. I grew up in a tiny town on Cape Cod. When I was twelve, we went to Boston for the Saint Patrick's Day parade and I thought I had died and gone to heaven. I mean, people looked so different. I heard other languages for the first time. And people were talking about . . . fucking foreign policy! Well, not at the parade." Nadine smiled, remembering a dim pub called the Black Rose, where she overheard two students arguing about bombings in Northern Ireland while her father tried to order her a Coke. "Woods Hole," she said, "they talk about clamming and boats. They don't want to know what's going on off-Cape."

"Something to be said for that," said George. "A simple life."

"I guess. But it isn't for me."

"I hear you," said George, and they tapped their cans together, a toast. George sat back and studied Nadine. Nadine touched her neck. "Back to the story," she said.

"Right," said George. "Right. So I started researching South Africa. I finally found a *Newsweek* article explaining what Thola had meant by *MK*."

"You were ten, reading about the MK?"

"Wild, huh? I read that they sent kids to Mozambique and Angola for military training, and I was hopeful, but I saw on my light-up globe that neither spot was near the Bay Area."

"No," said Nadine, laughing.

"I read that the MK were given guns and hand grenades, taught how to fight, and then sent back into South Africa. The idea of Thola as armed and dangerous only made her more attractive, of course."

"Of course," said Nadine, thinking of Sammy again, the biker whose tattoos and bad attitude had been his best charactcristics.

"I went around singing the ANC anthem, which I'd found on a Time-Life cassette of world music. I still remember it. *Nkosi Sikelel . . .*"

Nadine winced at his off-key rendition. "I get the picture," she said.

"At this point, my mother no longer thought my crush was so cute. She did not appreciate my singing African songs, and she threw away my FREE MANDELA T-shirt. She said it was the nanny, but I knew better."

"What about Thola?" said Nadine. "Did she ever write back?"

"Not until I was in seventh grade."

"What did the letter say?"

George put out his cigarette. "I have it," he said. "You can see for yourself." He went into his bedroom, returned with a time-worn piece of paper.

"You saved it, all these years?" Nadine asked.

George shrugged, gave the paper to her.

Hola George,

Thank you seven times for seven letters. I am very happy to have them. I am very busy with school and dance, of course, but I do think about you and about your nice mlungu home in America. My cousin (Albert) is home you will be glad to know. Things are not good and happy here, but we have faith. During the day there is fighting in the streets, nyaga nyaga, which means trouble, as I am sure you appreciate. The area around my house and in my house is safe for now. Two friends are dead, and I sing for them and I pray for them. They have not died for nothing.

In school, we are learning about white man history and also science. At ballet school I am becoming a master of the jeté and Albert teaches me the toyi-toyi. You should see me. Do not worry that I will fall in love with a Freedom Fighter, George. I told you before and tell you once more I do not have time for such things. When there is a free South Africa you will hear from me. You can write again and tell me more about this Alcatraz. Also, how did the San Francisco Ballet Gala Benefit of your mother go? I hope well. Send prayers for me and for you I will do the same. My sister Evelina says hello and she would like to come to America. Unfortunately, she is clumsy, and can never be a ballerina.

Nkosi Sikelel' iAfrika,

THOLA

(The Lion)

"This was what—fifteen years ago?" said Nadine.

"Right," said George, taking the letter back and folding it carefully.

Nadine leaned forward. "How did you reconnect?"

"I wrote to her all through high school; and then during college, I finally saved enough to come over. Kevin set me up with this apartment about a year ago. Maxim was headed to Bucharest, and wanted to make some extra money by renting out rooms."

Nadine nodded and sipped her beer. "Go on," she said.

■

Fourteen

Geroge worked in the campus bar during his junior year in college, and by summer he had saved enough money to buy a ticket to South Africa. (His parents had refused to supplement the "African girlfriend fund," as his father called it.) Though there had been other women for George, he still pined for Thola. When the plane landed in Johannesburg, George felt something in his gut. He looked out the window at the dusty, red earth. He thought, grandly, *I am home.*

He arrived in Cape Town four hours later, and called Kevin Holderman, whose number he had written on a square of notebook paper. Kevin, an energetic older man, drove him to the Nutthall Road house. "Okay," he said, "here's Thola's address, and the keys to Maxim's car. Ask around Site C in Sunshine township. Everyone knows Tholakele. But watch your back."

"I can't thank you enough," said George as he walked outside with Kevin.

"Listen," said Kevin. "You've got to be careful. It's illegal for blacks and whites to mix."

"I know," said George. He muttered, "Fucking ridiculous."

Kevin lit a cigarette and stared into space as he inhaled. The trees around them were vibrant. "It's the way things are," said Kevin, finally.

"That's a stupid thing to say," said George.

"Why don't you soak it all in," said Kevin, "before you start casting judgment."

. . .

It was afternoon in Cape Town, but the middle of the night at home. George felt woozy from cigarettes and lack of sleep. He went outside and found the yellow Tercel parked in the middle of a pile of weeds.

There was a map on the passenger seat. Styrofoam cups and fast-food wrappers littered the car. One of the back windows had a bullet hole. It took a few tries, but finally the car started. George picked up the map, which was marked with red X's. Cape Flats was a blank expanse, but Maxim had filled in some of the streets. He had noted *Sunshine,* so George started the engine and drove.

After about ten minutes, the streets of the city, lush and land-scaped, ended, and then the townships began: tiny shacks and concrete blocks lining the road. George followed the signs to Sun-shine, but found himself lost on a street filled with animals, peo-ple, and garbage. He passed brightly colored tin buildings. On one building, QUEENS' HAIR SALON had been painted in red, fol-lowed by a list of services, including RELAX, S-CURL, BLOW, and HOT WATER. A few blocks away, he found Thola's address.

As soon as he stepped from the car, George noticed how many people were watching him. From windows and yards, from the makeshift bar across the street, men and women stared openly. He had never felt so conspicuous. He was scared and guilty for being scared. He hadn't even showered before coming to see Thola, he realized, pushing loose strands of hair back into his ponytail. He felt ashamed.

George walked past a row of concrete buildings. Laundry hung on a line, and a few empty plastic buckets had been overturned to make stools for women who sat and gazed at him. The buckets, George learned, were for human waste. There was no plumbing in Site C. There were no electric lines: there was no electricity.

Thola's house, a corrugated-iron shack with horizontal windows, was surrounded by a dirt yard, which had been carefully
swept. There was a spindly tree and a walkway made of stones. In
the chilly afternoon, smoke curled from a fire in the backyard.
George swallowed. The sky above him was closed in by smog. He
approached the metal door and knocked.

An older woman with close-cropped hair opened the front
door. She looked tired, her shoulders folded forward. "Hello,"
said George, with way too much enthusiasm. "I'm here to see
Thola! My name is George. I'm a friend of hers from America!"
He grinned, and the woman looked at him levelly. She stepped
back, indicating that George should come inside, and spoke to
someone in the back room. George could not grasp what she was
saying; he later learned she spoke only Xhosa.

On the wall, framed pictures and cutout newspaper articles had
been hung. George recognized the girl in the photos: Thola. He
smiled.

"Welcome," said a woman in a green headdress, offering a tray
with a teapot and a mug. "Thola is not here. Thola is at work."

"She got a job?" said George. "I didn't know. That's great!
That's really great."

A young girl at the kitchen table snickered. She wore a school
uniform, plaid skirt with an oxford shirt. Her hair was pulled into
two braided pigtails. When she looked up, George could see that
one of her eyelids opened only partway. In front of her was a math
textbook. "Where is she dancing?" said George.

"She is not dancing anymore," said the girl, looking at George
angrily. "She is a maid."

"A maid?" said George.

The older woman pushed a mug of weak tea into George's
hands. The mug was very hot, its handle broken off. George
switched it from hand to hand, trying to ignore his scalding fin-

gers. The woman spoke in Xhosa. "She says it's a good job," said the girl, rolling her eyes.

"Well, that's wonderful," said George, trying to feign enthusiasm.

"We have heard many times about you," said the woman in the green headdress. "I am Tholakele's aunt, September. This is her mother, Fikile, and Evelina, her sister." George looked long at Fikile. He could not believe the stooped, round-faced woman was Thola's mother. He tried to catch her eye, to smile, but Fikile looked into her tea.

"Howdy, partner," said Evelina. She was trouble, George could tell.

"Where does Thola work?" said George.

Fikile spoke, and George stared, trying to find Thola in her. September translated, "A fine home in the city. Twelve Serpentine Avenue."

"Oranjezicht," said Evelina, naming a suburb not far from George's apartment.

George sipped from his mug. "I sure am glad to be here," he said lamely. "Will you tell Thola I came by?"

Fikile giggled like a young girl—George was startled to hear such an innocent sound from Thola's world-weary mother—and spoke softly to her sister. "She says that Thola was right. You are handsome, for an American," said September. Fikile hid her smile with her pudgy hand.

"Thank you," said George. He didn't want to leave, but couldn't think of anything else to say. "See you very soon, I hope," he said, moving to the door.

Evelina followed George to his car and asked for a ride to a friend's house. George agreed, and then saw two boys walking toward them. "Start the car, please," said Evelina tensely.

"What's the matter?" said George. The boys looked about ten years old.

"Please start the car at once," said Evelina. "*Tsotsis,*" she said, after George had pulled away. "They are the hoodlums." She added, without emotion, "They raped my friend." George opened his mouth to ask questions, but could not decide where to begin.

Evelina directed him through the narrow, busy streets. Finally, she told him to stop outside a small house. "Studying?" said George as Evelina reached for the car door.

"Yes, studying," said Evelina flatly.

"Well," said George. "It was great to meet you."

"I feel the same," said Evelina, and she slammed the door, looked both ways, and ran to the house.

George couldn't help himself. He drove out of the townships with relief and followed the handmade map to the leafy suburb of Oranjezicht. He was shocked by the contrast between the townships and the stunning suburbs a few miles away. As he drove, the road wound up the side of Table Mountain; some homes would have views of the sea.

Twelve Serpentine Avenue was a white house with an elaborate garden of frangipani and hibiscus. It was surrounded by a high metal gate, and signs warned of alarm systems and guard dogs. George sat in his car, and then he saw a figure outside the gates, underneath a blue gum tree. His heart beat quickly as he got out of the car. He approached the figure, who he knew, just knew, was his Thola.

Her eyes were closed, and she leaned against the trunk, smoking a cigarette. George watched her, the planes of her cheekbones, her lips. He had dreamed of her for years, and now here she was, more beautiful than he had imagined. She wore a gray uniform, and her hair was cut close to her head. Her ankles were crossed, her feet wrapped in ugly shoes. She wore a thick cardigan pulled over her chest.

Thola opened her eyes. Outside the gates of an opulent home, years later and on the opposite side of the world, they saw each other again. George knelt before her, and she smiled.

"Ah," she said slyly. "My Prince Charming. At last, you have arrived."

"Jesus," said Nadine. "That's quite a love story."

"Have you ever been in love?" asked George.

"No," said Nadine quietly.

"I'm sorry," said George. He reached across the table, but before his hand touched Nadine's the front door banged open. A blond man in his thirties entered the room. He was thin and unshaven, and wore jeans and a black T-shirt, three cameras around his neck. There was dirt smeared on one of his cheekbones, and with his wild blue eyes and bony frame, he looked a bit frightening. Nadine felt the hairs on the back of her neck rise. His sweat smelled of spice. "Motherfucking Cape Flats," he said.

"This," said George, "is Maxim."

Fifteen

Maxim: his muscular arms, unshaven cheeks stubbled with rough hair. A cigarette between his fingers even before he had climbed out of bed. On Nadine's first morning at the house on Nutthall Road, he wandered into the kitchen as she was making a pot of coffee. His jeans hung low on his hips.

"That coffee's crap," he said.

Nadine wore pajama pants and a tank top. She turned. "What do you suggest?" she said.

"Come with me. For the day."

"Where?"

"Yes or no," said Maxim, walking toward Nadine, pinning her with his eyes.

"Yes," said Nadine.

In the Bo-Kapp neighborhood, Maxim bought Nadine a syrupy coffee. She drank it too fast, and ended up with a mouthful of grounds. "Forgot to mention," said Maxim. "Don't drink the last sip."

Nadine looked at him darkly.

"You're fucking gorgeous," he said.

Nadine blushed. She lined up her notebook and pencil on the table. "Where are we headed?" she asked.

"We drive around," said Maxim waving his hand toward the city. "We look for trouble."

"The townships," said Nadine.

"Yes," said Maxim. "It's like the coffee," he said. "Once you taste the real thing, the rest is shit."

Nadine thought of her disappointing stories so far: a long interview with the man who monitored the penguins at Boulders Beach, the group of Germans on a wine tour. She had even stooped to writing an article about shopping for African handicrafts.

"I'm ready," she told Maxim.

Maxim drove the Tercel out of town, onto the highway. He explained that the murder of Jason Irving had been just the tip of the iceberg. "These kids are tired of waiting for equality, so they're turning to violence." Quietly, he added, "One of the kids who killed the American was Evelina Malefane."

"I remember the name. A little girl, right? With pigtails."

"She's Thola's sister," said Maxim. "She went to jail a month ago."

"Thola? You mean George's girlfriend?"

"She's a lot more than George's girlfriend," said Maxim.

"What does that mean?"

"It's complicated," said Maxim. He put on his blinker and drove off the highway. The air was thick with the scents of urine and spoiled meat. The streets were riddled with potholes, and then the pavement stopped and mud tracks began. Morning sun glinted off streams of waste that ran along the road. Makeshift houses were crammed together: pieces of welded iron without plumbing or concrete floors. Trash was simply everywhere: wet rags, cardboard boxes, discarded food wrappers, newspapers.

"Don't tell me it's complicated and stop," said Nadine. "I want to understand. That's what I'm here for, damn it."

Maxim raised an eyebrow. Children came running toward the car, banging on the windows and yelling in English and Xhosa. "Can I explain tonight," said Maxim, "over dinner?"

"Okay," said Nadine. There was no time to savor the invitation; Maxim rolled down the window.

"*Hola,*" he said, stopping.

"*Hola,*" said one skinny kid, opening the back door of the car and clambering in. Maxim explained later that the township thugs liked to pretend they were a real part of the resistance movement, and so adopted the Spanish greetings that guerrilla fighters had brought home from training camps, where many teachers were Cuban. "You looking for bang bang?" said the boy, smiling too widely from the backseat. Nadine shot Maxim a nervous look.

"Anything happening?" asked Maxim, putting his hand on her knee to calm her.

"You have petrol, com?"

"I'm a journalist," said Maxim. To Nadine, he said, "He wants the gas for Molotov cocktails." Maxim's hand was warm on her knee.

"You want the *nyaga nyaga,*" said the boy, "you give me something."

"Here," said Maxim, pulling a ten-rand note from his cigarette packet.

The boy took the money and a cigarette. Maxim lit the cigarette. The boy had long eyelashes and acne-pitted skin. He wore a white sweatshirt that said HOOK 'EM HORNS. He was very young, not yet a teenager.

From the backseat, the boy directed them down alleys and past a food stall, where piles of fatty meat lay glistening. A man in a blue shirt and a sleeveless argyle vest tended the coals of an enormous barbecue. Kids of varied sizes filled the streets; one girl in pink track pants sucked a lollipop provocatively, her hair poking in all directions. There was a heavy stench of blood, and the ground was wet: lunch had recently been slaughtered.

Finally, the boy extended a skinny arm, pointing to a long, concrete block in the distance. "The hostel," he said. "There's the bang bang for you, com."

"Okay," said Maxim, handing the boy another ten-rand note.

"I'm Mikey," said the boy. "Ask for me if you need anything, okay?"

"You got it," said Maxim.

"Watch yourself, white boy," said Mikey, starting to laugh. He seemed drugged; Maxim later told Nadine that Mandrax, a banned tranquilizer, was heavily used in the townships. The kids mixed Mandrax and marijuana, smoking it out of a bottleneck. They called the concoction "white pipe." Mikey jumped out of the car and ran back down the road.

"Put this on," said Maxim, pulling a bulletproof vest from the backseat. "It can get ugly."

"What about you?"

"Shit," said Maxim. "When my time comes, it comes."

"I feel the same way," said Nadine, not sure if this was true.

They drove toward the hostel, which was surrounded by people. Maxim explained that much of the township fighting was between blacks and blacks—members of Mandela's ANC party and the rival Inthaka party. The two groups were split along ethnic lines as well as by geographic origin: many Inthaka supporters were Zulu, and had moved into fortress-like hostels to be near jobs in the city. It was rumored that the government was funding and inciting the Inthaka fighters in order to weaken the ANC resistance. "In short," said Maxim, "it's bloodshed all around."

"Bang bang," said Nadine.

"Precisely," said Maxim. He turned to look at her, and a slow smirk moved across his lips. "You love it," he said.

"Yeah," said Nadine.

"Thank you," said Maxim, looking skyward, clasping his

hands together. "You have brought her to me at last." Nadine smiled, and Maxim looked back at her. He moved his hand slowly up her thigh. She lifted her chin, never breaking her gaze from his.

There was the sound of a gunshot, and Maxim turned away. "Showtime," he said, his voice husky. He opened the car door and moved toward the sound. Nadine followed. She was used to ugliness, but running toward gunfire was something new. The streets were mobbed. Dozens of men were chanting and shooting, trying to gain access to the hostel. Finally, they broke down a locked entrance and dragged a man out, surrounding him and beating him with sticks and stones. Maxim crouched behind a garbage can, his camera clicking and whirring. Nadine stood farther back, protected by a makeshift barricade, taking it in.

An older woman in a turban headdress walked by Nadine. "What's going on?" asked Nadine. "Why are they beating him?"

"He is a traitor," the woman spat, her arms crossed. She watched the scene with apparent relish.

Nadine could not look away. Her mind spun. She wondered if the anger around her would result in a better South Africa, or just a bloody disaster. Could Jason's death—and violent outbreaks such as this one—possibly end apartheid?

The man cried out, panicked. Maxim told Nadine later that the crowd thought he was a Xhosa spy, hiding in the Zulu hostel. It would be impossible to tell the man's ethnic group until his passbook was examined. Nonetheless, people attacked him viciously. The man fell to the ground and was quiet. Someone yelled, "Poyisa!"

Both sides scattered amid screams and gunshots. A tank crunched over the sandbags set up to barricade the area. From inside the tank, white police fired randomly. The group surrounding the man dispersed, but some were shot and fell to the ground.

Maxim ran, pulling Nadine alongside. They hurried into the Tercel, and Maxim put the car in gear, pressing the gas to the floor. In the rearview mirror, Nadine watched the scene. The Zulu man did not rise. His blood formed a thick puddle on the ground.

"Fuck," said Nadine.

"Hold on," said Maxim. He sped out of the townships, driving until he reached a dazzling Camps Bay beach. People sunbathed and swam in stylish bathing suits. Rows of shops selling beachwear sparkled in the sun.

"I don't . . . ," said Nadine.

"Follow me," said Maxim.

He climbed from the car and stripped to his cotton underwear. His body was ropy with muscle, his skin pale. "We'll swim," he said, and Nadine nodded.

Pulling off her jeans, she followed Maxim into clear waves. She dove underwater, trying to cleanse herself of the township smell. The cold water ran along her arms and legs, and she heard the thudding sound of her heart.

Nadine surfaced, water over her forehead and over her shoulders. The sun was hot and bright, but she shivered. Maxim stood in front of her, so near she could see the stars of gold in his blue eyes.

They looked at each other. Maxim lifted his arm and touched Nadine, tucking her wet hair behind her ear. Nadine felt blood rush to the surface of her skin. She wanted Maxim to pull her closer, to kiss her and keep kissing her.

Maxim's fingers moved down, touching her neck, her collarbone, the soaked fabric of her shirt. When he reached her breast, she breathed in sharply and closed her eyes. "Nadine," whispered Maxim. His arms were strong around her, and he pulled her close.

"Yes," said Nadine. Maxim kissed her hard, the waves running over them. He held her aloft, she wrapped her limbs around him, she opened her mouth. His touch was rough, as desperate as her own. His fingers found lace underwear; he ripped it from her body.

"Yes," said Nadine. She thought, *So this is love.*

Sixteen

■

The phone rang at five AM. Hank's Nantucket living room was filled with a murky light. The television was on, muted. Wrenched from dreams, Nadine picked up the phone. "Hello?"

"Nadine Morgan?"

"Hello?" She blinked away the image of Maxim's face, the memory of his body.

"This is dispatch. Taxi's on the way to your house."

"It's not my house, it's—"

"Lady, you call a taxi?"

"I did, yes."

"Well, it's on the way."

"Thanks."

Nadine pulled off the blanket and sat up. She recognized the movie on television: *On Golden Pond.* Outside the window, Nadine could see a minivan pull into the driveway, headlights sweeping the snowy lawn.

Nadine splashed water on her face and brushed her teeth, washing her hands with Hank's peppermint soap.

She had fallen asleep in her travel clothes, and her bag was jammed full and zipped. In the kitchen, Nadine picked up the phone and hesitated, then held it with her chin and dialed Hank's condo in Falmouth. The phone rang, and she thought of the sound echoing through the apartment. She could almost see Hank, his dark eyelashes, his olive skin. He breathed heavily when he slept, sometimes muttering or sighing. The phone called to Hank, but he did not answer.

After three rings, Nadine hung up. She found a pencil and a legal pad. She touched the pencil to the paper, trying to find the right way to say good-bye. *You were right,* she wrote. *The story on Jason Irving was just what I needed.* She stared at the note. She added, *There is something about South Africa that I just can't put behind me. I hope that someday—* Her pencil stopped. She wrote, *we can . . .*

Nadine bit her lip. The pencil was still. Finally, she tore off the sheet and threw it in the trash bag. She turned down the thermostats and stepped outside. Hank's front door closed behind her.

Nadine put the trash bag in the bin at the end of the driveway, tossed an empty whiskey bottle in the recycling. The air was frigid; her hands ached. The driver stepped from the car and walked toward Nadine, taking her bag. He stowed it in the trunk, then held the door open, and she climbed inside, breathing in the scent of men's cologne. The driver, a heavyset man, settled himself in his seat.

"No need to talk," he said to Nadine, and she nodded.

In the Nantucket airport, Nadine bought a weak coffee. She called Hank's office and left a message with his answering service: "Please tell him I—Nadine—Please tell him Nadine went to South Africa and she will call soon. And tell him I said thank you. For everything."

"South Africa?" said the woman incredulously.

"Yes," said Nadine. "Tell him I'll call soon."

"They got phones over there?"

"Yes," said Nadine. "They do have phones."

When the flight was announced, the few early travelers boarded the prop plane to Boston. Nadine was seated across the aisle from an older couple. She glanced at them and felt a shock, then turned and stared, unable to believe her eyes. It was Jason's parents, Krispin and Sophia Irving. Krispin, wearing a pale blue sweater and wool slacks, read a newspaper. Sophia wore what looked like silk pajamas with a soft gray wrap.

The plane lifted into the air, and Nadine saw Nantucket Island below them, a sandy shoe in a dark sea. She felt an unfamiliar sorrow leaving the island: she had always been so happy to leave Cape Cod. Now she wanted to be in Hank's warm bed, sipping coffee and planning the day. Maybe he was right, she mused. Maybe Nadine really did want a more settled life, a couch, a bedside table piled high with books.

Sophia Irving's hands emerged from beneath her blanket and she tipped a bottle of cream into her palm, setting the bottle down on the tray table and rubbing the lotion into her face with her fingertips. When her skin shone, she produced a red eye mask and slipped it over her face. She leaned back into the plastic seat, exposing her throat.

"Excuse me," said Nadine.

Krispin looked up from his newspaper. Outwardly, he looked prosperous and confident, but his eyes were dull. "I don't mean to intrude," said Nadine. "My name is Nadine Morgan, and I'm a reporter. I'm, well, as it turns out, I'm going to Cape Town. To cover the TRC hearings."

"You're from Nantucket?" Krispin asked.

"No," said Nadine. "Actually, I—"

Sophia Irving pushed her eye mask up with an angry motion. "I don't mean to be rude," she said sharply, "but this is a difficult time. We'd like some privacy." Krispin looked at Nadine apologetically.

"Of course," said Nadine. "I'm sorry." She thought quickly about which angle to use, and then said, "You're incredibly brave. I just wanted to say that. It's amazing, what you're doing." Sophia did not look at Nadine, but Krispin met her eyes. "If you ever

want to speak with me, you can leave a message at this number."
She gave Krispin her Associated Press card, knowing she could
call for messages.

"I'll be clear: leave us alone," said Sophia, staring at her
latched tray table.

"I see," said Nadine, trying to think of something else to say.
Finally, she moved to an empty seat at the back of the plane, across
from the bathroom. She flipped open the in-flight magazine, staring at an ad for a Houston steak house. What the hell was she
doing, she wondered, reading about *succulent cuts* and *hearty
homemade sides.* Why wasn't she at Hank's, waiting for his return?
She was surprised to feel an ache, missing his tangled hair, the way
he hummed as he chopped vegetables for dinner. Her wrist
throbbed, and the picture of a rare piece of meat made her stomach turn. She closed her eyes, but opened them with a start when
she felt a hand on her shoulder.

"Nadine Morgan," said Krispin. He cleared his throat.
"Here," he said, handing Nadine a manila envelope. "This is a
copy of Jason's journal. He wrote so well, you'll see, even when he
was very young. Maybe he would have been a reporter, too."

"Thank you," Nadine said.

"This is a tough trip for my wife," said Krispin. "It's tough for
both of us. But Jason . . ." His clear, blue eyes teared up. "He
wouldn't have wanted her to . . . I'm sorry."

"Please," said Nadine, "go on."

"I can still remember her," said Krispin. "The way she
was . . . before . . ."

Nadine nodded, the words forming an opening paragraph in
her mind. She willed Krispin to continue.

"I hope this trip helps her," he said. He took a breath and
stood. "I hope you can write something. Something wonderful."

"I'll do my best, I promise," said Nadine, holding Jason's journal tightly. "Jason," she said. "He was a remarkable person."

"You knew him?"

"No," said Nadine. "No, I just . . . I've read about him."

Krispin looked long at Nadine. "We're staying at the Hotel Victoria," he said. "Come and talk to me. I want—" He looked away, out the window, at the clouds. "I want Jason to be remembered. I want this pain to amount to something."

"Of course," said Nadine.

Krispin nodded briskly. He patted the envelope on Nadine's tray table and went back to his seat.

On the twenty-one-hour flight to Johannesburg, jammed between a Liberian mother and her infant and a woman with a ruddy complexion, Nadine pulled out the envelope Krispin had given her and opened it. Krispin had made color copies of his son's journal, as well as everything from his birth certificate to his "Good Attitude Award" at Camp Becket in the Berkshires.

Nadine had to bite back tears as she took note of particularly moving information: Jason's dreams, his love of musical theater. She rubbed her eyes, thinking that the painkillers must be affecting her. She prided herself on never getting her emotions mixed up with her work. Sure, this boy had grown up near Nadine, but she hadn't known him. He was simply, she reminded herself, the subject of an article. Nadine forced herself to turn the pages.

She closed Jason's journal and took a melatonin tablet. Though the Liberian baby screamed every half an hour or so, Nadine slept for a while, and then watched three movies in a row. By the time they reached Accra, Ghana, Nadine had a splitting headache and her joints throbbed. In the tiny bathroom, she took some Demerol. She ran a damp paper towel over her face as the plane refueled and stewardesses sprayed the walkways with aerosol cans. The floral-scented antibacterial made Nadine's headache worse.

By the bathroom, two men in camouflage pants discussed their upcoming hunt. "I'm taking a lion *down,*" said one.

"Stewardess cut off my scotch," said the other.

"I'm taking a lion *down,*" said the other. "Well," he said, seeing Nadine, "what have we here?"

She pushed past him and sighed: ten hours until Johannesburg.

Seventeen

NANTUCKET TO STARDOM
MY PERSONAL JOURNAL

Today I was discovered. For my whole life, I've dreamed and hoped it would happen, and then it did, right after the dress rehearsal of the sixth-grade musical, *Guys and Dolls*. I rocked "Sue Me" and even Mr. Mancussi said, "Good enunciation, pal." I slid across the floor like it was ice and I was in the Ice Capades. I threw my heart into my arm movements. I even tried to be passionate about my kiss with Louisa Jelly (who totally needs to work on her enunciation. The only song she rocks is "Adelaide's Lament," because she's *supposed* to have a cold in that one). By the end of the show I was gross and sweaty but I felt good because I knew I had done my best.

I do not like taking showers in the nasty Nantucket Elementary gym, so I was still gross and sweaty when I met the talent agent. (Will have to work on this part for the movie version . . . maybe I can have a dressing room with a private *clean* shower?) He came right up to me and said, "Excuse me, but are you represented by a talent agent?"

"What?" I said, but then I played it cool. I said, "No, I am not currently represented by a talent agent." Thank goodness I had practiced for this moment in the downstairs bathroom mirror.

Mrs. Jelly, the costume designer and also Louisa's mom,

came over and said, "Nice job, honey. Let me take your hat."

I nodded and the hat flew off just like I had practiced in front of the downstairs bathroom mirror. I caught it between my thumb and forefinger and handed it to Mrs. Jelly. I gave her my special wink, just like the one that Frank gave the audience in *Our Town*. "Such a ham bone," said Mrs. Jelly. "Be sure to give me your little suit," she added, before leaving me alone with the agent.

"I've got to say, I'm surprised you haven't been discovered yet," he said. (Maybe he didn't hear the "little suit" comment? I hope not, please I hope not.)

"Really?" I said.

"Can I buy you a hot chocolate?" the man asked. "I'd love to discuss your future. You are a unique talent."

This is my real story. I am not making anything up. So I promise, I stood in the hallway, next to the row of dented lockers, and this man said, "You are a unique talent." It was just like I had imagined it, except I thought I would be outside in the snow when it happened for some reason, and I didn't imagine Rosemary Carmichel eavesdropping while she got *To Kill a Mockingbird* out of her locker.

I said, "Hot chocolate? Wow." I wish I had thought of something better to say. But I'm writing the truth as it really happened, and the truth is that I said, "Hot chocolate? Wow." Like most parents, Mom and Dad had not come to the dress rehearsal. I was supposed to call home for a pickup, but I thought fast and decided I could tell them that I had gotten a ride home with a friend. They didn't know I had no friends.

For some reason, I already knew that I wouldn't tell my parents about the talent agent. It just seemed like something that could be all mine, and I didn't want them worrying and ruining it for me. I told Mom once about how I prayed every night to be a star and she looked kind of sad and said, "You're my star, lovebug, no matter what." Which means she doesn't think I can be real star. I don't need that kind of negative energy! I changed out of my costume, and we walked down the steps of my school.

So this talent agent is super handsome. He looks like Frank Sinatra, the original Nathan Detroit and my idol: tall and with really, really blue eyes. His eyes are the color of the pond behind our house when it freezes and I can dance on it. "My name is Malcon," he said, "like *Malcolm,* but with an *n.*"

And I go, "Wow."

He took a puff of his cigar. (How did I know? In my dreams, he had a cigar, too!) At this point, we were walking along Surfside Road. The air tasted salty, and the first of the summer people were crowding the island, their BMWs and Jeep Cherokees parked all over the sidewalks as if they own everything, because, I guess, they do.

Malcon had talked about hot chocolate, so finally, as we passed Windy Way, I said, "Where are we headed?" I'm thinking, maybe Cumberland Farms? Do they have hot chocolate? My dream did not include Cumberland Farms.

"Oh, I'm sorry," said Malcon. "I have some hot chocolate in my car, if you'd like, and then I can give you a ride home."

I knew that Mom would not want me to get in some man's car. She had told me enough, *Don't take candy from strangers, Don't talk to strangers, Don't get a ride from a stranger, just call me.* To tell you the truth, Mom is a little paranoid. For one thing, there really aren't any strangers on

Nantucket. Hello, the whole island is fifteen miles long. Yes, okay, there are some weird dudes who hang around outside Island Spirits, and Mr. Mancussi said Nantucket has the worst heroin problem in Massachusetts. But it's not like Malcon was offering me heroin! Officer Brad came to school last year and showed us heroin and burned pot so we could smell it. He showed us angel dust and "rock," which is what people call crack cocaine. My favorite part was Ginny, the drug-sniffing dog. She can smell drugs in someone's luggage, but also she was really cute and licked me on the knee.

Anyway, I told Malcon that hot chocolate in his car sounded cool. I was sort of surprised that a big-time talent agent would drive a maroon rental car, but I guess you never know.

We got in the car. There was a six-pack of Budweiser in the backseat, and Malcon offered me one, but I was like, no thank you, I'm eleven. I did have a sip of Dad's St. Pauli Girl one day while we were fishing, and it tasted like ginger ale gone bad, in my opinion. There was no hot chocolate that I could see.

We drove out toward my house. Malcon started talking about my dance moves, how I have an elegant style. My facial expressions, he said, are very realistic. He also commented on my ability to keep a tune, though not on my enunciation. "I chose you out of all the other kids," said Malcon. "I'll make a long story short," he said, "I think you have a future in show business."

I am so glad I spent all those hours preparing in front of the bathroom mirror! I kept it cool. I was like, "Thanks, Malcon. I appreciate it."

"I mean it," said Malcon. And he turned toward me,

and looked me straight in the eye. I had a weird feeling in my stomach. It was a little bit like feeling scared, and also like feeling really happy. Maybe they are the same thing? Dad always says you have to challenge yourself, but he's talking more about trying out for the baseball team, I'm pretty sure, and not about a man in a maroon Buick sitting really close and staring at you. Malcon said, "Are you familiar with *American Superstar?*"

I felt like I was having a heart attack. Being on *American Superstar* is my most secret, most important dream. I tried to be cool. I said, "Yes." I decided that Malcon did not need to know that my parents won't even let us get a television and I have to watch *American Superstar* next door, while pretending to listen to our hundred-year-old neighbor's war stories. (Doesn't Mr. Mullen ever wonder why I only come over Thursday nights from eight to nine PM?)

And Malcon said, "Local auditions are next weekend in Mashpee. My agency would cover your ferry ticket, of course."

"Oh," I said. "Wow. Okay. I just have to talk to my mom and dad."

"Right," said Malcon. But he seemed disappointed. I always seem to say the wrong thing eventually.

"What?" I said.

Malcon sighed. He pulled the car over in a sort of dark section of Quidnet Road. It was a little creepy, but having your life change is supposed to feel scary, right? Right. So Malcon puffed on his cigar and opened another beer. "Sometimes," he said, looking moodily at the can, "parents can be threatened by their children's impending stardom."

This was a new perspective on things. The truth is, Mom and Dad have never really supported my acting career. I guess I always thought it was because they were afraid I wouldn't make it, but maybe they are sort of threatened. I mean, if I got on *American Superstar* I would have to move to Orlando, and even though Mom and Dad are always talking about seeing the wider world, I think they mean more like, the Acropolis. I think they kind of look down on teen stardom. They tell me I can be anything I want to be, but when I talk about being in a boy band or practicing my dance moves, I see how they look at each other. Why is sitting in a drab office any more important than doing the electric slide in front of a million fans?

So I looked at Malcon, and I said, "I know what you mean."

"It's up to you what you tell your parents," said Malcon. "I want you to practice that number, 'Sue Me.' But maybe less with the splayed hand shaking."

"Okay," I said, though I was a little hurt. I thought my hand stars were pretty rocking.

"I'm happy to meet with you and practice anytime," said Malcon. "I'll give you my card, and you can call me day or night."

"Okay," I said.

"Now I'm always going to be honest with you," said Malcon. "And I expect you to always be honest with me."

"I will," I said.

"You need to be your very best. You need to sing at the auditions like you have never sung before. Like an angel."

"I will," I said, "I promise I will."

"Why don't you plan on meeting me at the Hy-Line dock in Hyannis next Saturday at one?" he said.

"Perfect," I said. "So you don't need, like, a permission slip?"

Malcon laughed. I liked his laugh, it was really low in his neck. It was a dramatic laugh. "Don't need a permission slip in the Big Leagues, kid," said Malcon.

"Oh," I said, "okay." And then Malcon drove me home and parked in front of my house. The living room light was still on, and I knew that my parents were waiting for me.

Malcon handed me his card. The card said, "Malcon Bridges, Talent Scout. P.O. Box 3601, Boston, MA 02103. Phone/Fax 617-845-2390."

Boston! Clearly, Malcon was the real deal.

"Malcon," I said, as I climbed out of the Buick.

And Malcon said, "Yes?"

"Are you coming to the show this weekend?"

"I'll do my level best," said Malcon.

"That's what my dad says," I said. I hadn't meant to say it out loud.

Malcon seemed to see something in me. He looked at me for a while and then he said, "I'll be there, kid. In the back row. You can count on me."

I blinked so I wouldn't cry. "Good night, kid," said Malcon, and he touched my head with his hand, brushed my hair off my forehead. "You're going to be a star," he said.

Eighteen

A fter what felt like the longest trip of her life, Nadine saw Hank's green duffel appear on the luggage carousel in Cape Town. Around her, puffy-faced travelers claimed their bags with authority, but when the duffel passed by, she just stared. On the second revolution, Nadine stepped forward, cutting off a heavy woman in stirrup pants.

"Hey!" said the woman. There was a large penguin printed on her T-shirt.

"Sorry." Nadine grabbed her bag and pulled. It thumped onto the floor, narrowly missing a child's foot. Over the airport PA system, the Go-Go's sang, *Va-Cation, all I ever wanted! Va-Cation, had to get away!*

Nadine felt woozy, and bent over, putting her hands on her knees. "Are you all right?" said a kind voice: Krispin Irving. Behind him, Sophia stood with her arms crossed over her chest. Five wheeled suitcases were lined up next to her, and she wore a floral sundress—Nadine had seen the same one at the Lilly Pulitzer store—and sandals.

"Do you need a ride?" Krispin asked. "We're staying at the Victoria . . . we could drop you off." Sophia glared at him, her lips in a thin line. She spun around and walked toward the exit, past one billboard advertising wine and one with a picture of a starving baby.

Nadine hadn't made reservations, but quickly came to a decision. Though she usually stayed at the cheapest place possible, she reasoned that a few nights at the sumptuous Pink Vicky would

help nurse her back to health and give her better access to the Irvings. The Victoria was a colonialist-era hotel in the center of the
city, made to cater to the tastes of Americans and Europeans on
safari. "Thanks," she said. "That would be great."

Airline workers in bright jumpsuits watched the arrivals lazily.
With her good arm, Nadine lugged her bag behind Krispin as they
passed through the security gate, heading toward a man who held
a sign reading IRVING.

"Welcome to Cape Town! I am Abdul," said the man, sliding a
pair of round sunglasses over his round face. "I will be your driver
for your pleasant stay," said Abdul. Underneath his nose, there
was a skimpy black moustache. Abdul hustled them outside the
airport.

The Cape Town air was the same: drenched with sunlight and
the mingled scents of ocean and car exhaust. Nadine felt a momen-
tary vertigo. She planted her feet on the sidewalk and breathed
deeply.

During her ten years in Mexico, Nadine had often imagined
her return to South Africa. One of the ways she fell asleep at night
was playing the scene in her head: walking outside the airport,
hailing a taxi, driving to the Nutthall Road house. Her dream always stopped as the house came into view. If she wasn't yet asleep,
she rewound and replayed, walking outside the airport, hailing a
taxi, stepping inside, giving her address. Before the taxi turned
onto Nutthall Road, she could imagine Maxim was still inside the
house, slouched in his favorite chair, studying his photos, waiting
for her. Before the taxi turned, she had not yet failed him.

Abdul opened the door of his black Mercedes. On the seat, a
copy of the *Cape Argus*—just one edition now—lay next to a foil
packet of Simba potato chips. Nadine looked at Sophia, who was

combing her hair. "For God's sake, go ahead," said Sophia. Nadine opened the bag and dug in hungrily.

"It's not even breakfast time," said Sophia, disapprovingly.

"May I have some?" said Krispin. Nadine handed him the packet. Abdul pulled out of the airport and turned onto N2, the highway leading to Cape Town. Outside the window, there were marshy-looking fields on either side of the road. Krispin reached out to take Sophia's hand. She let him take it.

Nadine gazed at Table Mountain. It was over three thousand feet high, and Nadine had forgotten how she loved its enormous presence, cragged and beautiful. The top was absolutely flat, and in the morning, pale shadows ran down the shale and sandstone, spilling over green hills at the base. The light changed depending on the time of day, the time of year, the weather.

"What on earth is that?" said Sophia, pointing to the ethereal white cloud covering the mountain. The cloud seemed to cascade like a waterfall.

"We call this the Tablecloth," said Abdul.

"My God," said Sophia, "it's utterly terrifying."

Abdul chuckled. "As long as you are in the city and not on the mountain, you are safe," he said. After a moment, he added, "Well, safe from the Tablecloth."

"But assholes with rocks," said Sophia, "watch out."

There was an uncomfortable silence. Abdul looked puzzled. A few minutes later, he announced, "We are passing through the townships."

On either side of the highway, metal shacks glinted in the sun. Laundry hung from clotheslines, and groups of kids played along the road, some kicking a soccer ball, some just milling around. "Now that Mandela is president," said Abdul, "everyone moves to the city. There aren't enough houses or jobs." On their right, men assembled large concrete boxes. A ratty banner read, N2 GATEWAY

PROJECT. The air was stale, and smog hung overhead. The townships were more sprawled than in Nadine's memory, but they had
been created for blacks by the white-run government long before
Mandela's presidency, despite Abdul's implications.

Nadine remembered visiting Thola's house in the townships.
Nadine had arrived in Cape Town a month after Jason Irving's
death, and was stunned when Maxim told her that Thola's sister
was in jail for Jason's murder. Hungry for a story to put her on the
map, Nadine decided to convince Thola or her mother to speak
on record about Evelina. Nadine didn't want George interfering,
so with all of a new reporter's brio she weaseled Thola's home address out of him and borrowed Maxim's car, ignoring both men's
warnings not to go to Sunshine alone.

Fikile, Thola's mother, answered the door. Her hair was gray.
She wore a purple tunic of some sort, layers of clothing. Fikile
folded her arms across her chest at the sight of a white woman
with a reporter's notebook. "No," she said, with less anger than
exhaustion. "No interview, sorry." Her few English words encour-
aged Nadine.

"But I'm a friend of Thola," said Nadine, trying to look as
earnest as possible. This wasn't a lie, exactly: Nadine had been living with George and Maxim for a few weeks, and she saw Thola
regularly, though by no stretch were Nadine and Thola friends.
Not yet.

Fikile looked confused. "Can I come inside?" said Nadine. "I
am also a friend of George."

"Ah, *George,*" said Fikile. She smiled wide, her plump cheeks
expanding, and her entire stance changed. Her arms fell open,
and she gestured for Nadine to enter the house. "George," she repeated. "George and Thola," she said. She laughed.

"Yes, yes," said Nadine, nodding feverishly. "George and
Thola!"

"George and Thola," said Fikile. Fikile and Nadine faced each other, smiling energetically. Nadine couldn't imagine for the life of her how she was going to get from this exchange to a front-page exclusive.

The house was dark. Along one wall, pots and pans were organized and scrupulously clean. A cheese grater, propane stove, and ceramic bowls lined the top shelf. A shirt on a hanger was suspended above a bed, and a homemade curtain on a string was pulled away from the windows.

The walls were covered with newspaper cutouts of Thola, dancing or posing in her leotards. She was dazzling: tall and elegant, with impossibly perfect posture. When she walked into the house Nadine shared with George and Maxim, they all lost their breath for a moment. Thola was like that: she sucked the air from a room. It was thrilling to be around her, but also exhausting.

Fikile pointed at the lumpy sofa, and Nadine sat. After bustling in the kitchen, Fikile returned with a tray of tea. Nadine and Fikile sipped tea and nodded periodically, their expressions growing strained. Nadine voiced a few questions—*Do you miss Evelina? Is Evelina being treated fairly in jail? Do you feel that Sunshine is unsafe?*—but Fikile just stared blankly, topping off Nadine's tea. Finally, Nadine accepted that Fikile didn't speak English, didn't want to talk, or both. George had told her that Thola finished work around five, but it was six, and Nadine was sure Fikile had better things to do. Nadine stood, and Fikile rose, too, smoothing the fabric of her wrap.

"Okay," said Nadine. "Nice to meet you. Thank you for the tea."

Fikile nodded. She looked relieved that the visit was ending. Nadine let herself out, then stood in the parched square of yard. The township violence had only escalated in the two months since Jason Irving's murder, and she felt pinpricks of fear as she walked quickly to her car. She had botched completely her goal of securing the first interview with Evelina's family, and as she drove back to Observatory, the whites-only suburb where she lived, she was crushed.

Thola was at the Nutthall Road house, reclining like a queen across their living room couch. George massaged her feet as they watched *Sgudi 'Snaysi,* a Zulu-language sitcom. "Hello, Nadine," said Thola, when Nadine walked inside.

"Oh for God's sake," said Nadine, "here you are."

Thola smiled wide and reached for a pecan from a bowl on the coffee table. "Here I am," she said. She sat up and rolled her head to one side, stretching her lovely neck. "Shoulders," she said to George, and he began to rub them.

"Listen, Thola," said Nadine, summoning her courage. "I want to interview you, officially. I want to write a different kind of story." Nadine swallowed. "I want to write the story that will change Evelina's life."

George snorted, and Nadine glared at him.

Thola evaluated Nadine, her eyes narrowing. "I don't know about that," she said.

"Will you think about it?" said Nadine.

"Sure," said Thola. "I'll think about it while I clean toilets in a white man's house."

George laughed appreciatively. Nadine's face grew red, but she spoke evenly. "Thanks, Thola. I'd be grateful."

"No charge to think about it," said Thola.

Krispin peered out the window of the Mercedes as they drove past the townships. "How many people live here?" he asked.

"Millions and millions," said Abdul.

"Do you live in a township?" asked Sophia.

Abdul laughed politely. "Oh no, ma'am," he said. "I am a Muslim, ma'am, mixed race."

"Just the blacks live in the townships, then?" said Sophia.

"Oh no," said Abdul. "It's a complex situation, ma'am."

"Well, where do you live?" asked Sophia.

"In the Bo-Kapp, ma'am. I can take you there if you like. It's a mixed area." Nadine smiled, remembering weekends with Maxim in the Bo-Kapp. One morning, strolling through the colorful streets—the homes and mosques were painted in pastel colors—they heard jazz notes. Nadine and Maxim followed the music and found a group of kids in an alley. The kids wore tracksuits and baseball caps; their brass instruments flashed in the sun. Maxim leaned against a building with Arabic letters spray-painted on it and pulled Nadine to him. Nadine listened to the music, her arms around Maxim's waist.

"Well, every area's mixed now," said Krispin. "Isn't that right, Abdul?"

Abdul laughed again. "If you say so, sir," he said.

The road led out of the smog and into bright air laced with eucalyptus. The shacks were replaced by low, green bushes and stucco houses with ceramic roofs. Abdul drove higher and higher, and then, in a flash, the Atlantic Ocean came into view.

Krispin said, "Ah," and squeezed Sophia's hand. The water was light blue and vast, huge ships and metal machinery lining its edge.

"I will take you to a restaurant by the sea for dinner," said Abdul. "A restaurant called the Green Dolphin."

"That sounds perfect," said Krispin. He turned to Sophia. "Do you think he went there for dinner?" he said. "The Green Dolphin?"

"Oh, Krispin," said Sophia, "who the hell knows." Nadine cast a quick glance at Sophia, taking in her weary expression.

"We have an Outback Steakhouse," said Abdul proudly. "We have the Body Shop."

Sophia began to cry quietly. Krispin pulled her to his chest and closed his eyes.

"On your left," said Abdul, "the Cape Town City Hall." He gestured to a building lined with cream-colored columns and ornate engraving, a clock tower at the top. Palm trees surrounded the building.

And then they were barreling down Long Street, with its sagging balconies and seedy restaurants. They turned onto Orange Street, and then Abdul slowed and with gravity announced, "The Victoria."

Nadine remembered the enormous pink pillars, the brass letters spelling THE VICTORIA HOTEL. A man stood in front of the pillars, tiny in comparison. He wore a blue suit jacket with an insignia on the front pocket and a beige pith helmet. Nadine had been to the Victoria once before; Maxim brought her to the hotel bar to celebrate her twenty-sixth birthday. They felt out of place among the white elite, overwhelmed, and moved to a rattier locale after one glass of champagne.

The man leaned down to Abdul's car window. "Welcome to the Victoria," he said. In his hand, he held a clipboard. "Name, please."

"Mr. and Mrs. Krispin Irving," said Abdul.

"And, um, Nadine Morgan," Nadine said, leaning forward.

"Oh yes, Irving," said the man in the pith helmet. "Of course, of course." He waved them inside, and Abdul put the car in gear. Past the gate, the road was brick and lined with palm trees. The clatter and noise of the city faded as Abdul drove into an oasis of picture-perfect calm.

The Victoria was made up of many pink buildings, some with private pools, some with balconies. Abdul pulled up to the main lobby, where three men in uniforms waited. "Good morning," said one, opening the door of the Mercedes. Another man grabbed luggage from the back of the car, and the third simply stood by, hands folded across his chest. "I will leave you now," announced Abdul. "I will take you to dinner tonight at seven PM."

"Lovely," said Sophia, "We'll see you then." She turned to Nadine. "Good-bye," she said firmly. "Have a nice visit. Krispin, I'll see you inside. I do not want you to have anything further to do with this reporter. I hope I make myself clear."

"Sophia," said Krispin.

Sophia was shaking with rage. She closed her eyes and drew in a breath. Then, eyes open, she spoke to her husband. "I came here at your request," she said, spitting the words. "I am going to face the animals who killed my son. For you, Krispin. I don't want to be here." Her voice rose, and her shoulders shuddered. "*I don't want to be here,* do you hear me? *I will never forgive the—*" She stopped and covered her face with her hands. After a moment, she regained her composure, and let them drop. "I deserve to ask for something," she said.

Nadine opened her mouth, but Sophia walked away, passing through the hotel doors.

"Mr. Irving," Nadine said.

"I'm sorry," said Krispin. "I'm not going to be able to speak with you. Good luck, Ms. Morgan."

"Mr. Irving," said Nadine, feeling her story drain away. "If you'd just meet me for a drink . . ."

"Didn't you hear her?" said Krispin, looking at Nadine with pity.

"But," said Nadine, "we could . . . there's a coffee shop . . ."

"I said no. I'm sorry," said Krispin, turning away.

Nadine stood with her duffel between her legs. "You are not the child of the Irvings?" said Abdul.

"No," said Nadine. "The Irvings' child is dead. He was killed here, in Cape Town."

"Jason Irving," said Abdul. "I should have known."

"Yes," Nadine said.

"Do you need to go somewhere, ma'am?" asked Abdul.

"No," Nadine said. "I'll stay here. I can call a taxi if I need one."

Abdul looked at Nadine blankly. "You cannot take another taxi," he said. "It is very dangerous."

"Okay," Nadine said.

"Listen to me, ma'am," said Abdul. "You cannot walk outside the Victoria. You will be at risk. Street children. They sniff the glue."

"Okay, thanks," Nadine said, opening her wallet and handing Abdul a five-dollar bill.

"You don't listen," said Abdul, "but you should listen."

Nineteen

Nadine walked into the cavernous lobby, the porter wheeling her duffel before her on a large brass stand. The lobby smelled of eggs, bacon, and Pledge. A white woman behind the front desk looked up as Nadine entered. The woman was flanked by huge floral arrangements. "Good morning," she said cheerily. "Nice flight, hey?" Her accent, almost Dutch, was Afrikaans. Most whites in South Africa were either Afrikaans, descendants of Dutch settlers, or *soutpiels,* "salt penises": descendants of English settlers with one foot in Europe, one in Africa, and their *piel* hanging in the salty sea. Maxim's family was Afrikaans.

"It was long," Nadine said.

"How many hours?" asked the woman. Her name tag read JO-HANNA.

"Twenty-one to Johannesburg," Nadine said, "a layover, and then three hours here." Nadine looked at the Tanzanite jewelry in a lit-up glass case on the wall. A plaque read, VISIT OUR GIFT SHOP.

"Is it!" said Johanna, shaking her head. "Are you checking in, then?"

"Yes," said Nadine, placing her MasterCard in front of Johanna's manicured nails. "The least expensive room available, please." She would have to call Eugenia, beg for her expenses. Ian had been clear in his refusal to send her abroad until spring.

"We're out of superior rooms," said Johanna. "For the same rate, I shall give you a luxury suite."

"You know," Nadine said, "that's the best thing to happen to me in a very long time."

"I'm so happy," said Johanna.

The elevator was a tiny library filled with books on two sides. They were leather-bound classics. Nadine touched *Othello,* tried to pull it off the wall, and found that the books were glued together, fake.

Her suite was bright and sumptuous, with elephant and tiger prints on the wall. The giant bed had a canopy spilling over it; when Nadine looked closer, she saw that the rich fabric was patterned with men smoking opium pipes.

In the suite, an arrangement of flowers, giant eggs with stubby petals, had been placed in a crystal vase. They were proteas, the national flower.

Nadine ran the taps of her enormous bathtub and stripped off her travel clothes, piling them next to the bed. She put Jason Irving's journal on the mahogany desk by the window. Nadine knew she should begin working the phone now that the Irvings were refusing to talk. She sank into bubbles, willing herself to think about new angles, possible contacts.

Instead, she thought of Hank. She wanted to have him next to her, to pull his solid body into her arms. She had convinced herself she was happy alone for so many years, but now the lie was plain. What was the point of a giant tub—Nadine could stretch both her legs out completely—without someone to slide in beside her? The slow contentment Nadine had felt in Hank's house was gone now, and she was left with the unmoored, nervous feeling that she had convinced herself was inescapable. But what if she didn't have to feel the dull sense of loneliness as each day scraped by? The possibility of something else filled her with yearning.

When the water in the bath was cool, Nadine climbed from the tub. The sun outside her hotel window was too bright. She moved to close the curtains and discovered two wrought-iron doors leading to a balcony, which was appointed with a table and two chairs. Table Mountain was visible to one side, Lion's Head to the other. Nadine put on a thick terry-cloth bathrobe and sat outside for a while, staring at the busy streets.

Long after Nadine left for Mexico, bloody fighting had continued in South Africa. In desperation, the apartheid government finally released Mandela in 1990. He fought tirelessly to end apartheid, and was elected president in 1994. Nadine had seen the election on television: township residents, who had voted for the first time in their lives, watched the ballot counting with thunderstruck expressions. They danced in the streets when their beloved "Madiba" actually won. Ten years after Nadine's departure, South Africa was tasting a fragile peace. The city before Nadine had changed completely, and yet here was Nadine, still alone, still running, the same.

Twenty

NANTUCKET TO STARDOM

This morning was crazy, as usual. I woke up with a really good feeling buzzing around in my chest, and I wanted to run downstairs and tell my parents all about Malcon and the auditions. I was halfway down the stairs when I remembered the pinched look my mom gets when she thinks I'm going to lose or be humiliated. She got it when I told her I needed head shots to send to Cheerios for the "Face of Cheerios Contest." Yes, we went to the photographer, and we sent the pictures in, but every day when I begged her to go get the mail that little line between her eyebrows got deeper.

She was right: I never heard back from Cheerios. And I was upset, but I got over it (after a few months). She was also right about the Dance USA video I made her take of me and the Barbizon Modeling School Catwalk Summer Camp in Worcester. But that worried look just keeps on coming, when she picks me up at school and sees me standing alone, when we drive by a birthday party I haven't been invited to.

My dad says, *Let him stick his neck out, for Christ's sake,* but my mom says, *I just can't bear to see him sad.* She calls me her sweet baboon and she always wants to give me a hug and smooch my cheeks. She wants me to sit next to her when we watch movies and put my head on her shoulder. Okay, I like it, too. I love the smooches and the sweet baboon. But I don't want her to worry every time I take a chance!

So I decided not to say anything about Malcon or the audition. The kitchen radio was really loud—it was Dolly Parton singing "Here You Come Again." I went downstairs, and there was Mom in her fuzzy green robe twitching her bottom back and forth. When she heard my footsteps, she whirled around and sang—*totally* off-key—as loud as she could, "All you have to do is smile that smile and there go all my defenses!" And she held her arms open like I was going to rush right in.

I said, "Mo-om," and rolled my eyes as disdainfully as I could. She smiled at me and kept right on going. "Here you come again, looking better than a body has a right to and shaking me up so . . ."

"Mom!" I said. "Please stop right now."

And then—I kid you not—*Dad* came into the kitchen in his Brooks Brothers boxer shorts. And he sang right along with her! Talk about a bunch of ham bones. It was just too much before breakfast. I turned and tried to run back upstairs. But Dad followed me, grabbed me around the waist, and swept me up like I was a kid. He dragged me back to the kitchen and made me sing along, even forcing me to solo during the chorus, singing into a wooden mixing spoon.

"We should start a band," said Dad, out of breath from shimmying. "Like the Partridge Family."

"Like the Jacksons," said Mom.

I rolled my eyes again and gave them the Loser sign, but they didn't even know what it meant. Now I have to go: Dad and I are going to try for bluefish on Tuckernuck Flats. At least the radio on the boat broke, so no more scary tunes.

Twenty one

C ape Town was seven hours ahead of Boston, so Nadine had to wait to call Eugenia. She told herself she didn't want to wake Hank, and her father was snug asleep with Gwen, but Nadine thought of Lily, who might be up by five AM. She picked up her phone and, with the help of the hotel operator, dialed the number she knew by heart.

"Hello?" Lily's voice was sleepy but clear.

"Hi," Nadine said. "I didn't think you'd answer. It's me."

"Hey you," said Lily, "I heard you're shacking up with the good doctor."

"Actually," Nadine said, "no. I'm in South Africa."

There was a silence. "I beg your pardon?" said Lily, finally.

"I'm looking at Cape Town out my window."

Lily sighed. "You never change."

"Why should I?" said Nadine.

"I'm not even going to dignify that question with a response," said Lily.

"You're the one who's changed," said Nadine. "You don't want to hear about anything beyond—"

"I have changed, Nadine," said Lily angrily. "And I know you're afraid of ending up like your mom, stuck on the Cape. But you can't just keep . . . running away!"

"Why not?"

"Nadine," said Lily. "Dr. Duarte is a wonderful man. You really blew it this time."

"I left a message for him. I'm going to call him," said Nadine. "I just didn't want to wake him up."

"He doesn't know?" screeched Lily.

"I'm here for a trial," said Nadine. "It was a last-minute assignment. I had to get here, it was one of those things—"

"One of those things," said Lily.

"My God!" said Nadine. "Isn't anyone proud of me? What I do is important!"

"And what I do doesn't mean a damn thing."

"Lily—"

"Bo was sick yesterday. He had a fever of a hundred and one and was breathing funny. I took him to see Dr. Duarte. He said you were staying out on Nantucket. He was so happy, Nadine. He said you were so damn great, blah, blah."

Nadine was silent. In the background, she heard a baby begin to cry.

"But guess what?" said Lily. "I told Dennis you'd just screw him over. And I was right."

"Oh, Lily," said Nadine. "What can I do to make things better between us? I miss you, you don't know."

"I know," said Lily quietly.

"Why can't you love me the way I am?"

"Because this isn't who you are," said Lily. "This is you being afraid of being who you are."

"That doesn't even make sense."

The baby's cry grew louder. "I have to go," said Lily.

"Oh," said Nadine, "okay."

"I know you feel sorry for me," said Lily. "You feel sorry for me and my boring life. But you know what? I'm going to go hold my sweet baby. He's going to be okay, by the way. What are you going to do?"

"I'm," said Nadine. "I'm . . ."

"Right," said Lily. And she hung up the phone.

Nadine held the receiver in front of her, and then started

laughing. "I'm going to mix a delicious gin and tonic," she told the buzzing line. "And I'm going to drink it on my snazzy balcony. That's what I'm going to do." She tossed the phone into its cradle with a flourish and walked over to the wooden bar, which had every sort of liquor and every sort of glass, from champagne flutes to cognac snifters.

Two drinks and a Demerol later, after making a list of possible stories, she called Eugenia in Boston. "Babe," said Eugenia. "It's been awhile. I heard you got beat up."

"I did," said Nadine. "Chiapas. But listen. I've got a hot story, and I want you to publish it."

"I heard you're a basket case."

"I'm fine," said Nadine. "Listen." She reminded Eugenia about Jason Irving's 1988 murder, played up the fact that the Irvings were about to meet his killers face-to-face. "The Irvings' testimony," she concluded, "could decide whether or not Jason's murderers are given amnesty."

"What's the deal?" said Eugenia. "Are they just unlocking the jails over there?"

"No," said Nadine. "It's a case-by-case basis. The crimes have to have a clear political motivation, for one thing. And the TRC has to feel that the criminals are telling the truth. People have been refused amnesty. What the Irvings have to say could make all the difference."

"You think they'll speak at the hearings?"

"Hard to say," said Nadine, imagining Sophia's pursed lips, her angry tirade.

"I always knew you'd go back to South Africa," said Eugenia. Nadine heard her draw in on a cigarette. "I've got a stringer in Johannesburg," said Eugenia, "but the Irvings won't talk to anyone.

It's a good piece either way, but if you can get the Irvings on record, this could be big."

"Eugenia," said Nadine, "I flew over with them! I have Jason's journal in my hand right now."

"You're my gal," said Eugenia.

"I need money," said Nadine. "I had to stay in the same hotel as the Irvings."

"No problem," said Eugenia. "This is front page. 'Parents Decide Fate of Son's Killers.' I love it."

"They're not exactly—"

"This," continued Eugenia, "is the kind of stuff that sells papers."

"I suppose," said Nadine, pouring a third drink. She realized the tonic was gone, shrugged, and poured more gin. "Thanks, Eugenia."

"Honeybun," said Eugenia, "you've always got a place at the *Trib.*"

"That's good to know."

"Send some other stories, too, while you're there. Some of the other trials, maybe."

"Will do," said Nadine.

"I'm not even going to ask why you're not with Ian on this one," said Eugenia.

"Great," said Nadine.

"Get quotes from the kid killers," added Eugenia. "A rock, wow. You can't make this shit up."

Nadine hung up and lay back on the bed. She grabbed Jason Irving's journal and opened it to a random page. *Today I leave for South Africa,* Jason had written. *It's finally time to see the place I've dreamed about.*

Nadine's notes fanned out around her, scrawled pages, and she thought of lying in bed with Maxim, his photos overlapping with her papers. She had felt full of purpose in those days, so sure that what she was doing was right. One day, Nadine picked up a photo of what looked like the interior of a kitchen. Light from a window hit canisters of flour and sugar lined up on the counter.

"What's this?" she said.

"A house near my parents' farm," said Maxim. Brought up on a farm outside Johannesburg, Maxim was bound to his family and his country by a mixture of love, guilt, sorrow, and hatred. Maxim had been raised by a black "mammy." His mother was wan and distant, and his father was baffled by Maxim's desire to "liberate the natives."

Nadine examined the photograph. It was the end of a long day, and Maxim wore only jeans. She touched his chest.

"It's a sad picture," she said. "Why is that?"

"A woman was killed in that kitchen," said Maxim. "Mrs. Robertson. She was a widow, used to hire me to help around the house."

Nadine stared at the photo. She and Maxim had been lovers for a few months, and she knew by now that if she waited, the story would come.

"That's the other side of things," said Maxim. "The blacks want the land back. Some group of thugs—could have been her own workers, but probably resistance fighters—beat her to death, just left her lying in the kitchen. She might have been there for days. My mum stopped in for a cup of tea and there she was. They took the jewelry, money, her china."

"Your mom found her?" said Nadine. "I'm so sorry, Maxim."

Maxim stared straight ahead. "Could happen to my parents, too," he said. "Their farm, it isn't near anything. Cut the phone lines and that's that."

"Jesus."

Maxim's shoulders slumped. "My mum said, she said to me, 'Just don't let me die alone, Max. Don't let someone find me when they come in for a cup of sugar.' "

"So you call every night."

"That's got to be the worst," said Maxim. "Dying—passing over—all alone in your fucking kitchen."

"You're going to live to one hundred," said Nadine, running her fingers through his flaxen hair, "a grouchy old grandpa who won't turn on his hearing aid and carves wooden animals all day."

Maxim leaned down, rested his head on her stomach. He took her hand. "A tumbler of whiskey at my side?"

"Yes," said Nadine, "I'll share it with you."

Twenty-Two

NANTUCKET TO STARDOM

Last night was opening night. I was nervous, but it was really fun to be backstage with all the other actors, getting ready for the show. Some of the other boys refused to wear makeup. Amateurs! I even knew what I was doing—I've tried out Mom's lipstick. The eye shadow was new: all Mom has in her travel bag is lipstick and some crusty mascara. Maybe I'll give her a makeover for Christmas, instead of a Whitman's Sampler. Mom could totally use a makeover. People always talk about how glamorous she is (probably because she's not from Nantucket) but I wish she'd get permanents at Hot Locks Salon and Spa, the way the other mothers do.

And finally, showtime. My heart was aflutter. My fedora was askance (new vocab from the Word a Day calendar). I peeked out at the audience and let me tell you, the Nantucket Elementary Auditorium was packed. I didn't see Malcon or my parents, but basically the whole island was sitting on folding chairs. And suddenly, I wasn't nervous anymore. I knew I was going to be fantastic. I was—as Malcon said—a star.

Gerald Smith said, "This doll has captured my attention," and I knew my cue was coming. The lights were hot on my face, and my eyes burned. I said my favorite line with all the feeling I could find: "Polka dots! In the whole world, nobody but Nathan Detroit could blow a thousand bucks on polka dots!" and the audience laughed. It was so awesome.

The show went by fast. "Sue Me" brought down the house, but in no time the final curtain fell. All that work, and opening night was over. When I took my bow, the applause thundered over me. I didn't even mind how sweaty my suit was.

So there, I thought, as clapping rang in my ears. *So what if you pick me last for medicine ball. Who cares if no girl asked me to the Sadie Hawkins dance and I had to get all dressed up and hide out at Mr. Mullen's? I'm not different, I'm special.*

I had imagined all the jocks would be in the front row, crying because they were so sorry they punched me in the stomach when I walked by them in the hallway, but I wasn't disappointed that the front row was full of old ladies from the Nantucket Senior Care Center. I bowed again and again.

And I mean, if I was excited about opening night, imagine how I'm going to feel at the Oscars. Or when I win *American Superstar,* or at least rock the house at the Mashpee Mall Regional Auditions.

We all went outside in our costumes and ate cookies in the hallway and Mrs. Jelly gave the girls bouquets. What is the deal? Boys can't get roses? I was really jealous of freaking Louisa, who doesn't even enunciate but got a sweet bunch of long-stems.

And then came Mom, all smiles in one of her weird-o outfits, complete with some sort of cape. Sometimes, I do wish she'd wear a nice pair of slacks and a cardigan, like everyone else's mom, instead of shopping in Boston and

New York. But anyway, she was so happy. I said, "Where's Dad?" and she got that line between her eyebrows.

"There was an important call," she said.

"It's opening night."

"He'll be here tomorrow night, honey. In fact, he could be arriving any minute."

"I know," I said. "I just really wish he had seen me."

"I can't wait to tell him all about it," said Mom. "You were astonishing." She tried to gather me in but I pulled away from her. For some reason, I was totally bummed. I guess the excitement of the night wearing off and all.

I said I had to go get changed and she said, "Of course, honey." She looked sort of lonely there in the hallway, and I told her there was cider and she said, "Oh cider? Great!" But Mom is no actress.

In the backstage dressing room mirror, I stared at myself. *I should dye my hair,* I thought: *a nice chestnut, maybe, or platinum like Marilyn Monroe.* While I was putting on my sneakers, Mom came in. She smiled, and sat down on the floor Indian-style. "Come here," she said. I sat on her lap and she wrapped her arms around me. It felt nice. She rested her cheek on the top of my head. "I'm sorry about your dad not being here," she said. "He loves you, baby. I love you."

I was just starting to feel okay again when Bret Williams burst into the room. "Whoa-ho," said. "Looks like I'm in-terrupting something!" He said it in a creepy tone, like Mom and I had been making out.

"Dude," I said. I stood up really fast, my shoulders still warm from my mom's hug. "We were just—"

"Whoa-ho," said Bret. "I can *see* what you were *doing!*" He left, letting the door slam behind him.

"Wait," I said, to the door. I looked at Mom, who was sitting on the floor looking confused. All of a sudden I was angry at her, in her fancy outfit. Who did she think she was? "I'm not a *baby*," I said. I pushed the door open and ran into the hallway. "She's such a loser!" I said loudly, but no one was listening.

And what do you know, but I felt a hand on my back. I turned around, and it was Malcon Bridges.

He said, "Hey kid," and then he handed me a rose. It was a little bit wilted—I think it was one of the ones they sell at the checkout lane at Stop & Shop—but it was a rose all the same. Malcon moved his hand to my shoulder and said, "Fine job."

"Thanks," I said to Malcon. "I'm really glad you're here."

This morning, Dad was waiting for me in the kitchen. "Son," he said. "I heard you were great last night."

"You look tired," I said.

"It was a late night," said Dad.

"Then why are you up?"

"Thought maybe we could get some doughnuts," said Dad. "And then take the boat out? We could even head to Muskeget, bring your mom home a bass?"

"Right, Dad," I said. "That's a great idea. I'll eat a bunch of fattening doughnuts and then go get all wet and cold and lose my voice before I have to go fit into my costume and sing the part of Nathan Detroit. That's a *brilliant* plan."

"What's that around your eyes?" said Dad.

I looked at my reflection in the microwave. "Mascara," I said.

"Oh," said Dad.

"I don't think you understand one thing about me," I said.

"That's not true," said Dad. "I understand that I let you down. And I'm trying to apologize."

We stared at each other, and then I got up without saying a word. I knew if I started crying, he'd say that I was just like my mom, prone to histrionics, one of his favorite expressions. I left him in the kitchen and came up here to write. Mom says it feels so great to write in your journal and get it all out, but I don't feel so great.

Twenty-Three

W hen Nadine woke, it was the middle of the night, and she stood on the balcony under the stars. The mountains looked sharp, and below, the city was quiet. Signal Hill was outlined against the sky, a slow swell. Lion's Head was a rocky thimble. Nadine could smell the ocean. On her room phone, the message light was steady.

It was midnight. Nadine thought of Hank, handing her a cold beer after a long walk on the beach. They'd made love and then eaten Triscuits and sharp cheddar cheese.

Back in her room, Nadine turned on the bedside lamp. She summoned her courage and dialed Hank's office. His receptionist told Nadine to hold, and then he came on the line. At the sound of his voice, joy coursed through Nadine. "Hey!" she said. "Did you get my message?"

"I did. I had no idea how much that article would inspire you," Hank said coolly.

"I'm in Cape Town," Nadine said.

"So I hear."

"This story is amazing. The *Boston Trib* is going for page one. I told you about Evelina . . . about Maxim . . ." There was only silence.

"I told you on the beach?"

Hank did not respond.

"Well, thank you," said Nadine. "Thanks for the article. The *Whaler* of all things."

"You're welcome," said Hank. "I guess I thought we'd talk about it when I got back."

"Oh."

"A little dinner conversation."

"Jesus," said Nadine. "It's more than dinner conversation to me."

"Clearly."

"Are you angry?" said Nadine. "I don't get it."

"Nadine," said Hank, "I'm speaking to you as a doctor. You shouldn't be walking around, much less walking around in South Africa."

"I feel fine."

"I doubt that."

"Jesus," said Nadine again.

"All right," said Hank. "Where does this leave us?"

"What do you mean?"

"If you don't know what I mean," said Hank evenly, "I'm going to hang up this phone."

"What did you expect?" said Nadine. "Did you think I would live quietly on Nantucket for the rest of my life?"

"For the rest of the week, maybe."

"Well, I guess you misjudged me."

Again, Hank was silent. Finally he said, "I guess I did."

"This is an important story," Nadine said, hollowly.

"I know."

"I'm staying at the Hotel Victoria," said Nadine, "if you need to reach me."

"I already tried," said Hank. "Looks like I wasn't the man for the job."

"What are you talking about?"

"Good-bye, Nadine," said Hank. "And you can pretend you don't get this, either. I fell in love with you. I don't know how it happened so fast, but there you have it. I miss you, and I'm sorry you had to leave. I wish you had chosen me, tried to give this a chance. But you clearly want something else. I wish you the best, really."

"I," said Nadine.

"Good-bye," said Hank.

"Listen," said Nadine. "Please."

"I'm listening," said Hank.

"This doesn't mean it's over."

There was a silence, and then Hank spoke. "No," he said, "you're wrong. In fact, Nadine, this does mean it's over. I don't want to love someone who's always packing her bags. That's not a life."

"I packed your bag, actually," said Nadine, trying to sound jovial. "The green duffel."

"It's yours," said Hank. "A parting gift. Take care."

"Hank," Nadine said, but the line was dead. Nadine slammed down the phone. Then she changed into clean jeans and a clinging silk top Hank had insisted she buy on Nantucket. In the bathroom, she pinned her hair awkwardly with her good hand. Breathing hard, she applied lipstick. The bar at the Vicky was a hangout for established journalists, and Nadine hoped she could still charm some leads, even in her bedraggled state.

She rode the elevator downstairs. The Planet Champagne Bar was located on a screen porch overlooking the gardens. Nadine went inside and looked around. South Africa might still be segregated, she thought, but at the exclusive Victoria wealthy blacks, whites, and so-called coloreds mingled freely.

Outside, clusters of fashionable people sat under the trees, smoking and talking softly. Nadine felt lonely and far from home, her wrist and head aching. A waiter in a tuxedo approached and handed her a cocktail. "What's this?" Nadine asked.

"A diamond fizz," said the waiter, who had a pale goatee. He placed the drink on a Victoria Hotel napkin. "Compliments of the gentleman at the bar." He inclined his head gracefully.

Nadine looked over and saw the back of a man's head above a

button-down shirt, close-cropped salt-and-pepper hair. One hand was on his knee, long fingers white against the dark fabric of his jeans. He sat with two other men, both of whom looked scruffy and intense. As Nadine watched, he turned and smiled, lifted his chin, as if to say, *Come closer.*

Nadine gasped. The ponytail was gone, but she recognized him in an instant. It was George.

Twenty-four

NANTUCKET TO STARDOM

Sorry, it's been awhile since I've written. I've been super busy, but today something happened that I need to write down.

I'll start with last week. Dad came to the Saturday-night, Sunday-matinee, and Sunday-night performances of *Guys and Dolls,* and then framed the review in the *Gazette,* which said I "channeled Sinatra right before the audience's eyes." I tried to stay annoyed at him, but after every performance he was waiting in the hallway with a huge bouquet of flowers. (Daisies, irises, a dozen roses for closing night.) Mom bought some vases and my room looked like a freaking flower shop. It was like sleeping in an awesome-smelling garden. When I'm famous, I'm going to have fresh flowers delivered to me every single day.

But the week after the show ended was rough. I wasn't a busy big shot anymore, just my usual self wandering around the hallways hoping no one would trip me or write FAG on my locker with Wite-Out. Mom says all the bullying will end and my time will come. I'm ready for that to happen.

Am I a fag because I like flowers and lipstick? What is a fag? I don't get it. I just know I'm not the same as everyone else. And my parents are always worried about me, always saying, *But maybe you'd like soccer* and *No you cannot have leather pants.*

Malcon has shown me something, something I always hoped was true. Maybe there's a whole world outside Nantucket where I do belong. Maybe my loserness is actually something great, and I don't fit in because I'm better. I decided I would discuss this idea after school with Joe and Kyla, my best friends and also the head stylists at Hot Locks Salon and Spa.

On Monday, Mom said, "See you at three," as she was dropping me off.

I took a breath and said, "No you won't."

"What?" said Mom.

"I have *plans*," I said. "I have my own plans, Mom. I'll be home at five."

I figured she would worry, or at least ask what my plans were. But instead she shrugged and said, "Okay, honey." She pulled away from the curb without even looking back.

Kyla was busy with a frosting when I arrived at Hot Locks after school, but Joe poured me a cup of tea and listened as I outlined my theory about Nantucket being the loser, not me. I knew that Joe had his own issues, what with his wife and the guy who plays piano at the Jared Coffin House, but he listened to me like my problems were new and interesting. When I was finished talking, he said, "I think you're absolutely correct. I do. There's someplace in the world where every man feels like a king." I smiled, and Joe stood up. "Check out the new *People*," he said, tossing me the magazine. "You will not *believe* what Madonna is up to."

I threw myself into practicing for the *American Superstar* auditions. Sometimes I wondered if I should sing something a little more modern, like "Shake You Rump" or "Nigga in da House." In the end, I decided I had to trust Malcon's judgment.

I figured I could tell my parents I had a Drama Club meeting on Saturday, or I was hanging out at Murray's Toggery, which I sometimes did, trying to suss out what the summer people were wearing. I was also a member of the fake Human Rights Club, which I made up as a way to explain all the afternoons I went to Hot Locks Salon and Spa after school. My parents liked Joe and Kyla, but always said they wished I would spend time with kids my own age.

You can imagine my horror when Dad came home with tickets to a Red Sox game for Saturday afternoon! He was all proud and excited, handing me a catcher's mitt wrapped up in a box and pretending to be something good, like a leather jacket. And as I was trying to muster some excitement for the mitt, Mom and Dad, their faces lit up like birthday cakes, handed me the baseball tickets.

Could he get me tickets to the traveling company of *Streetcar Named Desire*? No, he could not. How about *Cats* or *A Chorus Line*? No, sir, Dad spends his hard-earned money on tickets to some baseball game. Then he goes on and on about hot dogs and all the soda I can drink.

"I'm really sorry," I said, trying to look like I was. "But the Human Rights Club is having a rally on Saturday. We're protesting child labor."

"Oh well," said Dad. "I guess I'll have to take your mother." He smiled at her, and then she surprised us all.

"I'm sorry, honey," she said. "But I have plans on Saturday. I'm meeting a friend in Boston for lunch. Maybe I can see you after the game."

"A friend?" said Dad.

"Yes," said Mom. Her face was all red, and I realized with a shock that Mom—who I thought I could read like an open book—was hiding something.

What is going on? My hand hurts, so it's time to go. Kyla gave me an Alberto VO5 hot-oil treatment, wish my hair luck.

Twenty-five

As Nadine approached, George stood. "It's you," he said. His friends' fervent conversation halted. Nadine put her drink on the bar.

"It's me," said Nadine.

"As breathtaking as ever," said George.

"Thank you," said Nadine, though she knew her lank hair and weary eyes hardly added up to breathtaking.

"Boys," said George, "this is Nadine. A fellow journalist. We shared an Obs apartment a long time ago. Before. But Nadine moved on to bigger and better things."

Nadine tried to smile, and George's companions responded with serious nods. It was clear they had been discussing something depressing.

"Alphonse," said one of George's friends, a heavyset black man. He held out a weathered hand, which Nadine shook. "Al, for short."

"I'm Ernest," said the other man. His accent was Afrikaans.

"That's his name," noted George. "Not his personality."

"Ernest," Nadine said. "Like Hemingway."

"Haven't shot myself yet," said Ernest.

"Nor have I," said Nadine. She picked up her glass and took a sip.

Ernest guffawed. Like Hemingway, he was a white man with a belly and an overgrown beard. The muscles in his arms and chest were huge, and he was deeply sunburned.

"It's been awhile," said George. He looked older, all the naïve bravado gone, replaced with something hard and cold. "I take photos now," he said. "The novel didn't pan out. I'm just in town a week or so."

"I've seen your work," said Nadine. George had become well known for his unflinching portraits of war. He traveled around the world, chasing bloodshed. Though he hadn't won a Pulitzer yet, Nadine knew it was just a matter of time.

"Novel?" said Ernest, raising an eyebrow.

"How about today?" said George, turning to his friends. "Anyone get anything?"

"The esteemed Archbishop Tutu, eating a sandwich at the break," said Ernest. "I think it was ham, or egg and mayonnaise."

"I got another crying mother," said Al. "I got ten more crying mothers."

"They're digging up some bodies," said George. "Out by Vlakplass. They'll bury them right this time. Might be some good shots there."

"Will Mandela come?" said Al.

"Who knows," said George.

"Not like the old days, that's for sure," said Al, glumly.

"We miss the blood and guts," Ernest explained to Nadine. "We're vultures," he added, shrugging and sipping his beer. "Democracy makes for boring photos."

"Depends on the democracy," said Nadine.

"What are you doing here, anyway?" said George. "I thought you were following the Zapatistas in Mexico."

"Keeping tabs on me, are you?"

"Hard to miss you," said George, "when your name's in the paper."

"I'm covering a story. Jason Irving. His hearing is Monday."

"Don't we know it," said Al. "More journalists here for the dead American boy than for all the Africans put together."

"Don't mind him," said Ernest. "We're knackered. We've been following the commission all over the country." He shook his head. "I've been to almost forty public hearings so far, each one filled with hundreds of brokenhearted mothers and widows. I suppose it should add up to something."

"And brokenhearted fathers," said Alphonse.

"And sons," added George. "And men, electrocuted until they couldn't stand up."

"Ah, fuck," said Ernest. "I can't wait until the TRC is over. I call it the Truth, Retch, and Cry."

"How much longer?" asked Nadine.

"I think there are ten or so hearings left. Then the commission's report."

"And then we begin life in the new South Africa!" said Ernest. His tone was mocking.

"I need another drink," said Al. "Can we charge them to your room, Big Shot?"

"Why not?" said George. "It's on *Newsweek.*"

Al ordered drinks, and the three men fell silent. The room was dim, and the music was slow and sultry, some sort of jazz. "And you?" Nadine asked George. "How are you? How is Thola?"

"Oh God," said Al. George didn't respond, but drew in on his cigarette and blew smoke, facing away from Nadine. "Tell her," said Al.

"Tell me what?" said Nadine. She felt a leaden weight in her stomach.

There was an awkward pause. George continued to look toward the screen glass doors, toward the lawn and the sky.

"Hendricks faces the TRC in Cradock, right?" said Ernest. He looked at George, concern in his brown eyes.

"Hendricks?" said Nadine. "Who's Hendricks?"

"What about Gandersvoot?" said George, turning back to

them. In his voice was a warning. "That's tomorrow. And Thola's sister, Evelina, on Monday. The Cape Town hearing is chock-full of thrills." He looked at Nadine for a moment, their eyes locking. Ernest and Al exchanged a glance. "You've already written about Evelina, haven't you, Nadine?" Nadine met George's cold stare.

"George," said Nadine, "don't."

"You had an exclusive interview with Thola," said George. "The one chance to change minds. Isn't that what you said to Thola? You would *change minds* about Evelina?"

"George," said Nadine, sighing.

"But you dumped that story and ran off to Mexico, didn't you, Nadine? You barely had time to say good-bye. Not to Thola. Not to me."

"For Christ's sake," said Nadine.

"Not to Maxim," said George.

"Hey now," said Ernest, bringing his palms together. "What about a change of scenery?"

Nadine broke her gaze from George. "Where to?" she asked.

"A *shebeen*," said George.

"G," said Al, "I don't think—"

"She's been to them," said George, holding up his hand like a traffic cop. "She was here before," said George. "It's Disneyland now."

Al raised his eyebrows. "You're welcome to join us," he said, "but it's not a big deal. Stay here if you're more comfortable."

"Comfortable," Nadine said quietly, even the word making her feel hemmed in.

"You do like to be comfortable, don't you?" said George.

"I'm happy to stay here," Nadine said. "I don't feel very well, actually."

"She likes the champagne bar," said George.

"So do you, you bugger," said Al.

"Jet lag?" said Ernest.

"Most likely," said Nadine. "I have all the symptoms. I'm exhausted, and sort of sick to my stomach. Kind of dizzy, too."

"Sounds like my wife when she was pregnant," said Al. "All she did was sleep, throw up, and eat ostrich biltong."

"Nasty stuff," said Ernest.

"I like it, myself. Salty."

Nadine smiled, but as the men headed to the *shebeen,* leaving Nadine with empty glasses, she thought of Hank, and the way she had climbed into his bed without considering birth control. But you couldn't get pregnant from a few nights of unprotected lovemaking, Nadine told herself. Not at the wrong time of the month. Not at thirty-five years old.

There was a concierge on call at the front desk. He looked up with a subservient smile when Nadine approached. "Ma'am?" he said, "You have been enjoying a cocktail in the champagne bar?"

"Yeah," said Nadine, "listen. I need a favor."

"Anything, madame," said the concierge superciliously. "Anything at all. My wish is your command."

"Good to hear," said Nadine. "I need a pregnancy test."

The concierge looked stunned, and Nadine heard laughter. She turned around to see Sophia Irving, one arm over her chest, the other tossed out, a cigarette in her fingers.

"The plot thickens," said Sophia, laughing again and then walking with an exaggerated, drunken gait to the elevator.

"Mrs. Irving!" called Nadine, but Sophia stepped into the elevator and pushed the button. Nadine ran to her.

"Did you know that a little girl killed my son with a rock?" said Sophia brightly. Her eyes glittered: with alcohol or madness, Nadine wasn't sure.

"Please," said Nadine, but the elevator doors closed and Sophia was gone.

"One moment for your personal hygiene item, ma'am," said the concierge. He picked up the heavy black phone and spoke rapidly in yet another language Nadine did not comprehend.

∎

Twenty-six

NANTUCKET TO STARDOM

Is Mom in love with another man? This question has been worrying me for days. I once heard Bret Williams say that the only time moms go into Boston is when they're redecorating or having an affair. We are not redecorating.

Today Dad took the early boat to the baseball game with Mr. Mullen from next door, giving me a dejected look as I ate cereal in my pajamas.

"You want your hat?" he asked, holding a Red Sox cap.

"That's okay, Dad," I said. I was reading the back of the Special K box, studying the Ten Tips for a Trimmer Waistline. "Give it to Mr. Mullen."

"Son, I'd really like for us to hang out together."

"Yeah, Dad," I said. "Me, too."

"Maybe we could hit the whaling museum tomorrow." When I was little, I loved the whaling museum. It was a family joke that I made my parents talk about whales so much they wanted to move to Nebraska so we could talk about corn.

"Sure, Dad," I said.

"Well, good luck at that, um, meeting of yours."

"You, too," I said. I was preoccupied. Could I really replace two meals a day with bowls of thin flakes? I wasn't sure. I was considering the possibility as Dad closed the door behind him.

Meanwhile, Mom was primping. I wandered upstairs to find her on her hands and knees in the bathroom, rummaging through the cabinet under the sink.

"Mom," I said, "what are you doing?"

"Oh!" she said, standing up. She looked embarrassed. "Have you . . . do you know where my mascara might be?"

"I have it," I said. "For the play," I explained. "By the way, what ferry are you taking?"

"The ten fifteen," she said. "Why?"

I shrugged. I was supposed to meet Malcon at one, so all was well.

"Who are you having lunch with?" I said. If she said *a decorator,* I could really rest easy. And let's be honest: our La-Z-Boy living room could use an update.

"Oh, just an old friend," she said.

"A man or a woman?"

"A man," she said. She gave a weird little laugh and I felt a flicker of fear in my stomach. "Are you coming back tonight?" I said.

"Of course!" she said. She put her hands on her hips. "What do you think, muffin?"

I said I didn't know.

"There's nothing *nefarious* going on," she said. "You give me too much credit." *Nefarious* had been Tuesday's Word of the Day. "And never mind the mascara," she said. "It won't matter, anyway." She looked bummed, all of a sudden. She gestured to her stomach. "Mascara," she said, shaking her head.

Dad has a photo of Mom by their bed. In the picture, Mom is really young, sitting in some French plaza. (They went to Paris for their honeymoon.) She's wearing a miniskirt with a flowy silk top, and her legs are skinny. She looks like a model. But everyone gets old, right? What can you do? Some of the other moms are muscular as deer, spending all their time at the health club, but I think Mom's soft stomach is beautiful. So she spends her time reading books on the couch, so what? But I don't know how to tell her any of this in a way that won't make her feel bad. So I said, "You look great, Mom."

She snorted. "I have a mirror," she said.

I looked at my watch—I had three hours to do my hair before catching the noon ferry. "I can make you up," I said.

"What?"

"I know how. From acting class. I'll give you a makeover."

Her face scrunched up like she was about to cry or laugh. "Oh honey," she said. "That would be wonderful."

I did what I could.

Twenty-seven

T he Response One pregnancy test arrived with Nadine's
     room-service breakfast, nestled inside a linen napkin.
Nadine took the test in the bathroom. While she waited for the re-
sults, she called the front desk to ask for the Irvings' room. She
was connected, and when Sophia answered, Nadine said, "Mrs.
Irving, it's Nadine Morgan calling."

"Well, good morning," said Sophia.

"Good morning," said Nadine. "I . . . I was hoping perhaps we
could meet for lunch today, or coffee . . ."

"Should you be drinking coffee, dear?" said Sophia.

"I don't . . . I was hoping," said Nadine, "that we could talk
about Jason. About the trial. Would there be—"

"I think I made myself abundantly clear," said Sophia, her
voice growing hard. "You have no idea what I'm dealing with. I
assume you have no children, Ms. Morgan. Not yet, at least!" She
laughed again, a mean, loopy laugh. "My son's killers are going
on trial Monday morning, even though they have already been
found guilty. I am spending the weekend sightseeing. We're looking at penguins, and I'm going to drink this delectable Cape
Pinotage. I'm not talking to any reporters. Is that clear enough,
Ms. Morgan? Let me say it once more: Don't call again." Sophia
hung up.

Nadine held the receiver. She wanted to dial Hank, to say she
had made a mistake by leaving, or why didn't he hop on a plane
and come ravish her, or just say hello. Good morning, Hank. Or
happy middle of the night. Instead, almost by instinct, she dialed

Lily. Dennis answered, sounding sleepy and alarmed. "It's me," said Nadine.

"Nadine?"

"Yeah. I'm sorry, Dennis, I know it's late—"

"Are you okay?"

"I'm, well, not really. I mean, yes, I'm fine, but . . . can I speak with Lily?"

"Goddamn it, Nadine," muttered Dennis, but he woke Lily, whose voice was clear on the line.

"What is it?" she said. "Are you hurt?"

"No," said Nadine.

"Are you still in Africa?"

"Yes," said Nadine.

"What is it?" repeated Lily.

"I just took a pregnancy test."

"Oh," said Lily. "Whoa, sweetheart. Hold on, I'm making tea." Nadine heard the rustle of covers, Lily's padded steps to the kitchen, the beeping of a microwave, and the clanking of a spoon in a cup. "I'm ready," said Lily. "Talk to me."

"It's Hank, and I . . . I've been dizzy, and I'm late."

"What does the test say?"

"It's in the bathroom," said Nadine. "I'm scared to look."

"I'm with you," said Lily. Nadine felt a wash of relief. It was like college: no matter how bad the drunken mistake, calling Lily always made things better. Nadine started toward the bathroom, but the phone cord wouldn't reach. "Shit," said Nadine.

"Oh my God," said Lily.

"No, it's that . . . the cord won't reach."

"Oh for God's sake," said Lily. "Go grab the stick and don't look. We'll find out together."

Nadine did as she was told. "It's positive," she whispered.

"Holy Lord God," said Lily.

"Fuck me," said Nadine.

There was silence, and then Lily said, "Honey? What are you going to do?"

"I have no idea," said Nadine.

"You have to tell him."

"Yeah."

"But not until tomorrow."

"Really?"

"Yes," said Lily. "You know," she said, "if you need me, if you need help with anything, just come home."

"What should I do?" said Nadine.

"I can't decide that one for you."

"Is it . . . ," said Nadine. "Is it terrible?"

"Terrible?" said Lily, genuinely confused.

"You seem so tired," said Nadine. "You seem . . . kind of lost in it all."

"Yeah," said Lily, her voice growing pensive. "I guess I am. And you know what? It's scary, too."

"Tell me," said Nadine, sitting on her bed.

"Loving them, it's . . . the only word I can come up with is *anguish*. I love them so much I'm in anguish. I'm so scared something might happen to them. And it would be my fault. And then I would be alone. I mean, there'd be Dennis, but I'd . . . I'd be alone."

"Jesus," said Nadine.

"Yeah," said Lily.

"I'm proud of you," said Nadine. "I guess I never told you that."

"I'm proud of myself," said Lily. "You know, if you came home, we'd be in it together. And actually, Nadine? I think Dr. Duarte is a lot more like you than you think. He's smart, and he's done so much . . . he's funny, too. He was a pirate for Halloween. He had this parrot on his shoulder. And an eye patch."

"I mean really," said Nadine. "You think I should come home and marry Hank? I mean, honestly, Lily."

"Why?" said Lily. "Why is it so impossible?"

Nadine was silent.

"You got knocked up," said Lily. She started to giggle. Nadine couldn't help but join in, laughing so hard that her stomach hurt. Finally, they said good-bye, Nadine promising to call in a few days.

She washed her face and decided to get to work. The TRC hearings would take her mind off her decision, she hoped. She dropped the test into the wastebasket by her desk and rummaged through her duffel bag, trying to find something clean to wear. She might be knocked up, but at least she could send Eugenia a story about Friday's hearing, the trial of Leon Gandersvoot, a member of the apartheid government's "counterinsurgency." Men like Gandersvoot were told to take care of any uprisings against the government. They "took care" by torturing and killing suspected activists. Now the apartheid government claimed there had been no such command. Many whites in Cape Town, Nadine believed, didn't want to acknowledge that such things had taken place. They knew what had been done to keep them—the tiny white minority—safe in their bougainvillea-covered homes, but they didn't want to know. *South African TRC: Dragging dirty secrets to the surface,* Nadine wrote in her notebook. It made her feel better to flip open her notebook, to scribble. She knew how to be a reporter.

The Good Hope Centre was mobbed. Nadine climbed up the crowded steps, clutching the china mug from her room, which she was using as a take-out coffee.

She found her way to the press area, a bare room with a television surrounded by plastic chairs. The other reporters were animated. "It's unbelievable, really," a woman with a blonde pixie haircut said, after introducing herself as Ruth. "I can't believe Gandersvoot is going to walk in here and tell the truth. He'd be jailed for the rest of his life if it weren't for the TRC, but we'd never hear what he'd done, from his own mouth."

"We know what he did," said a bitter voice. Nadine recognized it and looked across the room to see George, holding a camera.

"Not the details," said Ruth.

"Fuck the details," said George. "Not worth giving Gandersvoot amnesty."

"I guess that's the question," said Ruth tiredly. She had been covering the hearings for a year, she told Nadine, traveling all over the country. First the victims had told their stories, and now the accused had their turn. The hearings were open to the public, and every one was mobbed. The audiences were primarily black: after being mistreated their whole lives, blacks could finally hear the crimes against them spoken of openly. The process was clearly taking a toll on the reporters, many of whom, though hyped up on caffeine, looked exhausted. "The problem with us South African journalists is that we keep bursting into tears all the time," said Ruth.

Today, she explained, Gandersvoot was being tried for the murder of a young man named Julian Hamare. Julian, a black high school student and activist, had been abducted, tortured, and fed rat poison. He returned home wheelchair-bound; his hair fell out from the poison. The second time he was taken from his parents' home in Guguletu township, he never returned. Julian's mother, Faith, had saved his hair in a plastic baggie for twenty years.

George approached Nadine. "We missed you last night," he said.

"I'm sorry," said Nadine. "I was tired."

"I hear you," said George. He rubbed his eyes with his finger-tips, then sighed and said, "Thola's gone. She's been gone a long time."

Nadine's knees felt weak. "What do you mean?"

"I mean she's gone," said George. "Come on." He wanted to get shots of Faith, so they went into the main room where the hearings would be held. Some five hundred folding chairs were filling quickly. Headphones trailed along the floor: the hearings would be translated into eleven languages. In the corner, a woman held a pitcher of ice water. She was, George said, a "comforter." Her job was to support whoever was testifying, victim or perpetra-tor. She supplied tissues, cold water, and human contact as neces-sary.

At the front of the room, the members of the Truth and Recon-ciliation Commission sat at tables covered with white tablecloths. Nadine recognized Archbishop Desmond Tutu, with his gray hair and oversized glasses. A banner above the tables read THE TRUTH SHALL SET US FREE.

Faith Hamare, wearing a blue polyester suit, her hair wrapped in a matching scarf, sat with ramrod-straight posture in the first row, next to three seats with sheets of paper on them reading VIC-TIM'S FAMILY. The bag of her son's hair rested on her lap. George knelt with the other photographers, taking pictures of the stony-faced Faith. Periodically, Faith held up the hair and shook it for the cameras.

Nadine walked to the back of the room. Ruth leaned against the wall, holding her tape recorder and a small pad, waiting for the hearing to begin. The noise in the room was deafening.

"Are you a reporter?" Ruth asked.

"Yes," said Nadine. "The *Boston Tribune*."

"Covering Gandersvoot?"

"Yes," said Nadine. "And Jason Irving's killers."

"Of course," said Ruth, resigned. "They fly you in and they fly you out. A dead American, big news."

"The Truth and Reconciliation Commission is big news."

"Have you read about it in the American papers, then?" said Ruth angrily. "Front page, hey?"

Nadine pulled her notebook out and pretended to look closely at the blue-lined sheet. On the day she'd flown from Nantucket, the *Boston Tribune* had featured a front-page story about renovations at Disney World.

"You know George, eh?" said Ruth. She tried—and failed—to conceal a smirk.

"I did know him," said Nadine. "A long time ago."

Ruth nodded. "Well," she concluded crisply, standing up straight, "he'll need you."

"Sorry?"

"You heard me. I'm glad George has someone to lean on. He's been carrying this by himself for way too long."

"What?"

"Tholakele. The whole thing. Oh, hold on. It's showtime." Ruth pressed the RECORD button on her tape recorder. Nadine squinted, failing to find George in the crowd.

All eyes were on a white man who made his way to the front of the room flanked by bodyguards. He was wearing a suit and striped tie and had a narrow moustache. His step was swaggering and confident. To Nadine, Gandersvoot looked like an accountant with a clear conscience.

Gandersvoot settled himself in a chair, took his oath, and poured a glass of water from a pitcher before him. He was ten feet from Faith, who stared straight at him. Gandersvoot's lawyers led him through his plea for amnesty. He seemed strangely removed as he described the day he took Julian.

"I was under orders," said Gandersvoot, his accent clipped. "I picked up Julian Hamare on the night of October twenty-ninth in Guguletu township."

"Where's Guguletu?" said an Australian reporter.

"Fifteen minutes from here," said Ruth.

"And where did you take Julian Hamare?" asked Gandersvoot's lawyer.

"I took him to Post Chalmers," said Gandersvoot.

"Where's Post Chalmers?" the Aussie asked.

"Do shut up," said Ruth.

"After that," continued Gandersvoot, taking a sip of water, "I shot him, and buried him in the river."

"The Fish River?" said a lawyer.

"Yes," Gandersvoot said. "The Fish River."

Faith's eyes had been dry until this point. She cried out hearing Gandersvoot's words, her wail filling the courtroom. She knew, at last, where her son's body lay. Pain fluttered in Nadine's gut.

"And why did you kill Julian Hamare?" asked the lawyer.

"I was told to kill him," said Gandersvoot. "He was a threat to national security."

"Now this is hard for me to ask you," said the lawyer, "but what happened at Post Chalmers?"

In a flat tone, Gandersvoot said, "He was tortured, at Post Chalmers. We burned his body, me and some other officers. We gave him a cup of sleeping pills so it wouldn't hurt, and we had a *braai*."

Murmurs of outrage rippled through the crowd. A member of the TRC spoke. "You put Julian Hamare's body on a barbecue grill?" he said. Around the room, spectators had their hands pressed over their mouths, eyes watering.

"Yes," said Gandersvoot.

"How long did you *braai* Julian Hamare?" asked another TRC member.

"Six hours," said Gandersvoot. "Maybe seven hours," said Gandersvoot.

"What did you do for six or seven hours?" said a TRC member. "Did you stay there, for *six* or *seven* hours?"

"We did, yes," said Gandersvoot. Nadine felt bile rise in the back of her throat.

"When the body was burned," said Gandersvoot's lawyer, "what did you do then?"

"We had had a bit to drink, as you will at a *braai*," said Gandersvoot. He seemed to think this would get a laugh, but the room was completely silent. Gandersvoot cleared his throat. "When the bones were cool, we disposed of them," he said.

"In the Fish River," said his lawyer.

"Yes," said Gandersvoot. He nodded solemnly.

Faith was silent, tears running down her face.

There was a break after Gandersvoot's testimony, and Nadine went back to the hotel. It must have been the lack of sleep—she sat on her bed and started to cry.

Nadine wanted to talk to Hank. She wanted to be in his Nantucket living room, telling him about the TRC, listening to his calm voice, his considering thoughts. She wanted to be taken care of. In Hank's home, Nadine had not felt alone.

She dialed his Falmouth number, but there was no answer. It was the middle of the night in Massachusetts, but the phone rang and rang. She tried the Nantucket number, and on the second ring, she heard his voice.

"It's me," she said.

"Nadine," said Hank. "Nadine. Is something the matter?"

"Well," said Nadine. "I'm pregnant."

There was a silence, and then Hank laughed. "I can't believe it," he said. There was joy in his voice.

"I know," said Nadine.

"Isn't this," said Hank, and then he said, "Maybe," and then, in a more professional tone, "How are you feeling?"

"Feeling? I feel sick. The stuff I'm hearing at the trials, it just makes it worse." She told him about Faith Hamare and her bag of hair.

Hank's voice became clinical as he instructed Nadine to stop taking the Demerol and find some folic acid pills. "Why don't you come home?" said Hank finally. "Why don't you come back, and we'll take it from there." Hank sounded hopeful: he had confessed how much he wanted children.

"I can't just . . . run away from this."

"But you can run away from me," Hank said darkly.

"That's not fair."

"Would it help if I came there? To South Africa?"

"No," said Nadine. "I don't know. I just feel like this is something . . . something I have to do."

"I don't . . . ," Hank said sadly, "I really don't understand you."

"I know," said Nadine. Neither of them hung up, but neither had a word to say. Nadine listened to Hank breathe. They were eight thousand miles apart.

After she hung up, Nadine opened her minibar and stared at the small bottles. Faith Hamare's lined face swam in front of her eyes. And Gandersvoot, who had committed such evil acts with such confidence: his sneer turned her stomach. She wanted a drink.

There was a rap at the unlocked door, and George walked in.

"I'll join you," he said, pulling out a gin. He drank it, and wiped his lips. "All right then," he said. "Ready for the afternoon testimony?"

"No," Nadine said.

"You're shaken," said George. "You knew this was happening, Nadine."

"Yes. But I . . . I don't think I can hear any more."

"Jesus, Nadine! You can't just ignore things that are hard to look at. You have to . . . to stare into them. Document them. Bear witness. That's our job, isn't it? What's happened to you?"

"It never used to bother me," said Nadine. "But now . . . I feel sick. I really do. I'm dizzy. I was beaten up . . ."

"So you can just fly in here. You can just . . . listen to the story of Jason's death and then fly home. The world is yours to play in as you wish. And there's not a price, right? Am I right? What's your expression? The world is your oyster."

"My expression?" Nadine said. "What are you talking about?"

"I was born in San Francisco," said George. "I could have lived the rest of my life in blessed American ignorance. I thought it was my right to be safe and happy, to love whoever I wanted, and marry and—"

"And have children," Nadine said.

"Sure, whatever I wanted. It was my right. But fate has a way of letting you know who's in charge."

"What happened?" Nadine said, leaning in to touch George's knee. "Tell me. What happened to Thola?" They stared at each other, and then George said, "I have something to show you."

"Fine," Nadine said.

"It's ten hours from here."

"Ten hours?"

"Yes."

"Jason's hearing," Nadine said feebly.

"It's not until Monday."

"George."

"Fine," said George. "Forget it. I should have known."

"No," Nadine said, looking at the phone. Hank's words hung in her ears: *I don't understand you.* Nadine looked at George; the dark planes under his eyes from lack of sleep. George understood.

"Let's go," said Nadine.

Twenty-eight

NANTUCKET TO STARDOM

Bear with me. This starts out sad, but it ends up being the best day of my life.

I got a ride into town with Mom, jamming my bike in the back of her Saab. I waved as her ferry took off. She looked really nice in jeans and a fitted T-shirt. She had told me all about the man she was meeting, someone she had been friends with before she had even known Dad. When I asked Mom if she was having an affair, she smiled and gave me a big hug. "No way," she said, and I believed her.

I sat on the steps of the Nantucket Juice Bar and looked at the boats. I started to think about where you could go once you got to the mainland. Florida, for example, or Los Angeles—big places, where you could be cool without having to know about baseball. I got really excited, thinking about traveling all over the world, like on tour, having my picture taken in Japan and Australia. I would ride in limos, and see exotic animals, like emu.

Then came the bad part, starring Roger Fell and his BMX bike. Roger was my friend until fourth grade. We pretended to be Indians in the cranberry bogs, fighting each other with homemade bows and arrows. Roger always won, and then we ate his mom's peanut butter oatmeal cookies, lying on the ground and watching the clouds. But now everything was different.

Roger called me a fag as he and his friends rode in, wearing shorts cut off below the knee and hooded sweatshirts. Their shins showed above their stupid sneakers with no laces and the tongues hanging out. Roger was wearing a wool cap that said AC/DC.

I ignored them.

"Faaaag!" yelled Tristan Morris. "Nice outfit, gay boy!" He filled his straw from his can of orange soda and blew it all over the paisley shirt I had borrowed from Kyla. They rode around in a circle, spitting soda on me. I kept my head down and didn't cry.

"Is that a banana in your pocket or are you just happy to see me?" said Roger.

"Come on, Roger," I said.

He sucked soda into his mouth, and spit.

I was red-faced by the time I ran from the harbor to Hot Locks Salon and Spa, and I just said, "Please hurry. I have to catch the noon ferry."

"The Mashpee Mall Regional Auditions!" cried Joe.

"My shirt!" said Kyla. They put their customers on hold and hustled me into a shampoo chair. Joe washed my hair while Kyla cleaned my face with a warm washcloth. They didn't mention my tears all mixed into the dried soda.

"Bastards," hissed Joe. He blow-dried my hair, adding styling gel for an even better look than before. Kyla rushed out and came back with a whole surfer outfit for me: Quiksilver T-shirt, baggy pants, and Adidas soccer slippers. "I'm sorry," she said. "Nothing was open but Force Five Watersports."

Joe folded his arms over his potbelly and looked me up and down. "I know," he said, snapping. "Sing Beach Boys!"

"I'm doing 'Sue Me' . . . ," I said.

"Wouldn't it be nice if we were older," sang Kyla, her palms open in front of her. Her dreadlocks swung back and forth.

"Then we wouldn't have to wait so looong," added Joe in a scary falsetto.

"No," I said. "Please. I'm doing 'Sue Me'!" They were silent. Even I could hear the hysteria in my voice.

"Call Mr. Murray," said Joe, finally. "Tell him we're opening the Toggery. One thing Mr. Murray's got, he's got seersucker."

Half an hour later, Joe, Kyla, and Mr. Murray watched me board the ferry. Mr. Murray loaned me the suit for free, and I bought a round-trip ticket with money I had stolen from Mom's purse.

"America's next superstar," called Kyla.

"Sinatra has returned," Joe yelled.

I held my white straw hat on tight, and stepped carefully to avoid messing up my suit.

Malcon stood in jeans and a red sweater at the end of the gangway in Hyannis. His face brightened when he saw me, and I made myself walk—not run—off the boat.

"You look fantastic," he said. He gave me a big hug, which was a little strange but okay.

"Thanks," I said. I was so glad I was not wearing soccer slippers. Malcon's sweater was cashmere, I could tell.

We reached the car, and Malcon opened the door for me. He slid into his seat and started the motor. It was a beautiful sunny day. We sped toward the Mashpee Mall.

I've been to Mashpee before, and to Boston. I have even been to New York. And on my tenth birthday, when my parents said I could pick anywhere in the world to go, I picked Orlando, where *American Superstar* is filmed. (I can still see Mom and Dad at Gatorland, watching them feed raw chicken to the alligators. They had wanted me to pick Paris or Rome, leaving travel brochures on the kitchen table, but when I stood up for my choice, they went gung-ho, even getting tickets to Wham! Tribute Night at the Hard Rock Cafe.) Still, this drive in Malcon's Dodge Neon was the most exciting trip of my life.

"You going to make me proud, buddy?" said Malcon. He put his hand on my knee and squeezed. He kept his hand there. It felt a little creepy, but I didn't say anything.

"Yes," I whispered.

There were hundreds of kids at the Mashpee Mall Regional Auditions, maybe a thousand. The auditions were held in the Gap, and the line stretched past mannequins wearing baggy pants. Malcon took me by the hand and helped me fill out the forms, signing his name wherever it said *Parent/Guardian*.

We waited outside for a long time, and then we sat in Gap Women, Gap Men, and finally Gap Kids. At last, a woman with scraggly gray hair came out and called for me.

I stood up. Malcon gave me a hug and said, "You're my star."

I followed the gray-haired lady into a big dressing room. The *American Superstar* judging panel was nowhere to be seen. In fact, nothing was in that room but me, the lady, and a plastic chair. She sat down. "Okay," she said. She sighed.

"Should I wait for the judging panel?" I asked.

"I am the judging panel," she said.

"Oh," I said. I cleared my throat.

"This is not what we call *off to a running start,*" said the lady. She folded her arms across her chest.

I don't know what came over me. I thought about Malcon holding a wilted rose. I thought about Dad and Mr. Mullen, yelling at adult men in baseball uniforms. I saw Joe, his potbelly, and the hope in Kyla's eyes when she handed me her paisley shirt. I felt filled with purpose. I fixed the lady with my Sinatra stare.

"Get ready, lady," I said. And then I sang.

I gave it my all. I went for the hand stars, I did the electric slide. I rocked that Gap dressing room like it was the Nantucket Elementary School Auditorium. I concluded with my arms open, heart and back of my throat exposed. "Sue me, sue me, what can you do me, I love YOOOOOU!" I sang, as I slid toward the lady on one knee. There was silence.

"Thanks," said the lady. She wrote something on her clipboard.

An hour later, she stood next to a mannequin in a bikini. She read a list of ten names, explaining that these kids would move on to the Boston auditions in a week.

Malcon had his arms around me as she called the winners. He winced each time, giving me a half hug. I didn't wince, because I freaking knew. I was the seventh name called. Malcon shouted and punched the air with his fist. He mushed me in a big hug. I decided I could get used to the feeling of stardom, and warm cashmere against my cheek.

Twenty-nine

"Are you going to tell me where we're headed?" Nadine said. The road had turned to a one-lane highway as George and Nadine left Cape Town behind.

"The Eastern Cape," said George. "I'm taking you to see zebras and maybe even an elephant."

"Hm," Nadine said.

"Hm is right," said George. He tapped a finger on the steering wheel. "Nadine," he said.

"What?"

"You smell the same."

"I still use Pert Plus."

George turned up the radio. "Today's Truth and Reconciliation hearings were dominated by a missing boy, and a mother who kept his hair for twenty years," said a smooth newscaster.

"Oh for fuck's sake," Nadine said.

"Don't worry," said George. "They won't say *braai* on the radio."

"Leon Gandersvoot admitted today that he abducted and killed ANC activist Julian Hamare, then buried him in the Fish River, Eastern Cape Province. Faith Hamare says she is happy to know the truth about what happened to her son." There was a crackle, and then a broken voice: "Can I forgive him? Yes. What else can I do? We are in this together." Then Faith's wail filled the car.

"Good God," Nadine breathed.

"In soccer news," said the reporter, "Black Leopards beat SuperSport United—" George turned the dial and found a station playing jazz.

"He'll get amnesty," said George, after a few minutes.

"What's the alternative?" Nadine said. "If you executed the guy, Faith would never have known what happened."

"What good does it do her?" said George. There was fury in his eyes. "What good does it do her to carry the facts around, the details, the time it took to *braai* her son?"

"I don't know," Nadine said.

"Compromise," George spat. "Forgiveness. Truth. Reconciliation." He shook his head. "Words," he said. "No meaning. Just words."

"But you have to try," said Nadine. "You know? If you don't forgive, you're just stuck. You just keep reliving the same moment. You can't be free. You can't ever be free to—"

"That sounds all well and good," said George. "Just forgive everybody. Move on happily. But you know what, Nadine? Some things are unforgivable. And that's just the way it is."

Nadine's eyes filled with tears. She dug her fingernails into her palm and stared out the window. The sun beat down, and Nadine prayed that George was wrong.

Thirty

■

"Have you seen *Endless Summer*?" George asked.

"What?" Nadine sat up, blinking. It was stifling in the car, and her legs were glued to the seat. Outside the window, glittering waves crashed over brightly dressed surfers.

"This is J-Bay, Jeffreys Bay, as featured in surf movies. As featured on T-shirts worldwide: Supertubes, the best break in the world."

"Oh," Nadine said. "I'm sorry. I was—"

"I need some food," said George shortly. "How about a curry?"

"Sure."

He pulled the car into a waterfront restaurant called The Mermaid. Men in wet suits ate scrambled eggs on the porch and squinted into the sun. George strode from the car to the door of the restaurant. His arms were strong and tanned. Nadine touched the pattern the car seat had made across the left side of her face. She had left her lipstick in the hotel, and without it she felt naked.

"As I said," said George, when they were seated, "the curry's great."

"Okay," Nadine said. The waitress arrived, and Nadine ordered buttered toast.

They ate in silence. Afterward, George disappeared, telling Nadine he was going for a swim. Nadine sat in the car, breathing in sand and suntan lotion, the fragrance of Cape Cod in the summer.

She saw an image from her childhood: Jim, making coffee one

warm Saturday morning. Nadine stood in the kitchen in her pajamas. "Can't you stay home today?" she asked. Jim turned to her.
She saw his face soften. "We could go to Toby's Island," said Nadine. Jim's shoulders caved inward, but then his face went cold
and he stood straight.

"Nope," he said, steel in his voice. "Got to work, dearie, you
know that."

He patted her head and shut her out, walking briskly down the
path to the car, opening the door, sliding in, and starting the engine. He turned right onto Surf Drive. Nadine watched until he
was out of sight, and then climbed the stairs to the turret, where
she would spend a lonely day paging through books. She wished
she were the one heading down the road, the one with somewhere
to go.

George came back, his hair wet, his jeans and button-down shirt
dry. "Had a skinny-dip," he explained.

Nadine offered to drive, but George shook his head. He
stretched his shoulders and neck before starting the car. "I don't
feel old," he said, "but my body does."

Nadine laughed. "Frightening, isn't it?" she said, "My back is
all in knots, and my shoulders . . . all the typing, I guess. Plane
rides."

"I hear you," said George. "It's my knees, bending down to get
shots." They headed toward Port Elizabeth, George staring
fixedly ahead. "I never thought about getting old," he mused. "I
don't like to think about it. This sort of life . . . it lends itself to a
sad old age. I mean, how long can you keep it up? Even now, I'm
fucking tired. And it's harder to sleep."

Nadine thought of her violent dreams, the way the images
stayed with her even when she was awake. "I know," she said.

"I never thought I'd be single, still," said George. Nadine could see the fine wrinkles around his eyes and mouth. Despite the air-conditioning, the car felt stuffy.

Nadine dreaded the answer, but asked anyway. Quietly, she said, "What happened to Thola?"

"I should have loved you," said George. He did not look at Nadine, and spoke matter-of-factly, as if to himself. "What would have happened if I loved you?"

"George," said Nadine. Irritation washed over her, and she rolled down the window.

"The AC's on."

"I know," said Nadine shortly. "I just need to breathe for a minute." She sipped the searing air, then rolled the window back up. She turned to George. "You had Thola," she said.

"I never did, not really," said George. He sighed. "I was ten years old, and somehow I picked the one person I could never have."

"Did she leave you for someone else?" said Nadine, casting wildly for a different ending to Thola's story.

"Oh God," said George. "I wish she had." He sighed. "When you arrived, Thola and I were trying to find a way to be together. We were happy, I guess."

"You seemed happy."

"I spent all those afternoons at the Waterfront, waiting for Thola to get home from work. You remember the Waterfront."

"Of course," said Nadine. It was a tin box of a bar in Sunshine, facing not the water but a filthy street. The outside of the *shebeen* was painted with a beach and pastel umbrellas. Inside, plastic tables were covered with oilcloth advertising Carling Black Label. Local men and boys, clad in bright sneakers and zip-up tracksuits, drank from enormous bottles. There was a pool table, a radio, a red metal lockbox for cigarettes, and a banner that read, CASTLE

BEER: PERFECTLY BALANCED TO SATISFY SOUTH AFRICA'S THIRST FOR SPORT.

"So I'd buy drinks for Thola's neighbors, some guys who became my friends. Eddie, who . . ." His voice trailed off. "Anyway, Thola would get home from work, change, and come get me. Sometimes she'd have a beer, but usually we hung out on those chairs outside her house. They had an old table. We'd make a fire and talk."

"That ratty patch behind the house. That's where I finally convinced Thola to let me interview her. Her mom was so sweet to me," said Nadine, remembering Fikile's smile, her apple cheeks. George stopped talking, and Nadine's mind wandered.

Nadine had been wearing shorts that afternoon; she could still feel the way the hot metal chair seared the skin on the back of her thighs. Fikile had placed a pitcher of water on the table, and Nadine drank from a cloudy glass.

"I think I can bring a unique angle to the story," Nadine began. "I'll write about Evelina from her family's viewpoint, try to make readers see her as a confused child. I was a confused child myself."

"George told me about your mother," said Thola. "I'm sorry about that, but what does it have to do with my sister?"

Fikile watched them carefully. She couldn't translate their words, but picked up on the tension. Clearly, appealing for sympathy wasn't going to cut it with Thola.

"It hasn't always been easy for me," said Nadine. "I guess that's what I'm saying."

"Ach," said Thola. "You think you can compare your life . . . to this?" She waved an elegant hand, indicating the garbage, the skeletal dog nosing the ground at her feet.

"No," said Nadine, "I don't—"

"I walked down the street today," said Thola, "in the city. I was shopping, hoping to find a book for George. Some novel he wanted . . . *The Portrait of a Lady?* He thinks he is this Henry James. So I buy the book, and I leave the store. I get a nice ice cream, a mango ice cream. Then I see this Boer man and his Boer girlfriend. They are walking on the sidewalk, and I am walking the other way. As he passes me, the man punches me in the stomach." Her eyes flashed. "He punches me, do you hear? I dropped my ice cream. And he kept walking. What would you do, Nadine?"

"Was there a policeman? Are you all right?"

"A policeman," said Thola. She rested her elbows on the table in front of her and bent her neck, running her hand along her hair. She took a deep breath, and then she looked up. "A policeman," she said, "would put *me* in jail for causing trouble. If I said any-thing—one thing—to the man, he could have me arrested. The man punched me, Nadine, and I bent over in pain. His girlfriend looked away. The man laughed at me, and I did nothing."

"He laughed?"

"I did nothing," said Thola. "And this is just today. Every day, I do nothing, and the anger gets bigger."

Nadine was silent. Fikile looked nervous as her daughter's voice escalated.

"That is why my sister raised the rock," said Thola. "That is why she brought it down." She stared at Nadine. "It was some-thing," said Thola, "and Evelina was tired of doing nothing."

Nadine met Thola's eyes. She remembered a summer after-noon when her mother was sick from the chemotherapy. The sound of her vomiting woke Nadine from a nap. She walked into her parents' bedroom and pushed open the bathroom door. Her mother retched, kneeling in front of the toilet in khaki pants and a bra, her hands on either side of the bowl. Nadine stood behind her mother, powerless. For a moment, her mother sat back, and there was silence. Nadine thought the worst was over, but then her mother started to heave again.

Nadine ran from the room and into the kitchen. Her beloved guppy, Table, swam in the Mason jar that was his home. The jar was filled with rocks and shells Nadine had collected on the beach. Nadine could still hear her mother's awful gagging. She picked up the jar and hurled it to the floor. It was better than doing nothing. The jar shattered, and Table jumped and flipped, trying to find water. Nadine watched the fish, its gills opening wide, she watched it die.

Nadine told Thola the story, and Thola listened. When Nadine was finished, Thola slipped cigarettes from her jeans: Marlboros, George's brand. Fikile reached for one and they smoked while Thola translated the exchange for her mother. At one point, Fikile let out a staccato laugh. "A policeman," she said to Nadine in English, shaking her head. Later, Fikile put her hand on Nadine's and squeezed. Then she spoke in Xhosa.

"My mother wants me to tell you about my name," said Thola.

"Your name? What about it?"

Thola sighed, drew in on her cigarette. Fikile met Nadine's eyes as Thola spoke. "My mother could not have a child," said Thola. "This was before her husband left. She prayed to God and she went to a *sangoma,* a witch doctor. The *sangoma* told my mother to be patient. One day, the *sangoma* brought a baby to my mother, wrapped in a flannel shirt. I had been abandoned, and my name means this, abandoned and then found. Not long afterward, my mother grew fat with Evelina and gave her a Christian name. My mother always wanted more children, but no more came. She says we may share her."

"What?"

"She can be your mother, too," said Thola. "If you want her!"

Fikile smiled, and Nadine felt teary.

"What," said Thola, "you don't want her?"

Nadine swallowed. "Yes," she said, "yes, yes, I want her."

Thola put her hand on Nadine's. "It's done," she said, her voice warming. "She is yours, and we are sisters."

Nadine nodded. Thola's hand was soft.

Thola drew again on her cigarette. "I will give you an official interview for your newspaper," she said. "But I want you to buy me lunch. And my mother. At a nice restaurant."

"Thank you," said Nadine.

Fikile spoke, and Thola laughed. "If you are her daughter now," said Thola, "she will insist you buy new shoes."

Nadine looked down at her stained flip-flops, and then at Fikile's clean pumps and Thola's pink ballet flats.

"Done," said Nadine. A week later, Thola left a present from Fikile on Nadine's bed: ballet flats, the same as Thola's. Nadine stared at the shoes. She knew Fikile hardly had the money for such luxuries. Nadine picked them up in trembling hands and slipped them on her feet.

The following week, Nadine picked up Thola and Fikile and drove them to Brendan's Café, a restaurant near her house in Observatory. Maxim was friends with Brendan, an up-and-coming chef who was happy to welcome both blacks and whites for lunch. Fikile giggled as they entered the restaurant and were led to a table.

"Hm," said Thola. "This tablecloth is not straight."

"Excuse me!" Nadine called to the boy with a brown moustache who hovered nearby. "Can you straighten the cloth, please?"

"Of course," said the waiter, bowing.

"I am getting used to this," said Thola regally. Fikile looked uncomfortable, her hands swimming above the table as if she did not know where to rest them. She had painted her nails bright pink.

"Mother," said Thola, opening her mother's laminated menu, "what will you choose?"

Fikile spoke in Xhosa, and Thola smiled. When the waiter approached, Thola said, "A beer for my mother, and one for me as well."

They ate prawns and potato samosas to start, and Nadine opened her notebook. "I grew up in Sunshine township, Cape Town, South Africa," said Thola. "My first word was *molo,* which means 'good morning.' I was always very beautiful and an excellent dancer with abundant grace."

Nadine smiled, taking it all down. Clearly, Thola had planned for this interview. Thola recounted her childhood, her trip to America, meeting George. "Now, where is Evelina's father?" asked Nadine, eyeing the last prawn on the appetizer plate.

"Next question," said Thola, taking the prawn for herself.

They ordered: steak for Thola and Fikile, a salad for Nadine. As she sipped her second beer, Fikile's cheeks grew rosy, and she swayed in her seat to the country music playing in the background. Brendan brought the entrées out himself, and offered salt and pepper from large silver mills. Fikile clapped when Brendan pulled out Parmesan to grate over her potatoes.

"Evelina was born with a crazy eye," continued Thola. "It was hard for her to be the sister of a famous ballerina, to be sure. The boys called us 'Beauty and the Beast.' " Fikile shook her head and nodded, cutting her steak primly.

On and on Thola spoke, through cheesecake and coffee. Nadine assiduously took notes. By the time Thola reached the day of Jason's murder, the café bill rested on the table in a leather folder. "I came home from my job," Thola said, "and my sister, she was in jail. They told my mother she murdered an American boy, but we could not believe it."

"Do you believe it now?" said Nadine.

"I believe it," said Thola, "and I think it will help to free our country. Do you see how much attention the boy's death has brought to South Africa? I am sorry for the boy and his family, but we must fight for freedom, whatever it takes. If killing white people leads to freedom, it is worth it."

The waiter approached, but receded when he heard Thola's tone. "Jason was against apartheid," said Nadine. "He was a teacher, Thola."

Thola stood, raising her chin. "It does not matter," she said. "Do you think the police asked Stephen Biko what he believed before they murdered him in jail? Did anyone ask me my opinions before they told me I could not go to college? What side are you on, Nadine?"

"I'm not on a side," said Nadine. "I want to present all the sides. I want the world to hear your side. Please, I'm sorry."

Thola sat back down. "This is a difficult story," she said. "So many important angles to discuss." Fikile yawned. "My mother needs to get home," said Thola, "and we will continue in the car."

"Okay," said Nadine.

"I want my struggle to be in the newspaper," said Thola. "The world has forgotten about us. Why aren't there American troops in our streets? What is Europe doing to help us? We are being treated like *animals*. Do you get this in your notebook? Black people are disappearing. Nobody knows where they go!"

Nadine was as exhausted as Fikile. She put the bill on her credit card, unsure how she would ever pay for it. Thola spoke of the resistance movement on the way back to Sunshine, pointing to the beautiful homes at the edge of the city—now surrounded by alarm systems and fences—saying, "A black family will live there, and there. No security fence or mean dog can stop the inevitable!"

In her bedroom, Nadine paged through her notes with a sense of defeat. Thola's words were practiced; she had avoided discomforting emotions. Nadine knew her interview hadn't revealed any underlying truths about Evelina. Still, she wrote for hours, first a profile of Thola and then an exploration of the ANC resistance movement. Maxim found her rubbing her temples and staring at pages and pages of disconnected words. Her last fax from Eugenia had read, *What about a lifestyles piece, N? Something about tribal music?*

With Maxim's help, Nadine finished her story in the middle of the night. She led with a recap of the murder, and then tried to explore the pressures that led Evelina to kill: the sense of hopelessness; the collective despair of generations of children told they had no chance at a brighter future; the belief that violence was the only recourse. Her last line read, *Only history will decide if Evelina Malefane is a murderer, a martyr, or a confused child. Perhaps she is a mix of the three.*

"Fikile. I feel so sad for her," said George, as they drove.

"What do you mean?"

He lit another cigarette. "When did you quit smoking?" he said.

"I haven't. Just a break."

"I see." George stopped for hamburgers at McDonald's, and turned north on a road called N10. He drove past signs for Addo Elephant National Park.

"No elephants?" Nadine said, biting into three french fries at once. She swallowed, but couldn't help asking, "Where are we going?" She felt a shadow of fear.

"Trust me," he answered. They had left the sea behind, and the land grew arid and empty. "This is the Karoo," said George, "The Valley of Desolation. This is where the Transkei and Ciskei homelands are located."

"What?"

"The apartheid government made fake homelands for blacks in the middle of nowhere. The Transkei and Ciskei are Xhosa homelands. People get picked up from cities and moved here, depending on tribe. Their neighbors might end up somewhere else entirely."

"I remember that now," said Nadine. She cradled her wrist in her right palm. Her pain had decreased every day, and she had stopped taking Demerol. Her head felt clearer, and her ribs no longer hurt, but in the evenings a dull ache in her wrist remained. They drove through vast, uninhabited plains. Black, flat-topped mountains loomed in the distance, while woody shrubs, wild mums, and giant aloe plants grew nearby.

In a shop by the side of the lonely road, they stopped to buy gas, cigarettes, and Cadbury Fruit and Nut bars from a white man wearing suspenders. He rang up their purchases, then returned to his book. Nadine squinted: he was reading *Our Man in Havana* by Graham Greene. Darkness fell as they drove. They listened to the radio for a while, and then the classical music faded to static.

Nadine took one of his cigarettes and lit it, but then put it out in the ashtray. She licked salt from her fingertips and looked over at George. Though he should have been looking at the road, he was gazing at Nadine.

"Can we stop for the night?" Nadine asked. The sky was black.

"Where?" said George. "There's nothing here."

Nadine looked out the car windows. The road snaked over empty plains and dry, scrubby hills. George was right: there was nothing, and they hadn't seen another car for an hour or so. Nadine felt a cramping pain below her stomach. Her wrist throbbed.

"Maybe we should go back," Nadine said, trying to sound relaxed.

"You remember that night? The night Maxim—"

"Of course."

"I went to meet you two at the Waterfront," said George. "We heard the explosion."

"I don't feel well," said Nadine. "I'm sick."

"Maxim ran out of the bar. The air smelled like something burning."

"Please, George."

"I heard gunshots and I ran to find you, Nadine. I couldn't find you, but someone told me Maxim had been shot. I drove to the hospital."

"Stop," said Nadine. "Stop it, George."

"Maxim was lying in that big bed. There were tubes, all these machines. I sat next to him."

"Please, George. I'm sick."

"Do you remember the tubes, Nadine? Do you remember?"

Thirty-one

Nadine remembered. Her feet in Maxim's lap, a large bottle of Castle beer in front of her. They had been planning a celebration for Maxim's upcoming birthday: a feast of Indian food at the house. "And what do you want for the big day?" Nadine asked him.

"You," said Maxim. "Maybe with caramel syrup?"

"I was thinking silk sheets," said Nadine.

George shook his head and covered his ears. "Please," he said, laughing, "I feel like I'm in a pornographic video." Suddenly gunshots exploded outside the bar. The lights went out, and the jukebox fell silent. "What the fuck?" said George, grabbing Nadine's arm.

She listened to Maxim's breathing. He touched her feet, moved them from his lap. They could hear sirens wailing, and more gunshots. Maxim gathered his cameras in the dark. Nadine spread her palm on his back: she could almost feel the adrenaline coursing through his veins.

He kissed her on the cheek, leaving the scent of his cigarettes. His bony nose, and the way he would burrow his face into her hair at night. His lips on hers, soft words: "*Tot siens, bokkie,* we'll have champagne tomorrow." *Bokkie*—his name for her— little doe. Her eyes adjusted to the dim light and she watched him go, his long back in a damp cotton shirt, rushing toward the action.

During the lull, when gunfire gave way to quiet, Nadine stood. "Don't go," George commanded, but she moved outside. She called Maxim's name. The gunfire started up again, and Nadine, her sneakers smacking the dirt road, her hair stuck to her neck with sweat, her nostrils filled with the reek of garbage and gunpowder, Nadine ran.

Maxim wasn't wearing a vest. He never wore a vest. As Nadine neared the commotion, she saw throngs of people outside a hostel. Police were firing at township residents, and they were firing back.

In the midst of the pandemonium, she saw Maxim kneeling by a sandbag barricade. He stood slowly and lifted his camera. Later, when the film was developed, Nadine would see that he had been capturing a man yelling at the police. The man's neck was ropy with tension, his mouth wide open.

When Maxim was working, he had told Nadine, he started seeing photographs, not reality. The worst sight did not affect him emotionally: it was his canvas—he thought of the light, the angle, shutter speed. Nadine watched him at work and was filled with pride. *He is mine,* she thought, and then she saw him stumble, and drop his camera.

He collapsed to his knees, looking with shock at his shoulder, which flowered red. As Nadine ran to him, he fell forward. He looked baffled. The bullet had grazed his collarbone, the bone where Nadine's cheek rested when they watched movies, entwined on the couch.

There was no ambulance. On Ncumo Road, Nadine stood and screamed, watched as blood bubbled from the wound. Fear coursed through her as she watched Maxim grow pale. Maxim, a stunned expression over his beautiful face. "What?" he said.

"Shh," said Nadine. She cradled his head in her lap, felt hot tears in her throat. She said, "Shhh, love, I've got you." The ground was hard and oily under Nadine's knees.

Near her, a woman wailed and rocked an infant who did not

move. Nadine directed her gaze to Maxim, trying to block out the other bodies, the stench of blood. An ambulance finally arrived, winding slowly through the crowd, and two men loaded Maxim into the back. "Are you coming, ma'am?" one asked, his fingers raking through his crew cut.

From the stretcher, Maxim gazed at her. "Nadine," he said. He held out a hand, and his palm fell open. Nadine hesitated for an instant.

"No room," said the other. "Meet us at the hospital."

The doors swung shut, Maxim's eyes searching Nadine's, his palm empty. Though the woman near Nadine held her infant up and screamed in Xhosa, the ambulance sped away.

Nadine pushed through the sea of people, finally finding a British journalist who had a car. "I need to get to the hospital," she pleaded, and he agreed.

At Groote Schuur, Nadine was ushered upstairs to a private room. Maxim lay in the hospital bed, eyes closed. George was hunched at his side. "Thank God," he said, standing. "He was asking for you, Nadine."

"How did you get here so fast?"

"The car," said George. "I looked for you."

"Here I am." Nadine's calm voice betrayed the fear in her spine.

Maxim opened his eyes. He blinked, unseeing for a moment, and then his pupils came into focus. His gaze rested on Nadine, and he seemed to relax. "Hey," he said.

"Hey," said Nadine, leaning in and touching her cheek to his.

"I'm okay," said Maxim weakly. "No worries, *bokkie.*"

"Thank God," said Nadine. She sat down in the chair George had vacated, and smiled at Maxim.

"Thank God if you must," Maxim said, coughing. "I'll thank the fine doctors at GSH." His mouth curved upward.

Awash in relief, Nadine kissed him hard on the lips. "You bastard," she said. "I was scared to death. You have to wear your fucking vest, Maxim."

"Nag, nag, and we're not even married yet."

"Yet?" said George. He leaned against the wall, his ankles and arms crossed.

"Be quiet," said Nadine. Over her shoulder, she said to George, "He's hallucinating."

"If I'm hallucinating, where's the caramel syrup?" said Maxim. Louder, he said, "For the love of Christ, someone give me a cigarette."

"Not a chance," said Nadine.

Maxim yawned. "Some wonderful drug is making me very sleepy," he said.

"Sleep, love," said Nadine.

"Okay," said Maxim. He raised his hand with effort, touched the ends of Nadine's hair. "So gorgeous," he said, and closed his eyes. Within minutes, he was breathing deeply.

Nadine let out a long sigh. George had found another chair, and he dragged it next to her and put his hand on her knee. "Fuck," said Nadine. "The last time I was in a hospital . . ."

"What?" said George.

"It was the day my mom died." George looked at the linoleum floor. "I was so angry at my dad," said Nadine.

"Why?"

"For letting it happen, I guess. Or for not being the one who . . ."

"For not being the one who was sick?"

"I don't know. Something like that." Nadine gathered her black hair, then let it fall.

"You need a psychiatrist," said George. His elbows rested on his knees, and he placed his chin in one hand and looked at her.

"I need a drink," said Nadine. The antiseptic smell of the hospital made her feel queasy and nervous.

"And a psychiatrist."

"Where's Thola?" said Nadine.

George shrugged. "One of her meetings, is my guess."

Nadine gazed at Maxim. He looked peaceful. "I hope she's careful," said Nadine.

"I know," said George. They sat in silence. An orderly came in to check on Maxim. She wore a starched uniform, and three gold bracelets on her dark wrist. Her eyes were swollen, as if she had been crying.

"How is he?" asked Nadine, her hand on the sheet that covered Maxim's thigh.

"He lost a lot of blood," said the orderly. She shook her head. "A terrible night," she said. They all nodded. "My father just called from Soweto," said the nurse. "My cousin was beaten up and taken away in a blue Kombi. They say he is a spy." She sighed, adjusted Maxim's tubes. "Maybe he is a spy," she said. "Who knows what is what?"

"I'm so sorry," said Nadine.

"You are American?" said the woman, looking Nadine up and down.

"Yes," said Nadine.

"A journalist?"

"Yes."

"My father," the woman said, lowering her voice, "he says Winnie Mandela was in the Kombi. My uncle saw her."

"Winnie Mandela?" said Nadine.

"Winnie Mandela, yes. The wife of Nelson Mandela. Mother of our nation, we call her."

"She was in the Kombi?" said Nadine. To George, she said, "I've been hearing rumors about her. She has some group of thugs living at the mansion. They call themselves the Mandela United Football Club. But no one has been able to prove anything."

"A terrible night," the nurse repeated, closing the door behind her. Nadine's heart beat fast. She turned to George.

"I know what you're thinking," he said.

"If I can get the uncle to talk . . . ," said Nadine.

George shook his head.

"I mean," said Nadine, "it's a three-hour flight. I'd be back by morning. Maxim, of all people, would understand."

"Nadine," said George.

"This could be the story," said Nadine. "The one."

"It's up to you," said George tightly.

Underneath the fluorescent hospital light—exactly like the light that had made her mother's skin sallow—Nadine stroked Maxim's face. "I love you," she said. She sat back, interlaced her fingers, let them sink to her lap. Maxim slept soundly. Nadine sat for a few minutes, then leaned forward. "Baby," said Nadine, "I'm coming right back. I'll be right back."

George exhaled, and averted his gaze to the floor. He pressed his lips together.

Nadine leaned close to Maxim, breathed him in. His clove fragrance, his hot skin. She kissed him. "I love you," she said.

"You have everything," said George quietly.

"I'll see you in the morning," said Nadine, standing and walking out the door.

In Soweto, the sprawling township outside Johannesburg, Nadine found the address Maxim's orderly had written on a prescription pad, but when she knocked, no one answered. The windows of the house were grimy and dark. As she smoked in her car, however, a boy approached. "You're a reporter?" asked the boy. His hair was shaved close, and he wore a soccer jersey and dirty jeans.

"I'm a white lady in a rental car with a tape recorder," said Nadine. "What do you think?"

"My father, he saw her," said the boy. His fingers clenched the edge of the car window, and he bounced on the balls of his bare feet.

"Who?" said Nadine breathlessly. "Who did your father see?"

"Mrs. Mandela," said the boy. "She was here."

The boy led Nadine to his home. When she stepped inside, a sheet separating the two rooms was pulled back, and the boy's father appeared. In halting English, he confirmed his son's story while his wife made tea.

When the interview was over, the boy asked Nadine to write down his address. "Please," he said, "you can send me a book on starting your own business?"

"Of course," said Nadine. The boy stood at the door of his house, his feet planted apart, as she walked away.

Nadine drove from Soweto to Johannesburg, her heart beating fast. She checked into a Holiday Inn. There was no answer in Maxim's hospital room, and no answer at the Nutthall Road house. For a moment, Nadine panicked, thinking Maxim might have taken a turn for the worse. But she told herself he was probably still asleep. Then, looking at the mirror above her hotel bureau, she called Renata, her old professor, in New York. Nadine watched her own face as Renata spoke excitedly.

"There have been rumors about Winnie for a while," said Renata. "They say she has a team of bodyguards surrounding her, that they'll kill for her. This is the first confirmation, Nadine. I'm calling the AP. This is your story."

Nadine booked the seven AM flight to Cape Town and wrote up her interview longhand at the plastic table in the corner of the room. A streetlight burned through the gauzy curtains. Nadine called to order something to eat, but the hotel had no room service. Her stomach rumbled.

A hazy dawn rose over Johannesburg. Nadine made coffee in the small pot, and the phone rang, interrupting her first cup. It was Ian Pauling from the Associated Press, offering a tidy sum for exclusive rights to Nadine's interview. "We're proud to run this piece," said Ian. "I'd like to talk more about your future with the AP."

"Thank you," said Nadine. "I'll fax my home phone along with the story."

"Talk to you very soon, Nadine," said Ian.

"Okay." Nadine hung up and squeezed her eyes shut, murmuring, *Yes.*

Below her South African Airways plane, Nadine saw elegant suburban homes with swimming pools and the gaping mouths of forgotten gold mines. She ate an apple yogurt and savored her success, leaning back in her seat and smiling.

She planned how she would tell Maxim, the details she would use to bring the night to him: the boy's thin fingers on her car window, the sleeping baby she had glimpsed through a hole in the sheet. The way the father's reverent tone as he talked about Nelson Mandela, his jailed hope, changed to bitter whispers as he described recognizing Winnie's face in the car. The boy taken in the Kombi had played tennis in the street, said the man, using a broken racket and a flat rubber ball.

Maxim would likely be laid up for a while, so in her imagination Nadine spent her new money on him, buying picnic ingredients, the red wine he loved, a wheel of Camembert. The plane descended, and the ocean shimmered, welcoming.

Nadine took a taxi from the airport to Groote Schuur. The hospital was busy. Orderlies wheeled stretchers and white men in lab coats bustled by, carrying clipboards. With her shoulder, Nadine pushed open the heavy door leading to the stairwell, and ran upstairs to Maxim, envisioning his excitement as he listened to her news. They would share breakfast and trade information like nuggets of gold. She would take him home, kissing him in the elevator, lifting his cotton gown. She flushed, and turned the corner to Maxim's room.

At the end of a long, wet hallway, Nadine saw someone slumped in a chair: George. His ponytail was loose, his eyes closed, mouth partway open. The floor had just been mopped; there was a pine cleanser stench.

George heard Nadine's approach, and sat up, lifted his head. His hair hung crazily around his face. As soon as Nadine saw his expression, she knew.

"Maxim?" she said. She reached the doorway, and saw the empty bed.

"No," said George.

Thirty-Two

Geoge stared intently at the road. The headlights swept across empty land until a sign came into view. It said, ANDRE V. HEERDEN. POST CHALMERS. HOLIDAY FARM.

"Maxim woke up, just once," said George. "It was the middle of the night. I thought I was dreaming. But I wasn't dreaming."

"What did he say?" Nadine felt as if she were suffocating.

"He said, 'Get Nadine. Where is Nadine?'"

She closed her eyes. "What did you tell him?"

George did not seem to hear her. "We're here," he said. His voice was low.

Barbed wire surrounded the property. George turned in and stopped the car. In the twin lights, a white building painted with red letters was illuminated: POST CHALMERS HOLIDAY FARM.

"It's closed," said Nadine. George rolled down the window and lit a cigarette. The air was warm and fragrant with sage. The rippling sound of cicadas rose from the trees and surrounded them.

"I thought you wanted to know what happened to Thola."

"I do." Nadine knew it was another story that would haunt her, but she listened.

"I had been trying to convince her to leave South Africa, for a while, anyway. You know that."

"Yes." Nadine clasped her hands, tried to appreciate this last moment, when any future for Thola was still possible in her mind: an apartment in San Francisco, a job with the London Ballet. Nadine had seen Thola dance only once, when she had waked in the middle of the night and walked by George's room on her way to the kitchen. George's door was open, and Thola was dancing in the soft light from the street lamps. Her movements were fluid and euphoric. It was the only time Nadine had seen Thola without her guard up. George was asleep and Thola danced for pure pleasure.

"Well, she wouldn't leave this fucking country. You know Thola, she wanted to fight, she was all fight and no . . . love. I don't know. Sometimes, I felt like the cause was more important to her than anything. More important . . . than me."

Nadine was silent.

"One night," said George. He paused, as if steeling himself, and went on. "One night—this was about a year after you'd left—she came over to the Waterfront, had a beer, but then told me she had to go. Her friend Botha was home. He had been away. I knew what *away* meant. I asked if I could come along. Of course, she said no."

Nadine couldn't seem to breathe deeply enough to fill her lungs.

George continued, "A white American was nobody's idea of an impressive boyfriend, especially a Freedom Fighter. God knows . . . I would have been shot if I had gone to one of her meetings. Anyway, I can still see her, standing outside the bar. She was wearing a pink dress, it matched her shoes. She was all spiffed up, and I was jealous." George took a deep breath and let it out. "I didn't kiss her good-bye."

He stared out the windshield. "In the morning," he said harshly, "my new housemate—he was a journalist, too, called Trey—he told me there had been an explosion in Sunshine."

"Oh, no," said Nadine.

"Yes. And Maxim's cameras were still lying around, so I had started taking pictures. I mean, how can you write a novel when right outside your door . . . well, anyway, I took a camera. I wanted to take pictures of the explosion. I guess I never figured anything would have happened to Thola. She was . . . I don't know how to say it."

"She was invincible," said Nadine.

"As it turns out," said George, "she wasn't."

Nadine struggled for air. "Just tell me," she said.

"I went to Thola's house, and Fikile answered the door."

"So Fikile was all right. Thola's house was all right."

"Yes. If only Thola had been home, with me . . ."

"George, don't."

He swallowed. "I stood there, in that room. All the pictures of Thola on the wall in her leotards . . ." He stopped.

"Where was she?" said Nadine.

"Fikile's sister September was there. She speaks English, re-member? She told me Botha had been MK, which was no big shock. He'd gotten some package from Zambia: a Walkman. Lots of them had been exiled, so I guess he thought it was a message from comrades or something. When he put the headphones on and pushed PLAY, his head exploded."

"And Thola was there?"

"She was still alive when the police came. They took her, neigh-bors saw them take her. Did I tell you she was wearing a pink dress? And those ballet flats, with the little bows. Did I say that al-ready? She loved those fucking shoes."

"George," said Nadine.

"Fikile, she went to a witch doctor. She spent all this money, and the guy tells her Thola's a zombie, not dead. I'm standing there in Thola's living room, and Fikile's asking me for more money to go back to the *sangoma*."

Nadine shook her head.

"I gave her all the money in my wallet. And then—I don't

know—I asked to take her picture. Fikile. She let me. She stood there, not crying, not anything, blank. So I took her picture, and then I left. In the street, I . . ."

"What?"

George spoke evenly. "I found one of Thola's shoes. I took a picture. A shoe in the yard of a burned-out house." His eyes were fixed, as if the sight were still before him. "Thola never came back," he said, finally. "I went wherever there was blood. Jerusalem, Croatia, Sudan." He took a deep breath and let it out. "It's been a long time," he said.

"I've seen them. Your photos. George, you're gifted."

"Ernest called me when Thola's killer applied for amnesty. Hendricks. He'll go before the TRC in Cradock next month."

Nadine could not see George; the darkness was complete. She leaned toward the open window, trying to taste something clean. "So what are we doing here?"

George didn't answer. "Can you sleep?" he said finally.

Nadine was curled in her seat, a velvet oblivion within reach. "Yes," Nadine said.

"Sleep," said George, and she did.

Thirty-Three

Nadine woke early, the sun hot on her face. George was sitting on the hood of the car, staring at the dilapidated farm. It looked bucolic, peaceful. Nadine climbed out of the car and sat beside him.

"Post Chalmers," she said.

"Yes."

"This is where they took her."

"That's what Hendricks said in his application for amnesty. Yes."

This was the place, this small farm in the middle of nowhere, this place that smelled sweetly of grass. The disappeared were brought here, then tortured by people like Gandersvoot. No prisoners left the Post Chalmers Holiday Farm alive.

"I try to get my mind around it," said George. "But I just can't . . ."

"We don't have to," Nadine said.

"Ah, America," said George. He put a cigarette to his lips.

"Are you going in?" Nadine said.

"What, to see where they beat her to death?" said George. "To see the animal pen where they lit her on fire, or put the wet bag on her head and suffocated her?"

"Yes."

His face was red. "To see where they put a condom on a metal pipe . . . ," he said. "Where they took electrical wires . . ." His voice broke. He turned to Nadine. "She could have spent the night at our house. In my bed."

"It's not your fault," said Nadine.

"I can't do it," said George. "I can't go in."

"So don't."

"But this needs . . . ," said George. "Someone needs to take pictures of this. To prove it happened. Nadine, I need you. I can't do it."

"No," said Nadine.

She looked at George. In the harsh sunlight, he looked a hundred years old. "You flew to Jo-burg," said George. "And I stayed with Maxim."

"What are you saying?"

George removed his camera from the case. He held it to the light. "I stayed with him," said George, "and you went to the airport."

Nadine closed her eyes. She opened them, and nodded. She took the camera.

Something happened to Nadine in the farmhouse. It wasn't just good-bye to Thola; she had said that long ago. It was good-bye to all of it. She walked through the dim rooms, saw the rusty instruments of torture, the walls painted in blood. Even the camera didn't protect her. There was a crack; she was broken. The echoing horror seeped inside her skin, inside her blood, inside her womb. She couldn't do it anymore. Good-bye.

In the patchy field behind the farmhouse, Nadine vomited into the grass.

They were silent on the drive back to Cape Town. Nadine drove, and George looked out the window. The placid landscape rolled by. Like Nadine, it said nothing of what it had seen.

At Jeffreys Bay, they stopped for gas. George took the wheel and drove to a beautiful beach, isolated at the end of a dirt road. "A swim," he said. They climbed from the car and dove in the water. George swam naked, and Nadine wore her underwear. Cooled, they lay on the sand with their heads next to each other. "Now it's your turn," said George, taking a strand of Nadine's hair and holding it in front of his eyes.

"I'm pregnant," said Nadine.

"You're not."

"Right," said Nadine, "I'm not."

"Nadine," said George, looking into her eyes.

"I'm not," said Nadine. "It was a joke."

George leaned over, his lips inches from Nadine's. "You're not the mothering type," he said. He laughed. "I've never even seen you *look* at a baby," he said.

"Right." Nadine's eyes filled with tears. She was suddenly jealous of Lily, who held her new baby with such easy authority.

George's lips touched her neck. "Marry me," he said, in her ear. "We're the same. No children. No settling. A more important kind of life."

"George," said Nadine. She felt a physical longing, but did not turn toward him. She thought of Hank, of sitting on his couch in front of the fire, the fragrance of garlic mixing with butter in the kitchen. She thought of waking to bright sun and new snow, Hank's dark hair on the pillow, his lips. The padded footsteps of a child in pajamas walking toward them.

"You don't have to answer. Not yet," said George.

As they drove, Nadine pictured Thola, the woman who should have been George's wife. Nadine had seen Thola for the last time after Maxim's funeral. Thola had not attended the funeral, of course: Maxim's parents would have been horrified at the thought of an urban black woman graveside, and Thola herself decided to stay in the city. "I can mourn him in my own way," she said. "I have no need to cause a spectacular." Nadine almost corrected her English, but then acknowledged that perhaps Thola's word choice was more apt than *spectacle* anyway.

Nadine and George had taken the Tercel from Cape Town to Maxim's parents' farm. Maxim's belongings, save for a few things they had kept—two cameras, a shirt that held his scent—were piled in boxes in the backseat. It was a long drive to Johannesburg and then through the countryside. They had to stop once and wait for a herd of goats to cross in front of them.

A long, rutted road led past the workers' quarters to the farm, a low-slung stucco home and several outbuildings. The death of Mrs. Robertson had not gone unheeded; Maxim's father had erected an enormous fence around the property, topped with circles of barbed wire.

Maxim's parents were polite but distant, gathering tightly around a blonde girl Maxim had dated in high school, before he had gone to Cape Town. The girl sobbed loudly though the prayers, which were in Afrikaans. As the coffin was lowered into the ground, Nadine's eyes—covered by enormous sunglasses on loan from Thola—were dry.

After the burial, they gathered in a high-ceilinged family room. A huge wooden table was surrounded by ornate furniture, and the floor was lined with tile. A chandelier hung over a roast leg of lamb. Mounted heads of animals watched them from the walls. It was hard to imagine Maxim in this place.

Nadine drank two cups of sherry and turned to a young cousin. "What are those?" she asked.

He pointed to each, saying, "Kudu, nyala, warthog of course, duiker, steenbock . . ."

"Lion," said Nadine, gazing at the snarling mouth. "Where do you even *get* such a thing?"

"Ja, you shoot it," said the boy. His cream-colored hair reminded Nadine of Maxim's. "You want to see the cool room?" asked the boy.

"What?"

"Where we keep the animal, skin it, you know."

"Oh no," said Nadine. "Thanks."

"Did you have sex with Maxim?" asked the boy.

Nadine blinked. "Yes," she said. She stood and added, "It was great."

"I knew it," said the boy.

Nadine walked outside with George and sat down on a step, staring at the rough grass leading to the fence. She balanced her plate of deviled eggs on her knees. "I'm moving," she said.

"What?"

"I'm moving to Mexico City. The AP has an opening in the bureau office there."

Outside the fence, three small girls played with a puppy. George sipped his sherry and lit a cigarette. An older woman approached the girls and hustled them down a path to a listing shack. The sun was setting, binding the sky in ribbons of purple and red.

"Well," said George, "good luck to you."

The next morning, Nadine was packing in her Nutthall Road bedroom when Thola burst in. "What's this?" said Thola, gesturing to Nadine's suitcases.

"I'm leaving. I got a job with the AP, in Mexico City."

"You're not finished here," said Thola. "Sit down and listen to me."

"I'm sorry," said Nadine. "I can't stay here . . . in this house."

"Get another place."

Nadine looked at Thola. "No," she said. She was suddenly very tired, and sat down on the bed. "I have to go where the job is," she said lamely. "That's what I do."

"Is that right?" said Thola.

"Yes," said Nadine.

Thola was silent. Finally she spoke, her voice bitter. "You cared so much about my sister, eh?" she said. "You promised my mother you would *change things* for Evelina. You were one with the struggle, right, Nadine? But now you don't need my sister anymore."

"That's not how it is," said Nadine.

"I know how it is," said Thola, rising and putting her shoulders back. She threw a newspaper on the bed, the *Boston Tribune.* Before she walked away, Thola said, "I know how it is to be punched by a Boer. It is nothing new to me."

Nadine picked up the paper, wondering where Thola would have gotten ahold of it, and saw the small story, tucked away in section three. The headline: EVELINA MALEFANE: MURDERER OR MARTYR? It was hardly the front-page exoneration Nadine had promised. She had hoped Thola would never see it. Nadine wanted to say something, to defend herself, but she didn't know how.

"Please," she said. "Thola, wait!"

Thola slammed the front door. From her bedroom window, Nadine watched Thola's graceful carriage as she walked down their front path, the lift of her chin. "Please!" Nadine said to the windowpane. "Wait . . . talk to me!"

Thola looked both ways and crossed the street.

As they drove from Post Chalmers, George turned on the radio, which was playing a transcript of the TRC hearing of Winnie

Mandela. "Did you know they called her 'Mommy'? The kids she kept at the mansion?" said George, his hand on the steering wheel.

"Yes," said Nadine.

"She refused to apply for amnesty. Claims she's completely innocent."

Nadine snorted. Her article, while the first proof of Winnie's involvement in the Mandela United Football Club, had not been the last. As more boys disappeared, parents had begun to come forward. In 1991, Winnie had been found guilty of kidnapping four youths, and sent to jail.

"The parents of Lolo Sono testified before the TRC that a blue Kombi took their son away. They said that Winnie Mandela was in the car. Their son was never seen again," said the announcer.

"Nicodemus Sono," said Nadine. "That's the man I tried to interview the night Maxim—"

"I want to hear this," said George, turning the volume knob. Nicodemus's voice filled the car.

"I am here today mainly to appeal to the commission," he said, "that if they could please help me find my son or if he has been killed, as this paper says, let me find his remains and I will exhume and bury him decently. Because this does not give me rest in my life. When he left he was already twenty-one. He should have been thirty-one this year. I don't know what to do. He is my only son."

The reporter continued, "Carolyn Sono also testified before the TRC." A woman's quiet voice spoke: "We are still not at ease. I am having nightmares, dreams, sometimes I hear knocks on the door, thinking that it is Lolo. When I am sleeping, I can see him flying from the sky, coming home, saying that Mom, I am back home. Then I will open my arms and try to hug him, and say welcome home. I am pleading with Mrs. Mandela today, in front of the world, that please, Mrs. Mandela, please, give us our son back. Even if he is dead, let Mrs. Mandela give us the remains of our son, so that we must bury him decently.

"Thereafter maybe we can rest assured, knowing that Lolo is buried here. I am facing day and night the ordeal of Lolo. If I hear that somebody is dead, I think that maybe that person that is dead may be Lolo, they are bringing him home. I had hoped that by the time the government was inaugurated, I thought maybe Lolo will be amongst the crowd and will come back home. But to no avail. I am pleading, please."

The announcer spoke, "Desmond Tutu, as well, appealed to Winnie Mandela."

Tutu's rich voice rang out in the stuffy car. "We are struggling to establish a different dispensation characterized by a new morality, integrity. Truthfulness. Accountability."

"Amazing," said George, gesturing to the radio. "The man is amazing. No one else could talk to her that way."

"I acknowledge Madikizela-Mandela's role in the history of our struggle. I speak to you as someone who loves you very deeply," said Tutu. "I want you to stand up and say: *There are things that went wrong.* There are people out there who want to embrace you. I still embrace you, because I love you. If you were able to bring yourself to say: *Something went wrong,* and say, *I'm sorry, I'm sorry for my part in what went wrong,* I beg you, I beg you. You are a great person. And you don't know how your greatness would be enhanced if you were to say, *I'm sorry . . . things went wrong. Forgive me.* I beg you."

Winnie's voice from the radio spoke: "I am saying it is true: things went horribly wrong and we were aware that there were factors that led to that. For that, I am deeply sorry."

"Finally," said George quietly. He pressed his eyes shut. The car swerved, and Nadine grabbed the steering wheel. George shook his head and opened his eyes. He slammed his palm on the dashboard and then took control of the car.

When they reached the Victoria, it was already night. George took Nadine's hand as they walked past the front desk. In the elevator, he said, "I'm on thirteen."

"Not a chance," said Nadine, pushing the button for her own floor. "I might fall asleep before I get to bed."

"You could sleep next to me," said George. He was quiet as the elevator rose. "It would be nice," he said, "to have you next to me."

Nadine leaned against him. She was tired, shivering-cold. "Okay," she said softly.

Fully clothed, Nadine fell fast asleep in George's bed. When she woke, it was barely dawn and she was ravenous. George had his arm around her waist. She moved it with care, and he slept on as she crept from his room.

Nadine took the elevator downstairs in her rumpled clothes, entering the grand, empty lobby.

"Hello, dear." Nadine turned and saw Sophia sitting on a velvet couch by the fireplace, which was full of smoldering embers. Sophia was dressed in a black suit and leather pumps.

"Sophia," said Nadine.

"She wants to meet with me," said Sophia, holding up a sheet of paper. "She came here, to the hotel."

"Who?" said Nadine.

Sophia read off the paper. "Fikile Malefane," said Sophia. "However you pronounce that."

"Evelina's mother," said Nadine, suddenly longing to see her. But Nadine had never lived up to her promises. She had not earned Fikile's generosity and warmth.

Sophia raised her eyebrow. "You've done your research," she said.

Nadine came closer to Sophia, sat next to her on the couch. Sophia's hair and nails were perfect, but her eye makeup was smudged and runny where tears had marred it. "Is it asking too much," said Sophia, "to have someone to blame?"

Nadine put her hand on Sophia's hand.

"My son," said Sophia. "My son, Jason. He loved to dance. Did you know that?"

"Tell me," said Nadine.

"He loved to dance, and he loved that band, the Grateful Dead. They sang all about peace and love. For God's sake, Jason should have been born in the 1960s. Lord knows I never belonged there, with all the hippies in the mud."

Nadine smiled.

"This lady," said Sophia. "This . . ." She looked at the paper again. "This Fikile woman. She wants me to speak at the hearing. To support her daughter's amnesty. To let the girl out of jail." Sophia stared at the letter, tears gathering in the corners of her eyes. "Jason didn't do anything," she said.

"No," said Nadine.

But Sophia wasn't listening. "I have been done a wrong," she said. "I have been wronged. My son is dead."

She began to weep. Nadine wished there was something she could say to make things right, to convince Sophia to forgive Evelina, to testify on her behalf. Sophia looked at Nadine pleadingly. "Can you see?" she said. "She wants me to talk with her. Mother-to-mother. But I can't. I just can't."

Nadine tried to think of an argument that would change Sophia's mind. Sophia's testimony could alter Evelina's fate, could save her from spending her adulthood in jail. But Nadine was silent. As always, she was silent.

Thirty-four

NANTUCKET TO STARDOM

Sorry. I got interrupted by Mom and her curried cauli-flower dinner, gag. Back to the story.

After my awesome audition, Malcon took me to the Hyannis Hearth and Kettle to celebrate. Over a big sundae, he made me tell him every detail of my performance. He listened to me, never interrupting, never looking worried or concerned.

When the waitress dropped the check at our table, Malcon said, "Wait. This is on me."

I didn't say that I had no money, or wallet for that matter. I just said, "Thanks."

"So," said Malcon, "how about coming over to my apartment and watching some videos?"

"I thought you lived in Boston."

"I do," said Malcon. "Right on Copley Square. But I keep a place here, in Hyannis. For business."

My stomach hurt a little bit. "Um," I said. "I told my parents I'd be home tonight. They'd be really upset."

"Another time, then," said Malcon. He drove me to the dock, and before I climbed out of the car he said, "So I'll meet the early boat next Saturday and give you a ride to the Boston audition."

"Okay," I said. "I can't believe it."

"You'll need to stay overnight," said Malcon. "We won't

be able to make it back for the ferry. My agency will cover a hotel room."

"Okay," I said.

"Hey," said Malcon, looking me in the eye. "I'm really proud of you." He leaned forward and kissed me lightly on the lips. I wasn't sure how to feel. The kiss was creepy, for sure, but Malcon was my talent agent and I wasn't going to mess it up. Men kiss each other in Europe, after all.

"Here's a few bucks," said Malcon. "Buy yourself a treat for the ride home. I'll see you next weekend."

On the ferry, I got a seat by the window. We pulled away from shore, and I watched the lights get smaller and smaller and disappear. Soon there was just dark water. I was, as Mom would say, on Cloud Nine.

I went to the snack bar to get a Diet Coke with Malcon's money. I wore my fedora. The cashier—a teenager with a unibrow—looked at me funny, but I didn't care. I bought the soda, and then turned around. In the fluorescent light, I saw a woman sitting at one of the tables. She was pouring wine from a little bottle into a plastic glass. In front of her was a box, wrapped in silver paper. She ran a finger along her hair, and pushed it behind her ear. I ducked down. It was my mom.

I sat a few rows away and watched her. She drank her wine and stared out the window. Once in a while, she picked up the package, examined it, and then put it back down. Finally, when her wine was almost gone, she opened the present carefully, peeling back the paper along the taped edge. In the box was a picture frame, but I couldn't see any more from where I was sitting. Mom stared at the frame with a tense expression. She looked at it for a long time. Finally, she drank the last of her wine. She stood up.

I looked the opposite way when she passed me. She threw her cup and the picture in the big trash can. Then she walked over to the stairway and began to climb. I guessed she was going to stand on the upper deck. She liked to watch Nantucket come into view.

The captain announced that we were about to dock. I didn't have much time. I ran over to the trash and pulled the frame out, then went back to my seat and held it under the light. In the frame was a picture of a big old farmhouse. I liked it. There was a big barn, and a sign that said, POST CHALMERS HOLIDAY FARM. It made me think of the time we went to the Barnstable County Fair and Dad and I milked the cows. The cow's teat things were warm. Mom watched us, leaning against a wooden rail and smiling. "My farmer boys," she said. Why had she thrown this picture away? On the back of the frame, someone had written a note:

FOR N,
THE ONE PICTURE
I COULD NOT TAKE
G

What was this about? I had no idea. But the picture would always remind me of making the top ten at the Mashpee Mall Regional Auditions—the best day of my life—so I decided to keep it.

The ferry docked, and I watched Mom walk off the boat. She looked like someone I didn't really know: someone a little mysterious. This had happened before, when she was picked up by a car to go on book tour, or when she went away for a girls' weekend with Aunt Lily. Usually, she was just Mom. But once in a while, she was somebody else, somebody with a whole life I didn't even know about.

I saw her walk to the Saab, start it, and drive away. I had left my bike chained to the stand outside the Nantucket Juice Bar. As I unlocked it, I felt confused. I was proud of my audition, so proud that I didn't even care that someone had written FREAK SHOW on my bike with Wite-Out. But I was also a little scared, the way I always was when Mom became the Other Lady, the lady who might have something better to do than hang out with me.

I rode to Quidnet Road under the stars, with the picture of the farm in my basket. At home, Mom had left a note for me to come and kiss her good night. From the doorway of their room, I watched my parents sleep, curled around each other like snails. I kissed them, and Dad said, "Climb in."

It would be warm under the comforter, but I said, "I'm not a baby," and I left them. I went to my room. I didn't write. I stared at the ceiling for a while. I felt angry at my mom for being the Other Lady. It made me want to have my own secret life.

Thirty-five

Nadine spent Sunday asleep in her room, the phone off the hook. On Monday, she ate breakfast in the hotel's Colony Room, next to an enormous mural of a black servant carrying a white party's picnic up a mountain. As she started into her plate of passion fruit, smoked salmon, and toast, George sat down across from her.

"Hey you," said George. "Have you been in hiding?"

"George," said Nadine.

"Yes?"

"George, that night . . ." Nadine couldn't look up. Her breakfast smelled strongly: cloying fruit, the burned edges of the toast. She felt bile rise in her throat, but she choked out the words. "That night, when Maxim asked where I was, what did you tell him?"

"You know," said George, his fork hovering over Nadine's plate as he decided what to take, "we can be married today. I know a judge. Something good, at the same time as all this sadness." He looked long at her. "You *were* joking about the pregnancy?"

"George . . ."

He nodded, as if something were settled. "I've put a call in to *Time.* They want to send me to Rwanda. You'll come along. Genocide. Call Ian, or whoever you're working for."

"Some honeymoon," said Nadine.

"We can join the mile-high club on the way over," said George, wiggling his brows.

In spite of herself, Nadine laughed.

. . .

She walked to the courthouse, past a throng of singing South Africans and a throng of foreign reporters filming the singing. Ruth smoked a cigarette in the reporters' room. "Another day, another dollar," she said when Nadine entered.

"I don't know how you do it," said Nadine.

"Nor do I," said Ruth. "My husband's going to leave me."

"What?"

"Nobody wants to hear all this . . . this shit. We knew, of course. We knew. But this . . ." She waved her arm. "My husband says it's too much. He wants to fuck someone who doesn't have these images in her head. Who talks about wallpaper and crown moldings."

"I'm sorry," said Nadine. She thought of Hank, who despite all the sickness he dealt with every day savored his life in the evenings, talking about his basil plants and baseball.

"C'est la vie," said Ruth.

Evelina no longer wore pigtails. Sitting between her lawyers, facing the commission, she stared straight ahead, her eyelid still half closed. She did not speak throughout the hearing. Instead, the monotonous voices of her lawyers detailed the way a crowd of young people stopped Jason's car and threw a brick through the window, chasing Jason when he tried to flee. The group chanted "One settler, one bullet," as they advanced.

Leaning against the back wall, her notebook flipped open, Nadine tried to block out the visions, but could not. Jason, falling down. Jason, attacked. And finally, Jason, dead, the final blows struck by pigtailed Evelina.

Evelina's lawyers insisted the killing had a political motivation. "South Africa is free today because of bloodshed," one lawyer said. He explained that despite her young age, Evelina had sympathized with radical ANC activists, and had taken their sayings to heart. "She truly believed that this killing would advance her country toward a fair and democratic government," he concluded, staring at a spot above the Irvings. "She is sincerely sorry for the death of your son, and asks with her whole heart for forgiveness."

Finally, Desmond Tutu announced the end of the day's session. "Tomorrow," said a female member of the TRC, "the Irvings may make a statement, if they so wish."

The courtroom was quiet, waiting for the Irvings' answer. Even Nadine found she was holding her breath. Sophia stood, and gathered her purse. She stared defiantly at the crowd. "We do not so wish," she said emphatically. Nadine saw an elderly black man's face fall, heavy with disappointment.

"It is my hope," said the TRC member, "that you will reconsider." Sophia did not speak. Krispin put his arm around her, and they walked past Nadine without looking at her. They would be escorted back to the hotel flanked by bodyguards.

Nadine looked in vain for George in the group of photographers trying to capture the Irvings as they walked down the courthouse steps. She took a taxi to the Victoria, planning to order dinner to her room, to lie down for a while. Her wrist hurt, her heart hurt.

The hotel lobby was crowded with a group of young men in ill-fitting suits and an old woman in a wheelchair. Behind the front desk, Johanna spoke shrilly. "I'm sorry," she said, her Afrikaans accent strong. "I have to ask you to leave right this instant." She was visibly upset.

"We need to speak to Sophia Irving," said one of the men, who wore a panama hat. "It is an emergency. I must insist. This is Fikile Malefane."

"I'll call the police!" said Johanna.

Nadine looked at the group, at Thola and Evelina's mother in a wheelchair. Fikile's face held more lines, and her cheeks were sallow and sunken. Fikile caught Nadine's eye, and she spoke in much-improved English. "Please," she said. "Help me, please. I need to speak to Mrs. Irving."

Johanna turned to Nadine. "Are they with you?" she asked.

"Oh . . . ," said Nadine.

Fikile stared at her. "Nadine?" she said.

Fikile's brown hands were cupped together. Nadine focused on them. She remembered her soft ballet flats, the scuffing sounds they made when she wore them. "Yes," she said. "Fikile, it's me."

"Can you help me, Nadine?" said Fikile.

Nadine stared at her but couldn't find any words. "No," she said, shaking her head and moving toward the elevators. She needed to lie down. Her mind reeled: what could she possibly do? "Nadine," said Fikile, her voice desperate. Nadine stepped into the elevator. As the doors closed, Fikile cried, "Can you help me, Nadine?"

Nadine slumped against the fake books lining the wall. She pressed her hands to her eyelids. When the elevator stopped, she rushed down the hallway to her room, where she could be alone. There was an envelope taped to her mahogany door. Nadine ripped it free and stuck her card in the door. The card didn't work. "Goddamn it!" she said. She inserted the card slowly, and the lock turned. Nadine sighed with relief.

In her room, she lay down on the unmade bed. The note was written in George's scrawled handwriting:

N,

*I TOLD MAXIM YOU WERE DOWN THE HALL, BUYING HIM
A COFFEE. I TOLD HIM YOU LOVED HIM.*

G

Thirty-six

NANTUCKET TO STARDOM

This morning, Mom said she was going to a big gala Saturday night. Her "old friend" is getting an award. He's a photographer, she said. "Am I invited?" asked Dad.

"Of course, hon," said Mom, but it seemed like she didn't really want him to come.

"I'll try to make it," said Dad. "I'll do my best."

"Great," said Mom. She usually ate Hostess mini muffins for breakfast, but this morning she was eating my Special K.

"What are you so happy about?" Dad asked.

"Nothing," I said. I have decided to keep Malcon and the audition to myself. I'm sort of afraid how Mom and Dad will react. I know they won't like the sound of Malcon, and they might be worried about me getting my hopes up again. I'll tell them about *American Superstar* after I win the Boston audition. I mean, they'll have to know if I'm moving to Orlando. In the meantime, I already told them I was having a sleepover Saturday night with my old friend Roger Fell.

"You know," said Mom, pointing to an airline ad in *The New York Times,* "we should all go to London."

"Why?" I said.

"I don't know," said Mom. "Maybe I'll write about it." This was Mom's excuse for any crazy trip she wanted to go on. Her first book had come out the year before. It was called *Give Me the Sun,* and was all about motherhood in different cultures. She had even gone to Africa for ten days, almost missing my birthday. The book was dedicated to me and Dad, and I tried to read some of it, but it had really long sentences and lots of footnotes.

"There's lots of great theater in London," said Dad.

"What about LA?" I said.

"Hm," said Mom. "Well, that's something to think about."

"Or we could go to Orlando again," I said.

"Orlando," said Mom.

"Again," said Dad.

Mom is acting weirder and weirder. She got her hair done at Hot Locks, and even her eyebrows look different. She went jogging yesterday, trudging along the beach in a Nike tracksuit. She ordered some fancy silver dress and a pair of matching high-heeled shoes. She started spending time again in her "office," which is really the third-floor storage room. She has a big poster in there. It's a man gazing at a red moon. She said she used to go to a museum in Mexico and stare at this painting. It looks creepy to me.

Mom said she was going to try writing a memoir about her journalist days. But when I brought her some Constant Comment tea, she wasn't writing, just sitting at her little desk and staring at the packing boxes that took up most of the room. I put the tea on her desk, and she looked up at me with tired eyes. "It's hard to know where to begin," she said.

The word of the day on Friday was *cryptic.*

. . .

I have started skipping school and practicing my routine all day in the salon basement. Joe paid to dry-clean my seersucker suit, and Kyla hemmed my pants, sewing a perfect seam. I am nervous and so excited about my Boston audition.

Man oh man. Today started out normal but now everything is a disaster. I am writing this on the ferry, sailing away from my old life. Well, not really *sailing,* but anyway.

Let me start at the beginning. This morning, I was practicing in my room when Mom came in. She was wearing the silver dress, and held her jewelry box. "Dangly earrings or pearls?" she said. But then her face froze.

I followed her gaze. She was staring at the farm picture, which was hanging above my dresser. "What's that?" she said, her voice low.

"It's a farm," I said.

She marched over and pulled it from my wall. "Mom!" I said. "What are you doing?"

She turned around. Her eyes were blazing—I had never seen her look this way. "You don't know one thing about this picture," she said. "I will not have it in my house. Where on earth did you get this?"

I lunged at her and pulled the picture out of her hands. I held it to my chest. "I saw you throw it away. On the ferry. I like it," I said. "I want it. It reminds me of . . . a really good day."

"The ferry?" said Mom, bewildered. But she couldn't take her eyes off the picture and her voice got strange. "Honey," she said. "Give me the photograph. I mean it."

"No," I said. My secret sat heavily in my stomach, like a huge hamburger. I wanted to tell her about the audition, about Malcon, but I was afraid. I was afraid telling her would puncture my dream like a big pin.

"I will tell you," said Mom. "Someday, sweetheart. But not now. Please. Just know that I need you to give me that picture. It doesn't belong—" Her voice broke. "It has no place in this house," she said. She rushed toward me and grabbed the frame. I wouldn't let go. She tried to rip it from my hands and I stumbled. The whole thing smashed and a shard of the glass cut me. Blood gushed out of my hand.

"Honey," she said.

"I'm bleeding," I said.

"Come here, honey."

"No," I said. The cut hurt and I was filled with a terrible anger.

"Honey," said Mom. "Come here, your hand."

"Get out of my room!" I screamed. We stared at each other for a minute, and then I said, "I hate you!"

My mom was always so strong, but I saw her face fall. "Don't say that," she whispered, and there was pain in her voice and I simply couldn't stand it. I grabbed my backpack and ran downstairs and out the door. I jumped on my bike and rode away as fast as I could. I finally understood that I didn't belong in that house or on this stupid island.

Mom tried to run after me in her new shoes. "Don't leave!" she said, and she was so pathetic that I hated her even more. I rode away and I said with each pump of the pedals, *I am never, ever coming back.*

Thirty-seven

Nadine stared at George's scrawled note, and then she threw it in the trash. She settled herself at her wide desk, opening her notebook and pulling the cap off a Hotel Victoria pen. She had to get to work, but the words wouldn't come.

In Mexico City, Nadine had a ritual. She would stuff notes into her backpack and head for Chapultepec Park, an oasis in the middle of the busy city. She would walk through the wrought-iron gates and settle underneath her favorite ahuehuete tree. The grassy spot afforded a view of the lake, where lovers pedaled in circles on rented boats. Around Nadine, Mexican families picnicked. She wrote in the shade of the tree, grasshoppers crawling over her papers, and rewarded herself with a fruit cup when the story was done.

Nadine tried to taste the fresh pineapple, mango, and jicama sprinkled with chili powder, but the thoughts of her shady refuge didn't help. Nadine opened Jason's journal to the last page, reading the entry dated April 6, 1988: the night before his murder. "I am discouraged," Jason wrote. "I think I am helping these kids, but then there are the bad ones, they're on Mandrax, all fucked up, they're angry. Sometimes I wonder if I'm even making a difference here."

Nadine swallowed, and read on.

"Most of all," Jason had written, "I am afraid that I will never find someone to love. I get so down, imagining a life without a lover, without someone to sleep next to at night. I have my students, and I have things to teach them. I guess I'm just lonely, at the end of the day." After this sentence, the page was blank.

Nadine looked down. Before leaving, she had hung the DO NOT DISTURB sign on her door: the cloth-covered trash can held both a pregnancy test and George's note. She stared into the can, trying to find meaning in its contents.

Hank's duffel bag was propped next to the desk, Nadine's clothes spilling out. She was always packing or unpacking, washing her underwear in hotel sinks, shaking out her cotton shirts. Nadine could not remember the last time she had folded clothes into a dresser drawer.

She thought of her father, more comfortable standing on the concrete floor at Falmouth Fish than in his home on Surf Drive. For a moment, she let herself love him. She was filled with the same fear that had made Jim force his shoulders back each morning and drive away from Nadine and his memories.

But one day, when Nadine was eight, he had turned the car around. Nadine was climbing up to the turret when she heard Jim pull back into the driveway. She ran to the front door and threw it open. "Daddy," she said, putting her hands on her hips, "did you forget your lunch?"

"Deanie," her father said, "did you know it's the first day of spring?" They looked out at the leafless trees, the chilling sleet beginning to fall. "I heard it on the radio," said Jim. "It's true."

Nadine could scarcely speak. She was filled with a fierce hope.

"I'm taking the day off," Jim announced. "Tell Clare to skedaddle. Your mom always said the first day of spring was a day to celebrate, and we're going to have a party."

Nadine stared at her father. How had he known about the spring parties? They had been something she had shared with her mother alone. Every year, on the first day of spring they dressed up and went for a fancy tea at the Dunbar Tea Shop in Sandwich. For two years, the day had passed without mention.

"Go on," said Jim gruffly. "Get in the shower, Deanie. I'm going to need some lessons before we head to Sandwich. Do I hold out my pinkie when I drink my tea?" He demonstrated, and Nadine erupted in giggles. Just when she had stopped hoping he would come back, he had surprised her.

Nadine shook her head; this was no time for reverie. She tried again to think objectively. But instead of a lead, she wrote, I'm just lonely, at the end of the day. Jason had not lived long enough to change the ending of his story. For Nadine, though, there was still time. She put down her pen.

Nadine walked to the door of her room, and opened it. In the elevator, she pushed the button for the eleventh floor. She stared at the book spines as the elevator climbed. There was *Tristram Shandy* and there, *The Collected Poems of Emily Dickinson.* When the gilded doors slid open, she strode down the plush hallway and knocked on Room 1102.

"I need to talk to Sophia," said Nadine, when Krispin stood before her.

"The hell you do," said Krispin. His bottle-green shirt was wrinkled and tucked unevenly into cotton pants. His hair, usually combed into an elegant mane, hung limply. He narrowed his eyes.

Nadine felt a rush of pity for Krispin, a man broken by circumstance, like her father. She took a breath, forging ahead. "I knew him," said Nadine. "Don't close the door. I knew Jason. He . . ." She swallowed.

"He *what*?" said Krispin.

"He and I were lovers," said Nadine.

Krispin's face crumpled as if he had been punched. He took a step back. "I can't . . . ," he said. "I always thought," he said.

Sophia appeared behind him, and put her hand on Krispin's shoulder. There was a light in her eyes. "Honey," she said. "Come in, honey."

"I thought he was—" said Krispin, shaking his head.

"Well, obviously he wasn't," said Sophia.

Nadine sat in a richly upholstered chair and told the Irvings about her love affair with their son. The story spilled out of her as if it were truth. "I fell in love with him the first time I saw him. He," she paused. "He took me to Camps Bay. Our first, our first kiss was on the beach."

Krispin, sitting opposite Nadine, slapped his knee. "My boy," he said. His eyes were full of tears.

"More," said Sophia.

"We were just friends at the start," said Nadine. "We had so much in common—I grew up in Woods Hole."

Sophia shook her head. "Woods Hole," she said, amazed.

"Your dad a scientist?" said Krispin.

"No," said Nadine. "He works at Falmouth Fish."

"Oh," said Krispin.

"Regardless," said Sophia. "Go on."

"So one day," said Nadine, "Jason bought some bread and cheese. He told me we were going to the beach for a picnic. Grapes, too. There were grapes. And wine. And smoked fish, and crackers."

"Some picnic," said Krispin.

"We went to Camps Bay," continued Nadine. "Jason spread out a blanket. A red blanket. We sat on the blanket and ate the picnic."

"A red blanket," said Sophia wonderingly.

"So we finished the wine. The sand was nice and warm. We went swimming in the waves. Well, and then he kissed me."

Krispin and Sophia were silent.

"I was with him in the hospital," said Nadine. She did not cry. "I was with him. I told him I loved him. It was . . . it was hard to watch him go. But I stayed, and I held his hand." Nadine closed her eyes, and saw Maxim's open palm. "I held his hand to my face," she said. "It was so soft," she said. "I stayed with him all night," she said. "I never left his side."

"He was always so sweet," said Sophia. "Even as a little boy. He was so kind . . ."

"He spoke once," said Nadine.

"But you can't keep them safe, you just can't." Sophia's voice was high-pitched, verging on hysteria. "What can you do? You just . . . you let them go."

"My God," said Krispin. He leaned forward, his giant watch slipping down his wrist. "What did he say?"

"He said he loved me," said Nadine. "He said he forgave the kids who . . . who . . ."

"Who killed him," said Krispin simply.

"He said he forgave them," said Nadine.

"You have to," said Sophia, wringing her hands. "You have to let them go."

"Sophia," said Nadine. "He would want you to forgive the girl. He would want you to speak to her mother. He would, I know he would."

Sophia was sobbing. She didn't seem to hear Nadine. She put her hand on Nadine's arm. "Oh, God," she said. "My baby." She looked at Nadine. "Did you know," Sophia said quietly, searchingly. "He loved pancakes. He had a freckle on his elbow. When he was little, when I gave him a bubble bath, I would say, 'Where's my favorite freckle?' and he would . . . he would bring his tiny elbow . . . he would lift it out of the bubbles . . .'"

"I know," said Nadine. "I remember that freckle."

Sophia nodded, overcome. "And his ears . . . ," she said.

"His ears," said Nadine.

Sophia opened her arms, and Nadine moved close. Someone else's mother held her tight.

Finally, Sophia sat back in her chair. She took the tissue

Krispin held out for her and dabbed her eyes. "Call the front desk," she said, her voice gaining strength.

"Sophia," protested Krispin.

"Do it," said Sophia. Krispin rose and walked to the bedside table. Slowly, he dialed, and held out the phone.

"Hello," said Sophia, taking it. She looked at Nadine. "Yes," she said. "No, listen to me. I want to see her. Yes, I said I want you to send her up. Room 1102. Thank you."

"Honey," said Krispin, "are you sure . . ."

"Shhh," said Sophia.

As they waited, the sounds of Cape Town filtered in through the open windows: honking horns, men yelling, the steady thrum of traffic. Nadine had once thought this noise would be the sound-track to the rest of her life. She had imagined, lying next to Maxim, that she would never leave this city. With every year, she would know Maxim a little better: she would comprehend the nuances of his country, and together they would alert the world to both the horror of apartheid and the fierce spirits on both sides of the fight. These were grand plans, and they were born of her love for one man. Nadine's dream of a life in South Africa died with Maxim. For a decade, work had filled the endless hours, but she could see now that there would always be another violent crime, a hungrier reporter.

Nadine's thoughts were interrupted by a knock on the door. "Go on and open it," said Sophia.

In her wheelchair, Fikile looked nervous. She was accompanied by the man in the panama hat. "I am Albert Malefane," said the man. "This is my aunt, Fikile Malefane."

"Come in," said Krispin politely. Fikile looked at Nadine as she was wheeled in the room. "Ah," she said.

Nadine smiled.

"You help me, Nadine," Fikile whispered as Albert gaped at the opulent room. He removed his hat. Fikile stared out the window. She said something in Xhosa.

"She says the whole city looks different from above," said Albert.

The two mothers sat facing each other. Krispin kept his arm around Sophia, and Albert translated for his aunt. "Her English is good," he explained, "but she wants to speak from the heart, and not worry about the vocabulary."

"Well, get on with it, then," said Sophia.

Fikile clasped her hands on the cloth that covered her knees. She looked straight into Sophia's eyes, and began to speak in Xhosa. Albert spoke a moment later. "I am thankful that you will speak to me," he said. "I know I have no right. Your son is dead, and my daughter is to blame. But she is not a monster. She is a girl who is possessed by anger. Her friends were raped and killed. She was not given a proper education. Her beloved sister, Tholakele, was taken by the government. She was killed by the government. Today, in the court, you see a woman named Evelina, and you hate her. But she is the baby I held to my breast. She is the baby I sang to sleep. Please look at me."

"I sang Jason to sleep," said Sophia. "I sang him 'Silent Night.' He hated being in his crib, always tried to climb out. But if I sang 'Silent Night,' he lay down and closed his eyes. I reached through the slats, and combed his hair with my fingers." She stared at a faraway place as Albert spoke to Fikile.

Fikile nodded, and reached out to touch Sophia's hand. Sophia met her eyes. Fikile cleared her throat and continued in Xhosa, Albert translating. "My Evelina took the life of your son. And the last years in prison have taken away much of my baby girl. A ghost is all that is left. We are both mothers who have lost their children."

"My whole life was my son," said Sophia, leaning toward Fikile. "I live in a nightmare. Every day when I wake up, I remember again that he is gone. All I want is to die."

"I ask for your forgiveness," said Fikile. "We do not deserve it, but I ask for it nonetheless. I beg you, from one mother to another. Can you forgive her?"

Sophia glanced at Nadine. Nadine realized she was holding her breath. She felt as if Sophia held her fate, as well. Sophia turned back to Fikile. She sighed, and her strength seemed to rush from her. "For my son, okay. For Jason, I forgive her," said Sophia.

Thirty-eight

■

NANTUCKET TO STARDOM

I have calmed down and found a new pen that works better. We are almost to Hyannis, so I don't have much time.

I rode my bike all the way to the harbor, leaving Mom in the dust. As soon as the ferry pulled out, I went into the bathroom. Joe had given me a sample tube of Aveda gel, and I used it to fix my hair before changing into my suit. My hand had stopped bleeding, but I wrapped it in toilet paper just in case. Here is some blood from my hand:

I stared at myself, trying to ignore the anxious feeling in my stomach. It was just the swaying boat. I gave the new me a confident smile in the bathroom mirror, and the man changing his baby next to me said, "Looking spiffy, there." I shrugged, and tried not to look at his baby's bare bottom.

We are docking, so I will write more after my audition. This means everything to me, so please God, let me win. If I don't win, I don't know what I will do.

The audition is over now. I feel like a different person. It's hard to write about what happened after I got off the ferry.

Maybe I can find a way to tell it without crying. I'll try. My hand feels better now.

Malcon was standing in the parking lot in Hyannis, leaning against his car. He wore another really cool sweater: yellow with cables running down the front. "Hey there," he said as I walked toward him. I said hi.

He gave me a hug, saying, "Did you tell your parents you're staying the night?"

"Yes," I said. I wasn't sure that Malcon was the answer to what I was looking for, but there he was, and he was better than going back.

"What's the story with the hand?" said Malcon.

"I cut it," I said.

"Let me see." Malcon took my fist, opened it carefully. He unwrapped the toilet paper, traced the cut with his finger. "Let's stop at a CVS," he said. "Clean this up."

"Okay."

"Do you want to tell me what happened?" said Malcon.

"No," I said. And he let it go. He took me to a pharmacy, and we cleaned the cut with cotton balls and hydrogen peroxide. Malcon put a bandage on and didn't mention it again, which I appreciated. As we drove, we talked about Elvis instead. In Malcon's opinion, Elvis's later performances were much better than his early ones. Malcon's favorite Elvis movie was *Charro!,* where Elvis had a beard. All I knew about Elvis was his Christmas album, which my Granny Gwen played every Christmas when we went to Woods Hole. She taught me all the words to the songs, and we even had a dance routine for "Santa Bring My Baby Back." But I didn't tell Malcon any of this. I just listened.

We drove past the Mashpee Mall, and Malcon honked. "Just wanted to mark the spot where you kicked ass," he said. We turned north and discussed the previous season of *American Superstar*. The cheesy blonde from Kentucky had won, but Malcon thought the Korean American boy had been better. We passed a bunch of rotaries, and then we reached the Sagamore Bridge. It loomed high above the water, fancy metalwork stretching like a crown. Malcon drove around the rotary really fast, merging onto the lane that headed off Cape Cod. At the entrance to the bridge, a sign said, WE CAN HELP. CALL THE GOOD SAMARITANS, and then a phone number.

"That sign," said Malcon, "gives me chills."

"Why?"

He turned to me. "It's for people who are about to jump."

"Oh," I said. "Jump off the bridge?"

"Yes, the bridge."

"You mean, like, kill themselves?"

Malcon raised his eyebrows. "Kid," he said, "you got rocks in there or what?"

"I don't get it," I admitted. "Why would someone jump off a bridge?"

Malcon shook his head, looking really old all of a sudden. "May you never know," he said, staring straight ahead.

We drove for an hour on Route 3 to Boston. We passed Plymouth, where I had gone on a class trip to stand in the rain and look at a rock. We passed Sam's Club, where Mom had taken me to buy a hundred-pack of Charmin and a million tubes of Crest. The city was on the horizon.

The truth is, I don't really want to talk about the auditions. There were so many kids at Gillette Stadium that I realized I wasn't so great after all. Maybe this affected my performance, I don't know. I'll say this: we waited for a really long time. The *American Superstar* judges were there. I didn't rock the house. I knew it even before I was done. Instead of feeling filled with fire, I was room temperature, and I couldn't stop thinking of Mom running after my bicycle. Chipe Basilia said, "Okay, thank you." And Johnny Thunder said, "Was that a Broadway tune?"

"Yes," I said. "I love Frank Sinatra!"

They all stared at me.

After a long afternoon, it was time to announce the winners. Even though I prayed and hoped each time the announcer opened his mouth, my name was not called. He finished, and people started packing up. It was over. I wanted to die. Malcon squeezed my shoulders and told me he was taking me to Quiznos' Subs for dinner. "You can have anything you want, buddy," he said. "I'm really sorry." He put his arm around me as we walked toward the exit.

"It's okay," I said, "really." But it wasn't okay. If I wasn't a star, then what was I?

"Tell you what," said Malcon. "After dinner, we'll get some ice cream and go watch movies in a hotel room."

"Why don't we just stay at your house?" I asked.

"My boring apartment?" said Malcon. "It's all the way over on Beacon Hill."

"I thought you said Copley Square."

Malcon stroked my neck with his fingers. "Right," he said.

I didn't like the way Malcon was talking to me. I didn't want his fingers on my neck. I missed my dad all of a sudden: I missed him so much I went cold. I remembered the way Dad used to take me whale hunting. Of course, you can't catch a whale from the beach, but we spent hours knee-deep in the water, pretending. Dad would point and yell, and we would run toward the imaginary whales with our driftwood harpoons held high. Sometimes Dad would be a whale and thrash around, grabbing me around the waist and dunking me. It must have been so boring for him, standing around in the tidal pools all day. Mom would sit on the towel with her book and call out, "Boys! Sunscreen!"

"Come on, buddy," said Malcon, holding open the door that led into the parking lot. I felt like maybe I shouldn't follow him. But here I was in Boston. I couldn't call my mom. Maybe I could call Aunt Lily from a pay phone?

Suddenly the loudspeakers crackled to life again. "Paging Harry Duarte," said a man's deep voice. "Harry Duarte, please report to the stage immediately. Paging Harry Duarte."

I glanced at Malcon, but instead of looking happy, he looked nervous. "Maybe I won," I said, excitement rising almost painfully in my chest.

"Harry Duarte," said the loudspeaker. I ran toward the stage, not even noticing that Malcon wasn't following me. My heart pounded in my ears as I pushed past throngs of disappointed kids. My name was echoed again and again as I neared the front. Visions ran through my mind, headlines proclaiming the regional winner who almost got away.

And then I spotted her, peering across the stadium with the same hope in her eyes that I felt in my rib cage. She looked beautiful under the spotlight, and as I got closer, I understood that in the same way I yearned for stardom, she yearned for me.

"Harry Duarte," said the man's voice again, and then my

own voice rose up. "It's me," I said, "here I am!" She put her hand over her eyes and scanned the crowd. When she saw me, she smiled wide.

"Mommy!" I said, and I climbed on the stage, burying my face in her weird-o dress.

Thirty-nine

I n her South African hotel room, in a lucid dream, Nadine went into labor. She felt radiating pain and struggled to sit up. She was on the couch in Hank's living room, where she had taken to sleeping now that she was big and uncomfortable. The Nantucket night was cold and clear.

By the door, Hank had packed a bag for the journey: hard candy and lotion and a CD of his favorite heavy-metal music. "Can't be too prepared," he had told Nadine nervously.

Hank slept in their bedroom, snoring. The ravages of South Africa—of Massachusetts, for that matter—never filled his dreams. He saw a broken bone and wondered how it could be healed. He didn't think about why it was broken, or what it would feel like if it had been his own leg. He did not lie awake at night, his stomach hurting after seeing an old man at a diner who looked frail and alone.

It was time to wake her husband. He would bundle up in his navy peacoat, with his gray wool hat. It was snowing in the dream, and they walked past the Nantucket Post Office. Suddenly, Nadine was inside the post office, a small boy next to her. They were picking up the mail, and the child had black curls and Ann's violet eyes. He turned to Nadine and said, "Mommy, where doggy?" The post office dog—a collie—appeared and licked the boy, sending him into a fit of laughter.

It was summer, then, and Nadine was on a giant sailboat. Krispin was at the helm, and Sophia handed Nadine a gin and tonic. Hank reclined next to Nadine, and Lily sat opposite in a polka-dot bikini. Lily looked the way she had during their sixteenth summer, happy and tan, and Nadine hadn't made any mistakes yet. The little boy appeared in a life vest. He climbed on Nadine's lap and settled his cheek against her chest. Jim waved from shore, and Krispin steered the boat to him. "Mommy, I'm hungry," said the boy. Nadine looked around for Ann, but then realized the boy was speaking to her. In Nadine's hand was a packet of peanut butter crackers.

Nadine woke, and made her decision. She wanted this baby. She wanted to raise him on Nantucket, Massachusetts. There were children who dreamed of living in a wooden house with a screen door you could leave unlocked without the fear of someone coming in and taking your mother away. There were children who wondered if such a place was real, if it was possible in the same world as theirs. Nadine didn't know what she could do to deserve the gift she had been given. For one thing, she could stop pretending it wasn't a gift, and start being thankful.

Hank would look at Nadine and see a mother. He would take a guest room and create a nursery. Nadine could live in his vision, she could try. She could stop pointing out the cracks in the ceiling, the horrors in the world. Maybe Nadine could find a drug and stop seeing them herself. Nadine could say to one child, *I've got you. You live in a great country. You are safe.*

Nadine could say it, and she could try to believe it, as well.

Forty

The next morning, Nadine sat next to Krispin and Sophia at the hearing. When they were called upon to make a statement, the Irvings stood. Sophia squeezed Nadine's arm, and she and Krispin made their way to the podium.

"It's hard to know," said Sophia, her voice small in the microphone. The audience grew hushed. "It's hard to know how you'll feel if something happens to your child. If your child is beaten to death for no—" She stopped, paused, then continued. "For a reason that doesn't make sense to you," she said. She looked at Fikile, sitting in the front row.

"But it's also hard for me to know what Evelina's life was like. What her days consisted of, what conditions . . . why she felt moved to do such a thing. I can't—I can't pretend to know that. My son, Jason, he tried to be a part of her world. He tried to help change her world. And he would want me to stand here. And he would want me to say, I am trying. Evelina Malefane thought . . . somehow . . . she wanted to do something to help her country. I don't know. But I am speaking for my son. I hope you will grant amnesty to Evelina Malefane, so she can make something of her life. Thank you."

She lifted her head and took Krispin's hand. They looked at each other for a moment, and then he embraced her. He cleared his throat, and said, "My son was a gentleman. He was a brilliant man. I will miss him every minute for the rest of my life. But punishing this—" He gestured to Evelina. "Keeping this poor young woman in jail doesn't bring Jason back. Nothing's going to bring him back." The sadness in Krispin's eyes hinted at unfathomable despair. Nadine realized she had moved her hands to cradle her flat stomach.

"Thank you," said Krispin into the microphone, and then he led his wife back to their chairs. Later that afternoon, Krispin bent to speak softly in Nadine's ear. "Grapes on the beach," he said. He patted her knee. "That was a nice touch," he said.

Nadine stopped to hug Fikile, and wrote down Albert's address so they could keep in contact. When Evelina was given amnesty, Nadine wrote with congratulations. Evelina moved back home with Fikile and began to make up middle school and then high school classes. Albert wrote that Evelina dreamed of working in a fancy restaurant like the one her mother would never stop talking about, the one where Thola made them fix the tablecloth.

Outside the courthouse, Nadine saw George sitting on a green bench. The sun was fierce; George squinted as he loaded film into his camera. When he saw her, he lifted it and began to take pictures.

"Stop," said Nadine.

He focused on her face. "I don't want to have to rely on my memory," he said. "I want evidence of this moment."

She sat down and looked directly at the camera. "What moment is that?" she said.

"The moment you tell me," he said, snapping a photo. "The moment you say *Yes, I'll marry you, George.*"

Nadine smiled wryly. "I'm going to the airport," she said.

George put the camera down. "Of course you are," he said. He snorted, a derisive sound. "Can't keep running, darling," he said.

"George, I'm sorry."

"I'll live," said George.

"I mean, about that night. I made a mistake. I should have stayed."

"It's done now," said George.

"I just wish I could . . . I wish Maxim—"

"It's done."

Nadine stood. "I'm going home," she said.

"You?"

Nadine put her hand on her stomach again. She thought of Fikile, the look in her eyes as she pled for her daughter. "Me," she said. "Believe it or not."

"I believe it," said George. He smiled forlornly.

Nadine kissed him on the cheek. "Good-bye," she said.

The air outside Logan Airport was chilly and dry. Nadine's hair—mashed from more than a day in airplanes—was filled with static, and she shivered in her thin sweater. A minivan stopped next to her, dislodging a pile of gray snow. The passenger-side window slid down. "Hey, stranger," said Lily.

Nadine grinned. She threw the duffel in the trunk and opened the passenger-side door. She was immediately hit with hot air that smelled of McDonald's. A high-pitched voice sang about the alphabet from the car stereo, and Nadine peered into the back, where Bo, Babe, and little Kristi were securely strapped into plastic seats. "I got you a Two-Cheeseburger Meal," said Lily, tossing the bag on Nadine's lap and pulling from the curb.

"Fantastic," said Nadine, unwrapping a burger with relish. The stereo blared, "S! I love the letter S! Slithery snakes and sweet cupcakes . . ."

"What on earth is this music?" said Nadine.

"Welcome to the rest of your life," said Lily. "Have you told him you're coming?"

"No," said Nadine. "I was afraid he'd tell me to fuck off."

Lily sighed and turned up the car stereo.

The ferry dock in Hyannis was already crowded with cars and people sipping hot drinks. Lily gave Nadine a kiss. "You're going to need this," she said, pulling a parka from the backseat.

"Wish me luck," said Nadine. "I'm a little scared."

"Oh please," said Lily. "It just gets harder from here."

"I'm ready," said Nadine.

Lily looked skeptical, but when Nadine opened the back door and kissed the children, Lily softened. "I love you," she said.

"I know," said Nadine. "Do you think I can do it?"

"I'm sure you can," said Lily. "And there's always Dark and Stormies." Nadine shook her head at the mention of their favorite drink, a mixture of ginger beer and dark rum.

Nadine embraced Lily and took Hank's duffel from the back of the minivan. She scrutinized the Steamship Authority weekend parking lot. Hank's green pickup truck was parked toward the front: Lily had guessed right that he would rush from work to board the evening ferry. Nadine bought a one-way ticket and a Snickers bar. She was terrified.

As she boarded the boat, she jammed her hands in the pockets of the parka. In each pocket was something square and hard. She pulled out two Moleskine notebooks. One was titled NANTUCKET; the other, NURSING.

On board she wandered from room to room, scanning the passengers. Finally, as the ferry pulled from shore, she saw him. He leaned against the rail on the upper deck, gazing out at the water. Nadine stood behind a metal door and watched him. He wore a fisherman's sweater, his hair still uncut and blowing in the wind. Nadine took a deep breath, and turned the knob.

There was no one else outside; it was freezing. Hank turned as Nadine approached him. He blinked, and happiness bathed his face. He smiled, then tried to hide the smile. He said, "Nadine?"

The horn sounded, and Nadine took Hank's face between her hands. She kissed him, and he kissed her back. His arms, his arms around her.

Nadine looked at Hank, tried to burn the image in her mind. She closed her eyes, sending the postcard to her mother.

Forty-one

NANTUCKET TO STARDOM
AND THEN BACK TO NANTUCKET, AGAIN

So my tearful reunion with Mom ended up on the six o'clock news, and now three reporters want to talk to me! But that will all wait until tomorrow. Tonight, I just want to write about the end of a really important day, and then I want to sleep.

As we walked toward her rental car, I asked Mom how she had found me. She had been a reporter, she said, didn't I remember? She knew how to find people. She laughed, and said it hadn't been hard: she had called Hot Locks, and Joe had told her about the auditions. Then she had flown to Boston. We climbed in the car, and she turned to me. "Why didn't you tell me about all this?" she said.

I said I didn't know. I wanted to tell her that I hated the worry line between her eyes. I said I was afraid she wouldn't let me go to Boston and meet Malcon. She got really tense and said, "Who is Malcon?"

I was silent.

"Harry?" she said quietly, and I told her.

She asked if he had hurt me, and I said no. She said she thought we should tell the police about him, and I wasn't sure, but I decided maybe she was right.

As we drove to the police station, my mom said some really nice things. She said that she was proud I had made it to the Boston audition. She was sorry if I felt like I couldn't confide in her, but I could. She said that she would try to tell me things, too, like if I wanted to know about the farm picture, or her life before she married my dad and moved to Nantucket. "I wanted you to think the world could be a certain way," she said. "I wanted you to feel safe."

"Okay," I said.

Did I want to hear about the farm picture, she asked. I said not really, not right now.

We sat in the police station and a policeman with a moustache asked me all about Malcon. He opened a book of black-and-white pictures and said, "Do you see him?"

"He didn't do anything," I said. "He's a talent agent."

But then I saw Malcon's face in the policeman's book. I touched the page, pushing Malcon's nose until my finger hurt. "That's him," I said.

Mom hugged me.

We called Dad from the policeman's office. I thought he would be mad, but he was just happy. "This house is way too quiet," he said. "Come home and let us know how it feels to be famous."

"I lost, Dad," I said.

"But first you won," said Dad. "Joe's sitting here telling me all about it."

"Joe's there?" It was weird thinking about Joe and my dad, hanging out having St. Pauli Girls in the kitchen.

"Joe thinks we should take you to see some Broadway shows," Dad continued, "or maybe you want dance lessons?"

"How about leather pants?"

"Don't push it."

"Okay," I said, sort of crying and giggling at the same time.

As we drove away from the police station toward the airport, it was dark. "Mom," I said. But then I didn't know what should come next. I wanted to tell her I was sorry. I wanted her to see that I had dreams that were bigger than Nantucket.

She put her hand on my head, combed through my hair with her fingers. It felt good. I wanted to tell her everything I had kept inside. But it's hard, even now, to explain my feelings. I love Mom and Dad, and they are doing their best. But there's something bigger out there for me, that's all I know. And the big thing might take me away from them.

"Mom," I said, "I'm growing up, Mom." She didn't speak for a little while. She was looking out the windshield, at the stars. She was looking beyond the stars. I closed my eyes and breathed in the smell of her: newsprint, soap, the ginger perfume she ordered from somewhere off-island. The wheels hummed on the pavement.

"I mean," I said. "I'm not going to stay on Nantucket forever."

Mom leaned her head toward mine. In the rearview mirror, we looked like ghosts, all lit up from the passing headlights. "I know," she said.

Forty-Two

The windows in the house were dark by the time Nadine reached home. Hank was dreaming, or awake, and listening for them. Perhaps she would tuck Harry in bed and she and Hank would make love. They would move together easily, warmly, and he would say *How I love you* in her ear. Or he would cling to her with the fierceness of the earliest years, when he still thought she might leave.

It was hard to stay still, to stay on Nantucket. But the quiet joys had filled her: the smell of apples in the fall, the way a gray sky could shine, dinner by the fire on chilly nights, summer days at the beach with plastic pails.

Nadine did not turn off the car. She watched her sleeping son. The moments were so clear: his hot weight in her arms, lips suckling her in the quiet hours before dawn. The last time he had nursed, and how she had mourned losing the ability to feed him. The evening he came upon her spraying perfume and exploded into tears: he stood in pajamas and cried until his face was mottled and wet. She and Hank walked out the door, Hank's hand on her back, steadying her, Harry's cries ringing out over the babysitter's soothing. For a year, Harry hid her shoes in the old grandfather clock so she could not go away.

Mom, he had said, *I'm growing up, Mom.* She had always known the time would come, but she wasn't ready. She looked at his nose, his eyelashes. He had lit the vibrant center of her life, and she knew that from this day on it would be a long farewell as he found his place in the world without her.

When she turned off the engine, when they stepped sleepily from the car and went inside. When he woke in the morning, when he made his own breakfast, when she sat in her office, staring at the page, remembering when it was enough, when it was everything. There was a day when he sat outside the door all afternoon, singing, telling himself stories, listening to her type, waiting for her to return to him.

This moment would end. The overheated car, the loving husband, the slow start of snow. This boy, beside her, asleep. The wind began to rise up, and Nadine waited.

Acknowledgments

M any books helped me in my attempts to understand South Africa. I was especially moved by the work of Nadine Gordimer, Greg Marinovich, Joao Silva, Antjie Krog, William Finnegan, Lisa Fugard, and Lynn Freed. The Voice by Vusi Mahlasela and music by Khayelitsha's the Moonlights, Cape Melodies, Jam Band, and Pace provided a glorious soundtrack to my writing days. Masha Hamilton—and her novels examining the intersection of love and war—inspired the character of Nadine.

The worst part about finishing a book is losing the excuse to call my brilliant editor, Anika Streitfeld, six times a day. I'll try to limit myself to four calls a day now, I promise. A. Michelle Tessler has believed in every crazy idea I've brought her; I am fortunate to have her representation and friendship.

Rebecca and Bill Johnson filled my Cape Cod nights with laughter and oysters. Becca and Andy Bunn, Jeanne Tift, the Great Escape Book Club, and George Eckstrom made a temporary stop into a home. Thank you to the McKay family for unwittingly allowing Nadine and Hank to fall in love in their Nantucket house.

For reading early drafts of this book, thanks to Wendy Wrangham, Sarah McKay, Kelly Braffett, Liza Ward, Ellen Sussman, Juli Berwald, Allison Lynn, Clare Smith, Clare Conville, Emily Hovland, and David Francis.

Thank you, Clay Smith, for the Avenue A Writers' Retreat and Restaurant.

Thanks to Don Filiault and Walter Sullivan for welcoming me

to the Beach Breeze Inn in Falmouth, Massachusetts, where much of this book was written. The Falmouth Public Library librarians made even the dreariest days bright, especially Kat Renna and Laurie McNee. Mary-Anne Westley called every morning (and some afternoons) and told me what she knew.

Tip Meckel, my great love, thank you for the scallops with white wine, and for bringing me home to Texas in grand style. WAM, you are the definition of joy. Let's build a house, boys.

In South Africa, I was helped immeasurably by Jennifer Patterson, Phillip Boyd at the amazing Dance for All (where Thola would have learned her moves), and Tertia Albertyn. Patrick Lutuli made his home, Khayelitsha township, come alive with his energy and wide smile, and it is impossible to believe that he is gone.

P.S.

Ideas,
interviews
& features . . .

About the author

Read on

Q & A with Amanda Eyre Ward

Amanda Eyre Ward talks to Masha Hamilton

Masha Hamilton: I've loved and admired all three of your novels, and each one probes different themes and settings. This time around, why did you choose to write about South Africa?

Amanda Eyre Ward: I've always been fascinated by South Africa. When I was in high school, I reviewed Alan Paton's autobiography *Journey Continued* for my high school newspaper. Paton is the author of *Cry, the Beloved Country*, and I was stunned by his descriptions of South Africa. It sounded like such a beautiful place, and I was moved by Paton's sorrow about what had become of his homeland. The world seemed very confusing to me. I wasn't happy and didn't have the power to fix things in my family. I think the fact that apartheid was such a clear wrong appealed to me. I wanted to fly to South Africa and do something to help. I thought I could help South Africans in a way I could not help myself. The first time I left the Eastern time zone, during my junior year in college, I flew to Africa. But I couldn't visit South Africa at that time – there were no study abroad programs. I went to Kenya instead. It took me seventeen more years to finally set foot in South Africa.

MH: That's something that intrigues me: the fact that our reach out into the world, often seen as idealistic, is of course well intentioned and generous of spirit, but scrape away the surface and you find it is often also motivated by very personal situations that have led to unmet yearnings. In your case, for example, an inability to fix things within your own family led to a desire to help South Africans. In *Forgive Me*, Nadine, too, has personal reasons that propel her into the world. Beyond that, I know the novel is inspired in part by a true story. What about that story captivated you?

AEW: I think the Truth and Reconciliation Commission is amazing. The concept of telling the truth and being set free could not be more unlike the justice system in the United States, where victims might never know the truth about an incident, as the accused have to focus on winning a trial, rather than seeking forgiveness. Amy Biehl was a twenty-six-year-old Fulbright scholar when she went to South Africa. I had dreamed of going, but Amy made the trip, devoting herself to teaching underprivileged students. One night, Amy was driving a student home in Guguletu Township when her car was surrounded by an angry mob. Like the fictional Jason Irving, Amy was killed by the same children she was trying ▶

Q & A with Amanda Eyre Ward
(continued)

◄ to help. Unlike the fictional Irvings, Amy's parents supported amnesty for Amy's killers from the beginning. The Biehls attended the TRC hearings and went on to found the Amy Biehl Foundation, which supports township children in a myriad of ways. I found the Biehls' ability to forgive their daughter's killers simply astonishing. Their story inspires me.

MH: They were able to understand that underlying conditions were more responsible for Amy's death than any individual, but I think that kind of comprehension is rare. Knowing the entire arc of the real story as you did, did you outline? How much research did you do before you began to write? Because you knew Amy's entire story, did you know how your own story would end before you began?

AEW: As usual, I had absolutely no idea where my novel was headed. I keep hoping that I will learn something and be able to save myself the trash cans full of mistaken routes. I rented a room at the Beach Breeze Inn in Falmouth, Massachusetts, and filled it with maps, photos, and index cards. I knew my characters, but I had no idea where they would lead me. For one thing, I thought Nadine and George were in love. The story changed over the winter as I wrote and watched the snow on the water.

MH: I think this is one of the magical aspects of fiction – that it forks off from the strict outline of the facts, and manages to go somewhere deeper and, I believe, ultimately more truthful. The characters begin to take over and dictate their own actions; at least that's always how it feels to me. So how did your visit to South Africa change the novel in progress?

AEW: I have a young son, and didn't want to leave him to travel to South Africa. I talked to everyone I knew who had been there, and tried to research the TRC online. People told me Cape Town was like San Francisco, so I tried to write the book imagining a San Francisco in Africa. It was ludicrous! In the end, I knew the book needed to appeal to a reader's senses to work – I needed to breathe in South Africa in person. I called my sister Liza and said, 'Would you come with me to Cape Town?' Without a second's hesitation, she said, 'Yes.' I bought the tickets about ten minutes later.

Liza took photographs and followed me wherever I wanted to visit. We also lucked into an amazing cab driver, Rashid, who drove us to places many drivers wanted to avoid. (Anyone visiting Cape Town should contact me for Rashid's phone number.) Our guide, Patrick Lutuli, introduced us to Khayelitsha Township, which was worse than I had imagined. I have travelled to some dangerous places, but I never felt afraid until I was a mother. Suddenly, I was no longer just responsible for myself. I lay awake for a few nights, thinking about the fact that one of the things I was most proud of – my ability to travel courageously – ▶

Q & A with Amanda Eyre Ward
(continued)

◀ wasn't necessarily a characteristic that made for a great mother. This journey into motherhood became one of the major themes of the book. By the time I was on the flight home, I had completely reimagined *Forgive Me.*

MH: How long were you in South Africa?

AEW: Only six nights. (I couldn't bear to leave my son for longer than that.) We stayed for three nights at the Mount Nelson Hotel, a gorgeous Colonial-era hotel with many swimming pools and luxurious rooms . . . men in pith helmets drinking tea, a champagne bar, the whole nine yards. Then we went to Khayelitsha Township, a slum a few minutes away, for three nights. It was quite an adventure.

MH: Was it difficult to find people to share their stories while you were in South Africa? I'm wondering if your experience mirrored Nadine's in that regard?

AEW: It was interesting. . . Many people were loath to talk about the past. This could be because many people I met were working for hotels or tour companies, and didn't want to focus on the dark side of South Africa. There's so much beauty to talk about too, so many amazing beaches, mountains, vineyards, and people. Parts of Cape Town feel like San Francisco, or Austin. Kloof Street is like South Congress Street in Austin, truly.

MH: Your comment about how not really feeling fear until you were a mother is one that resonates with me; I'm the mother of three and yet have not been able to resist diving into Gaza or visiting the poppy fields near Kandahar where farmers harvest opium. There is no doubt that I am more careful and cautious, though, than before I had kids. Nadine, of course, is not yet a mother as the novel begins. What was the easiest part of her character for you to explore – in other words, what felt most familiar to you personally – and what was the hardest?

AEW: As you know, Masha, speaking to you about your career gave me the idea of creating a character like Nadine. Our conversations about how journalists give up pieces of themselves to get an interviewee to reveal their truest story helped me so much in imagining what sort of a person Nadine would have to be to be successful in her field. She is also courageous – unafraid to drive right into a Mexican drug cartel or visit Subcomandante Marcos's jungle hideout – but so frightened to trust anyone or care about anyone other than herself. I can certainly relate to these traits. So much of creating Nadine's life was a simple process of research – where she would have been in the world at what age – but understanding her fierce independence, and trying to create the one man who might convince her to let her guard down, the emotional stuff, this was harder for me. One day, I was hiking out to Nobska Lighthouse in Woods Hole ▶

Q & A with Amanda Eyre Ward
(continued)

◄ and thinking about Nadine, and I realized she was a woman who had lost her mother. Then Nadine made sense to me, and I wrote the scene where Nadine and her mother, Ann, visit the same lighthouse toward the end of Ann's battle with cancer.

MH: This rings so true for me, Amanda: the idea that finding a way in, even a single point on which we can truly connect with our character, helps other less familiar traits become more understandable. I think that's true for journalists interviewing subjects as well as novelists getting to know their characters. Another important point you raise is how Nadine is courageous during moments many would find terrifying, and yet scared of things others find easy, such as being linked to (and possibly tied down by) a man. That brings us to Lily. She is a wonderful character. We see in many ways that her life, if more ordinary than Nadine's, is just as important and challenging. What can you tell us about the genesis of this character?

AEW: As a mother of two young sons, it wasn't hard to come up with the character of an overwhelmed mother, let's put it that way. I have many friends who are happily devoted to motherhood, and I admire them. But it's really hard to be home with toddlers; it's a whole indoor world.

MH: Yet you've made Lily very strong and well rounded, and I love that. I'd also like to know about the inspiration for the character of Thola, with her mixture of strength and vulnerability.

AEW: While researching the book, I learned about the Freedom Fighters who had left South Africa to train in Mozambique and elsewhere. They then returned to South Africa to fight against the apartheid government, and many were killed. *Forgive Me* began with the idea of a sheltered girl on Cape Cod, a girl who grew up to be Nadine, writing to a young South African girl, who was Thola. I envisioned Thola and Nadine as pen pals. Thola was always fully formed in my mind, a grand personality from the start.

MH: *Forgive Me* has a complex structure. Did you know how it would all come together?

AEW: Not at all. In fact, when I first told my editor about the book, I talked about South Africa and Nadine. We were sitting in her car, outside my hotel room in San Francisco. At the very end of our conversation, I said, 'Then I keep hearing the voice of this boy who wants to be a star.' I told her a bit about him, and my editor said, 'The boy is the heart of the story.' I remember going up to my hotel room thunderstruck. She was exactly right, so I picked up my hotel pad and pen and wrote, listening to what the boy had to say. Who he was and how his search for stardom would turn out all came later. ▶

Author photo by Jerry Baner

Q & A with Amanda Eyre Ward
(continued)

◄ **MH:** What are you working on now?

AEW: The stories all explore the search for love, whether in the embrace of a one-night stand, the gaze of a newborn child, or the safety of home. Characters include a 9/11 widow taking on the dating scene, a father on the Atkins diet, and an American woman in Saudi Arabia, planning her baby shower.

I'm also working on a new novel. I've been writing scenes from the characters' lives for a while now – the members of a colorful Texas oil family, a lonely new mother drinking whiskey at the Dorchester Bar in London, the daughter of a Mexican border guard – and the story is just starting to crystallize. This is a thrilling time in the writing process, when the pieces of a novel begin to shift and come into focus.

Masha Hamilton is the author of *The Camel Bookmobile.* ∎

Have You Read?

Sleep Toward Heaven

An unforgettable literary page-turner.

In Gatestown, Texas, twenty-nine-year-old Karen awaits her execution on Death Row. In Manhattan, Dr Franny Wren, also twenty-nine, plans her wedding and tries to resist the urge to run. In Austin, Celia, a beautiful young librarian, mourns her murdered husband. Over the course of one summer, fate brings the lives of these three women together, in a luminous story about the possibility of faith, the responsibility of friendship, and the value of life.

'Intimate, unflinching . . . very tough to put down'   PAM HOUSTON,
'O' The Oprah magazine

How to Be Lost

A spellbinding novel about sisters, family secrets – and love.

To their neighbours in suburban New York, the Winters family has it all: a grand home, a trio of radiant daughters, and a sense of security in their affluent corner of America. But when five-year-old Ellie disappears, the fault lines within the Winters family are exposed.

Fifteen years later, Caroline, now a New Orleans cocktail waitress, sees a photograph of a woman in *People* magazine. Convinced that it is Ellie all grown up, Caroline embarks on a search for her missing sister.

As she travels through the New Mexico desert, the mountains of Colorado, and the underworld of Montana, she devotes herself to salvaging her broken family.

'[*How to Be Lost*] invites comparison to *The Lovely Bones*'   *People* magazine

If You Loved This,
You Might Like . . .

FICTION

Cry, the Beloved Country
Alan Paton

An immediate worldwide bestseller when it was published in 1948, and perhaps the most famous and important novel in South Africa's history, this is the story of Zulu pastor Stephen Kumalo and his son, Absalom. Set against the background of a land and a people riven by racial injustice, it is an impassioned novel of searing beauty – a classic work of love and hope, and courage and endurance.

People of the Book
Geraldine Brooks

Hanna Heath, an Australian rare-book expert, is offered the job of a lifetime – the analysis and conservation of the priceless and beautiful Sarajevo Haggadah, rescued from Serb shelling during the Bosnian war. When she discovers a series of tiny artefacts in its ancient binding, she begins to unlock the book's mysteries. Hanna's investigation unexpectedly plunges her into the intrigues of fine art forgers and ultra-nationalist fanatics, and her experiences will test her belief in herself and the man she has come to love.

Inspired by a true story, *People of the Book* is a novel of sweeping historical grandeur and intimate emotional intensity.

NON-FICTION

Small Wars Permitting: Dispatches from Foreign Lands
Christina Lamb

Since leaving England aged 21 with an invitation to a Karachi wedding and a yearning for adventure, Christina Lamb has spent 20 years reporting from around the world and becoming one of Britain's most highly regarded journalists. This is a collection of her best reportage, following the principal events of the last two decades. Through the stories she tells – and her own development from a self-confessed 'war junkie' to a devoted mother – Lamb attempts to comprehend the human consequences of conflict in the countries she has come to know.

My Father's Daughter
Hannah Pool

Adopted from an orphanage in Eritrea and brought to England by her white adoptive father, Hannah Pool grew up unable to imagine what it must be like to know a blood relative. Then, unexpectedly, a letter arrived from a brother she never knew she had. Not knowing what to do, Hannah hid it away for ten years. Unable to forget it, she finally decided to track down her surviving Eritrean family. Frank, intimate, funny, and sometimes all too real, this is the story of one life, two families, and two very different cultures. ∎